the
other side
of the
bridge

the
other side
of the
bridge

A NOVEL

CAMRON WRIGHT

SHADOW
MOUNTAIN

Visit us at ShadowMountain.com

Library of Congress Cataloging-in-Publication Data

Names: Wright, Camron Steve, author.
Title: The other side of the bridge / Camron Wright.
Description: Salt Lake City, Utah : Shadow Mountain, [2018]
Identifiers: LCCN 2017041895 | ISBN 9781629724102 (hardbound : alk. paper)
Subjects: LCSH: Bereavement—Fiction. | Golden Gate Bridge (San Francisco, Calif.)—
      Fiction. | San Francisco (Calif.), setting. | LCGFT: Novels.
Classification: LCC PS3623.R53 O84 2018 | DDC 813/.6—dc23
LC record available https://lccn.loc.gov/2017041895

Printed in the United States of America
Publishers Printing

10 9 8 7 6 5 4 3 2 1

To ALICYN,
who offered persistent encouragement
and

JOHN SYLVESTER,
who instilled in me a fascination
for one day riding a Harley across the
Golden Gate Bridge

Faith—is the Pierless Bridge
Supporting what We see
Unto the Scene that We do not—
Too slender for the eye
It bears the Soul as bold
As it were rocked in Steel
With Arms of Steel at either side—
It joins—behind the Veil
To what, could We presume
The Bridge would cease to be
To Our far, vacillating Feet
A first Necessity.

—EMILY DICKINSON

chapter one

San Francisco, California, 2012

The damp metal nudges me forward, the waves open their welcoming fingers, the night's darkness offers to hide my shame. All whisper a single question that reaches up through the fog and catches in my throat. If I, Katie Connelly, were to jump from this bridge tonight, would my death matter?

Father Muldowney, my priest, says life is precious. He quotes a sixteenth-century monk who said, "'Midst all our frailty, fault, and sin, shines our heart, a light therein. E'er we must then stay the end, and cherish life to live again." I wonder if when the poet wrote those words, he knew what it was like to lose every person dear to him.

In truth, I didn't come to jump. I came only to glimpse death, to gauge his strength, to know what I can expect when it's my turn. I decide to crawl back over the railing and return home, but as I twist around, the steel beneath my feet trembles and I lose my grip. My feet slide out from under me and I stumble. I flail for the railing, but it's too late. I collapse into the clouds as the dank sea air rushes past.

I don't fear death—until my father calls from the bridge above.

"Katie, where are you?"

I scream for him as I descend, but the wind swallows my cry. I yell louder, but the sound falls with me.

"Katie?"

When they find my body, he will think that I jumped. I can't have him believe that I jumped!

More than anything, I want to live. I wish to be back with my father, to tell him he's important, to let him know that I love him—but my wishes are worthless.

After hitting the surface, I'll plunge deep into the blackness of the bay. For any hope of survival, I'll need to take a deep breath just before impact. I try to suck in air, but my chest tightens and my lungs freeze. I writhe and struggle. I tumble and fall, desperate for one more breath that never comes.

It's always the same when I awake. My sheets are wet; I shiver and my chest heaves as I gasp for air. It's a terrible dream, a horrendous nightmare, yet I despair every time I awake and it comes to an end.

In my dream . . . my father is still alive.

• • •

My birth name is Katherine Ann Connelly, though most people call me Katie. I work in the history department at San

Francisco State University as a research assistant. It's a solitary job, but it suits me.

In truth, I should be the one directing the research projects. At twenty-six, I have two undergraduate degrees and a master's degree I finished last spring. I didn't plan to live the life of a professional student. I've just been a tad lost since my father's death two years ago last April. He was a hard man to give up.

My boss, Professor James Winston II, has just handed me a research request. He's a good friend, a second father, and I'm sure he believes this assignment will help me in a therapeutic sort of way. He means well, but he should stick to history.

It seems the university was asked by the Golden Gate Commemorative Society to prepare a packet of information for the state's school system. Our portion will be a booklet titled *Our Heritage: A History of the Golden Gate Bridge*.

I'm concerned about this particular assignment because of my father and the memories it will dredge up. You see, my father worked on the bridge for twenty-nine years of his life. Professor Winston says that's why I'd be perfect, because I already know so much about the structure. Of course, he also tells me that I need to date, that I should find a good man.

The professor is full of nonsense.

Speaking of nonsense, I talk to him—my father, I mean. I have conversations with him as if he were still here. Sometimes, I even think I can feel him near. Other times, after I catch myself talking to a dead person, I realize that I may be stepping a bit over the crazy line, and I do my best to jump back. It's been a little over two years, and I know it's time to get over losing him—it's time I get on with life. I've even considered moving, getting away from the bridge, the university, the city, the memories. But each time I think that I've banked enough courage, I come up wanting.

I don't date much; I don't get asked. I'm sure it's my fault, though don't misunderstand: I look after myself, I watch what I eat and stay fit, and men do seem to find my athletic build and slim features attractive. The fact is, I'm miserable to be around—not in a rude sort of way, but in a lonely sort of way.

Enough about my better traits and back to matters at hand . . . I have until three today to get back to the professor before he assigns the project to another researcher. As I look over the project's notes, as I study the scope, I can see that I'd be perfect for it. I spent my childhood at the bridge. My father's stories about the structure have been ingrained in my head since I could crawl. I said that he worked on the bridge, but more than that, he loved the bridge.

My father also died there.

chapter two

Megan Riley—hair sopping, bath towel clinging—burst into the kitchen, beckoned by the howling smoke alarm. Her eyes darted around the room. No visible fire. No visible husband. Only Angel, their youngest, a petite child who had recently turned five. She stood peacefully beside the toaster admiring the rising smoke, like steam from the geysers they had visited in Yellowstone Park last summer, except today it was dark and sooty.

"Angel! Where's Daddy?" Megan hollered, pouncing toward the plug. There was no need. The appliance popped on cue, perhaps in surrender, to give up its burnt offering.

"Don't know, Mom," Angel answered with an innocent shrug. "But his toast is done."

Although the toaster may have ceded, the smoke detector was just getting started.

Megan tugged a chair beneath the alarm, balanced on it like a scantily clad circus performer, and fanned one-handed. The clamor did more than ignore her: the half-circle vents molded into the detector's puck-shaped face seemed to grin down.

Brad, barely sixteen and dark-haired like his father, turned the corner. He halted. His mother, dripping hair, tippy toes, clad in a tenuous towel, was flapping anxiously at the ceiling.

"Now, there's something you don't see every day," he deadpanned to Angel.

Megan ignored him, reaching instead with a single finger on her free hand toward the one button on the blaring contraption that would silence the racket once and for all—and then she would find Dave.

Just another inch and . . . her chair tipped backwards.

Megan screamed.

• • •

The trash in the kitchen was overflowing—yet again—and running it out to the large can in the garage, *before* Megan had to ask, seemed like a given. The toasting bread had started out frozen, the other children hadn't yet come down, and besides, he'd be back in less than two minutes.

In the garage, Dave straight-armed the can open and dumped, careful not to dirty his pressed shirt and silk tie. He dropped the lid, scooted back around his car, and then paused at the door. It was a beautiful thing, a BMW 650i coupe, purchased seven months earlier. Expensive? Sure, but it was his dream machine, the first sports car he'd ever owned. He was embarrassed at the time—to approach forty and buy a red sports car was such a cliché. Lately, he couldn't care less.

His thoughts were interrupted by a sound coming from the kitchen. *Was that the smoke alarm?*

It took only seconds after he'd pushed through the door for his eyes to scrunch, his forehead to furrow, his feet to spread. Light reflecting off the room had already traveled down his optic nerve to deliver the scene to his head, but his brain was having trouble sorting it all out. There was smoke in the kitchen, the smell of burnt toast, a deafening alarm—that all made sense. But why was Megan sitting in the middle of the floor with her knees pulled tightly against her chest, trying frantically to gather herself in a towel?

Brad was the first to speak. "Dad, I . . ." He raised his voice to be heard above the noise, but then the smoke alarm, perhaps growing bored, silenced itself. "Dad," he repeated, not wasting the moment, "I believe your toast is ready."

Dave's eyes were still looking for answers. He reached down to help Megan up, but she wouldn't reach back. Dave turned instead to his youngest daughter.

"Angel, I asked you to watch the toaster!" he chided.

Her tiny yet determined voice was adamant. "I did watch it, Daddy! I watched it the whole time!"

Silence swept the room—an eerie stillness, like one might expect in a death chamber. Then Megan, still double-clutching her towel, began to giggle uncontrollably.

• • •

The family had tried to schedule daily breakfasts together, but with people heading in so many different directions, it was not working out. Dinnertime hadn't been much better, with baseball, piano, and dance lessons all making their demands on the family.

While Megan finished getting ready, Dave checked his watch, then quick-stirred a pan of scrambled eggs.

Brittany, their middle child, entered, apparently completely unaware of the morning's fiasco, though Brad would contend she was unaware of *everything* but boys.

Dave scooped eggs onto her plate while Brittany settled into her chair. She was their child who never rushed—despite always being late. After all, it was only school. She had all day.

She tossed back her long brown hair, the color of her mother's, in a gesture that reminded Dave of Megan—and of the fact that his daughter was growing up.

"Did Mom tell you who I like?" Brittany asked.

"No. Should she?"

"I told her not to."

"So, who *do* you like?" Dave asked, taking the obvious bait.

"Promise not to tell?"

Dave tried to picture anyone who would care. He couldn't. "I promise."

"Jason Wilson. He's hot!"

"How old are you again?"

"Duh, Dad. I'll be turning thirteen in a year." Dave opened his mouth, but decided silence was his best ally.

Brad hustled back through the room. "I'm outta here." He

bent close to stare into Dave's eyes. "Dad, listen! Don't forget—game tonight—six p.m.—at the field."

"I didn't forget last time," Dave replied, every word protesting. "I was just running late."

Brad ignored the man to holler up the stairs. "Pick me up at three, Mom?"

Megan's voice echoed from a distant corner of the house. "Do you have everything?"

"Yeah. Try not to be late!" He snatched his baseball mitt, backpack, and the three remaining pieces of toast, and, like a tailgating teenager late to a party, he was gone.

Dave's phone alarm beeped. He would be late as well if he didn't leave now. Then, as if she'd been watching, Megan stepped in, dressed for the day and carrying Dave's coaching uniform. She folded it inside his briefcase and clicked the lid closed.

"I've got to run," Dave announced, picking up his suit coat.

"I know, honey. I'll see you at the game?" It was meant as a reminder, not a question. She continued, "We'll grab pizza on the way home after, if that's okay."

She leaned up to kiss him lightly on the lips, though his was a halfhearted kiss in return. He shifted his weight. It appeared he had something to say.

She waited. He remained silent.

"I love you," she added, pointing to his watch.

"Yeah, I know. I love you too." He took a breath, forced a turn, and paraded once again to the garage.

• • •

The car flaunted style, power, and sophistication. Dave let the leather surround him, rescue him, whisper its encouragement. Driving to work was one of the few moments of sanity he would have all day. He checked the car's clock, undecided as to whether he should slow down and savor the moment or press the gas pedal to the floor. He chose the gas.

He glanced in the rearview mirror and then eased his foot down. If he drove fast enough, it was harder for the anxiety to keep up. *Perhaps I'll just keep on going today,* he mused. *I'd miss my wife and family, sure, but at least I'd have my car.* His tease brought a grin.

Megan, on the other hand, was a minivan holdout, a vanishing breed of mothers who refused to join the modern age and trade up to an SUV. Though he appreciated her rebellious stance, what he couldn't grasp was her rationale—she actually liked her van. "It's practical, and I love the color," she would say.

Dave turned onto the New Jersey Turnpike.

She wasn't much younger than he—three years plus a month. Why was she so happy all the time when life had become so hectic, so crazy? And with burgeoning demands at the office, things were only going to get worse.

Dave was the dad, he was in charge—why, then, did he feel like the captain of the *Hindenburg*? Life was passing fast and it was all he could do to breathe. Some days were fine, but on other days, he felt like the desire had been sucked right out of him.

How could he explain it to Meg? She would retort with, *Life is short, so enjoy it.* But she still looked fabulous—he was the one growing old.

Ten more minutes and he'd be at the lot where he'd park his car to catch the train to Manhattan—he and a million other clones. On occasion, he'd brave city traffic and drive the entire way. He considered it today, but finding a place in the company lot this late would be all but impossible.

The train ride was the part of the commute he dreaded the most. It had become necessary when the firm had moved to Manhattan the previous fall—one more thing to complicate his life. He clicked on the stereo and selected his favorite playlist: Billy Joel.

Ironically, the song that played first was "Running on Ice."

There was always a new account at the office, more activities for the kids, run to this, late to that—and what did he have to show for it? More gray hair. He needed to slow things down, but how?

At times when he was alone in the car, Dave would sing along with the lyrics. Not today. Today he turned up the volume.

"Seriously?" he mumbled as he pulled into the lot. "Am I really going to be forty?"

chapter three

"Good morning, Mr. Riley."

Dave nodded his reply to the receptionist. She was new, and he couldn't remember her name.

When he reached his office, Gloria, his personal secretary, was thankfully not at her desk. It meant he could slip inside undetected to have a few more minutes to breathe. The room's solitude, however, was both a reprieve and a punishment. Every contemplative moment he spent motionless in his chair was a missed opportunity to get a head start on his day. He'd barely arrived and guilt was already piling up at his feet.

He turned his stare from the window to a company brochure on his desk.

Strategy Data International was smaller than the name suggested, middle of the pack when analyzing gross revenue. However, the company was respected and aggressive, and word on the street was that in the field of strategic marketing research, this was the firm to watch. Its newly appointed president, Ellen Brewer, had taken over from her father two years earlier. While children in many family businesses quickly drove their respective companies into the ground, Ellen was turning out to be an exception. With her conservative father out of the way, the man's only daughter had positioned the company for growth. Though she had initially been criticized by analysts as overbearing and inexperienced, her vision was proving brilliant.

Dave had never doubted. He'd known the woman long enough to be certain of one thing—Ellen Brewer would capture market share.

For fifty-two years the company had been headquartered in New Brunswick, just a twenty-minute drive from the Riley home in Jamesburg. Ellen's first executive decision had been to relocate corporate offices to Manhattan, closer to the big-money clients and with easier access to Washington, D.C. And in the few short months since the move, revenue had already increased by thirty percent.

While good for the company, the change had complicated life for Dave. He and Megan had talked about moving closer to the city to accommodate, but with children already established in school, sports, and other activities, it muddied the picture. Moves were hard on families, especially teenagers, and despite Megan's belief that the children would adjust, it didn't feel right to Dave. The entire situation remained a paradox—the anxiety of moving would wreak emotional havoc, but the pressures of staying were slowly doing the same.

The door opened and Gloria rushed in. "You're here! I didn't see you come in."

Not yet ready to face the day, but with no other choice, Dave pasted on a plastic smile and stood. His secretary didn't waste any time.

"Your ten o'clock called and would like to move your meeting to eleven. I hope that works because you have lunch at noon at the Lighthouse on 37th rather than at Pompanos. Ms. Brewer said she may be attending. She'll let you know in an hour. And your three o'clock with the new account . . . let's see, Ability Fitness Centers . . . has been moved to four."

"To four?" Dave protested. "I coach today. I can't be late or the kids will have me skewered."

"Do you want me to cancel?"

"I've canceled twice already. Keep it but be ready. I may need your help."

He watched Gloria's eyes roll, knowing she detested their routine when meetings ran long. She had barely stepped from his office when Brock Pelino strutted in.

Since joining the company five years earlier, Brock had become Dave's best friend. Ellen often teamed them up to handle important accounts, a pairing that had proved successful. The men worked well together, laughed at the same jokes, shared an appreciation of baseball and sports cars. Alike in many ways, they were also oddly different. Brock was slightly older, at forty-five, divorced, no children, and though he sympathized with Dave's family juggling act, Brock seemed happy to be married to his job.

In many ways it was an unlikely friendship: one man single, carefree, with little outside responsibility; the other buried in the duties of employee, coach, husband, and father, with never enough time to excel at any one of them. Perhaps it was a friendship that thrived because each envied what the other had.

"You hear the news yet?" Brock asked, almost giddy, as he closed the door. He loved office politics, lived for the gossip.

"You're dating the new girl in accounting?" Dave quipped.

"Seriously, we just landed the Yorkshire account."

Dave sighed, letting a hint of distress also escape. "That *is* good news." It was the right answer, but delivered in the wrong tone.

"Hey, c'mon. I thought you'd be thrilled. Our stock options are going to be worth a mint."

"Sure, if I don't drown first."

"Why so tense? You need a vacation," Brock added.

"Tell me about it."

Two quick knocks came at the door before Gloria entered.

"Your nine o'clock, is waiting. I've got the numbers ready." She handed Dave a folder. He glanced at his watch—five after.

"Thanks. Seat them in the conference room. I'll be right there."

"They're already there and waiting."

Dave straightened his shoulders. The gun had sounded and the day's race had begun.

He turned to Brock. "You want to continue this conversation

at lunch? Clients at the Lighthouse at noon. I think the waitress there has a thing for you," he added, trying to insert needed levity.

When Brock hesitated, Dave baited the hook. "Ellen will be dropping in."

"Look, normally I'd love to, but . . ." When Brock didn't bite, especially with the boss attending, Dave's eyebrows raised. Brock's explanation was simple. "I already have a lunch date with Jeanine."

"A woman! Of course, that explains it." Though the name sounded familiar, Dave couldn't place the face. He turned to Brock for help. "Jeanine?"

Brock headed for the door. Before closing it behind him, he let a smile slip. "She's the new girl in accounting."

• • •

Dave glared at the wall clock, expecting it to interrupt for him. Sadly it only glared back as Mr. Sorensen, a.k.a. King of Ability Fitness, continued to drone on about ruthless industry competition, the cost of labor, and how government regulation was killing business at all fourteen of his locations. Dave didn't care. The necessary points of discussion had been covered in the first ten minutes, and now the follow-up diatribe by Sorensen was not only making Dave late, it was boring him utterly to death.

Twice Dave stood to signal that the meeting had to end. Twice Sorensen stood, hardly taking a breath before sitting back down.

At five minutes before the hour, Gloria opened the door. She was a woman who hated to lie, and as such had waited until the last possible minute. She wasn't a moment too soon.

"Sorry to interrupt, Mr. Riley, but the senator is on the phone for you. Would you like to take the call?"

Dave bit his lip to suppress a smile, knowing her message was all but true. The year prior, the firm had hired retired autoworker Axel Senator to run the mail room.

Gloria continued, "Should I tell him you're with a client?"

Dave stepped into character, nodding to Mr. Sorensen. "Excuse me, I'd better take this call."

Dave pushed the blinking line on the phone. "Good afternoon, Senator," Dave began.

"Hey there, Mr. Riley. Gloria said you needed to speak with me?"

Dave pressed the receiver tightly against his ear. She obviously hadn't filled Axel in on the angle. "I'm fine."

"Well, I'm fine too, sir. Is there a problem?"

"What can I do for you today?" Dave asked back, wholly ignoring Axel's question.

"What?"

Dave didn't let the man's confusion slow him down. "I'm thrilled to hear your constituents are happy. It's amazing what we learn from market research, isn't it?" Dave turned in time to catch the look on Sorensen's face: saucered eyes, arching eyebrows, a mouth that puckered in childlike surprise.

Axel sounded equally amazed—or perhaps confused. "I don't

know what you're talking about, Mr. Riley. This is Axel in the mail room!"

"You'd like to meet?"

"Can't you hear what I'm saying? This is Axel!"

Dave let several seconds pass.

"I'm with a client, but, yes, I can leave right now." Dave offered Sorensen an apologetic shrug. "Of course, Senator, I'll be there immediately. Yes, I have the address in my phone. Good-bye to you too."

"What the—"

Click. Dave dropped the receiver to cut off Axel midsentence and then jumped to his feet. No time to waste.

"That was *our* senator?" a dumbfounded Sorensen asked.

"I like to think he's *everybody's* senator. At least that's how we think of him around here."

Dave grabbed his briefcase and jacket and then opened his office door. "He's a nice guy . . . you'll have to meet him someday."

Gloria already had the elevator open and helped shoo Sorensen inside. The man didn't let their herding slow down his enthusiasm. He continued speaking to Dave as the doors closed, "Call me next week when the marketing profile is complete. *We can do lunch.*"

While Dave normally walked the twelve blocks to the train station, today he waved down a taxi. He hadn't had time to change, so as the cab jerked away from the curb he opened his briefcase and removed his coach's uniform and shoes. If the driver noticed him changing, he didn't say a word. No doubt he'd seen worse.

When Dave pulled on his second shoe, his toe crunched something inside. Even before he'd fished out the wadded paper and smoothed it flat, he knew what it was. *"Just a quick note to say that I love you. See you at the game."*

Love notes. Megan had started writing them months earlier, to keep the *passion* alive. They would show up on occasion in un-expected places, and although he didn't keep track, lately they felt more frequent. He'd hoped the habit would run its course and die a forgotten death. It hadn't.

Dave had tried to reciprocate by writing messages back, but he felt like a copycat, not sincere. Sending flowers was his next attempt, but with work so hectic he'd often forget. Brock sug-gested Dave have Gloria schedule rose deliveries at the first of every month, like Brock did for two of the women he was dating, but for Dave, scheduled "love gifts" were so contrived they were self-defeating. Usually he did nothing, which only caused inade-quacy and guilt to smolder.

When the cab pulled up to the station, Dave stuffed the note into his pocket, swiped his card to pay the fare, and then bolted out the door. He ran in full stride for the train, weaving his way through the crowd, business suit wadded under one arm and briefcase in the other hand.

The uncooperative train seemed to crawl, and by the time Dave reached his car in New Jersey at the Park 'n Ride lot, he was already half an hour late. There were two other men who helped

Dave coach the team, but both were out of town for today's game. Dave had assured them he would take over, *no problem.* He was the man; he was in charge—and he wasn't even there.

He slid into the car, mumbled a quick prayer that policemen would be blind, and then he slammed down the gas. It still took twelve minutes more to reach the field.

After the car squealed to a halt, Dave bolted toward his team's dugout. He could see his guys up to bat. Woody Peterson was in the box, which meant they were already halfway through the batting order. Then Dave caught sight of Megan, clipboard in hand. She watched him approach and offered a quick wave. Angel was stacking baseballs into a pile at the far corner of the dugout.

"We're ahead, three to one," she glowed. "Christian is on third, and Woody is batting."

Megan turned to the field and hollered to the team, "It's okay, the coach is here now!"

Dave ignored the disapproving parent glances to focus instead on the batting order scribbled on the scorecard. It was all out of whack. "You put Woody up to bat after Christian?"

"Yeah, I sorted them by last name. It was easier that way."

"But . . ." He wasn't sure what to say.

"Don't worry, honey," she continued, reading his confusion. "Woody's small, but—"

Smack.

Both turned to see the boy's ball sail over the shortstop's head and drop shy of the left outfielder. Woody dashed for first while Christian slid home to score another run.

Megan beamed.

"Alphabetical order," Dave muttered to himself. "Who would have guessed?"

Brad was up next. He eyed Dave, nodded with confidence.

Dave called to him from near the dugout. "Keep that elbow up, Brad. Study the pitcher. You can see that he's tipping his pitches."

The pitch came high and outside. *Ball one.* Brad held steady while Dave hollered encouragement. "Watch the pitch, Brad. That's it, wait for the one you want."

The second pitch came in low. Brad let it go. "Not today," he mouthed aloud, "not today." *Ball two.*

The next pitch also trailed low, well below the strike zone, and Dave winced as he watched Brad swing. The pitch was low, all right, but not too low for Brad. He connected solidly, sending the ball over third base and toward the left field line. The outfielder raced at full speed and, seeing it would be close, laid himself out horizontally and extended his glove. It would be the play of the game—for one team or the other.

Brad won.

The ball touched leather but not enough to stop as it deflected off the mitt and rolled toward the fence. The prone outfielder sprang to his feet, but by the time he located the ball, it was too late. The runner on first touched home plate as Brad slid in at third.

By the end of the game, they were seven runs ahead—their

easiest win to date. Voting was unanimous: Brad and Megan shared the game ball.

After the equipment had been gathered, Dave, Megan, and crew headed toward the parking lot.

"Can you take Angel?" Megan asked. "Brad's coming with me. We'll pick up Brittany and the pizza and meet you at home."

"Sure. Let's go, Squirt."

Dave loaded the game gear while Megan transferred Angel's car seat. As he helped his daughter get properly strapped in, Megan drove away in the van before quickly circling back. *She must have forgotten something.* Dave waited for his wife to slow down and stop, but she didn't. That was when he noticed Brad behind the wheel. As the van passed, Megan held up Brad's new license from the passenger's seat for Dave to see.

Dave was speechless. In the rush of things, he'd completely forgotten that this was Brad's big day. Only Angel spoke.

"Daddy, Brad's driving. I think you should call the police."

chapter four

By nine-thirty Angel was tucked into bed, well past her bed-time. Another half hour had passed before the girl quit talking and drifted off to sleep. Dave waited for Megan at the Jacuzzi out on the back deck—one of the few places they could talk without interruption.

Dave studied her features as she slid into the bubbling wa-ter and closed her eyes: wispy hair curled across her shoulders, slender eyebrows balanced over a freckled nose, lips turned up just enough naturally on each end that she always appeared to be smiling. Even the kids joked that when Mom was angry, she stilled looked happy about it.

If asked about her appearance, Megan would be the first to point out the wrinkles now showing at the corners of her eyes. Dave would contend they only compounded her beauty with added badges of experience and wisdom.

"What?" Megan finally asked, sensing that she was being watched.

"I'm just thinking."

And he was. In the steamy solitude, his thoughts drifted to the first time they'd met, eighteen years earlier. *Psychology 102.* He was filling elective credits he needed to graduate; she was just beginning work on what would become an art degree.

Their first class assignment was to bring a picture showing something they feared. By a simple twist of fate, they'd sat adjacent that day, and as she'd laid her photo on the table, one taken in her early teenage years riding Disneyland's Space Mountain, he leaned forward and picked the curious photo up. It had caught his eye because sitting directly behind the wide-eyed, attractive girl screaming her lungs out from the front seat was Dave. Despite the resemblance, Megan didn't believe at first that it was him—until he recited the month and year the photo was taken.

It wasn't the only coincidence. It turned out their families had lived barely two blocks apart, their fathers had attended the same Rotary Club, and, despite multiple college scholarship opportunities elsewhere, each had selected the same university.

They dated for just four months before he proposed, and barely three months later their married life together started. Those had been carefree days . . . a far cry from the current rush.

"Do you think we're too busy?" Dave finally questioned, letting the thought that had been gnawing at him all week swirl with the steam.

Megan opened her eyes, then tried to whisk his worry away

the way she always did, with humor. "We have way too much happening to worry about questions like that."

"I'm not joking."

She considered him seriously, took a moment to answer. "Yes, I think we are. But it's by our own choice, isn't it?"

"But is it the right choice?"

"What would you cut out?" she asked. "Baseball? Dance? Piano? Better yet, which child should we sell?"

"I'm not sure," Dave answered, with no hint of a smile, before he clarified, "I mean about the activities, not the child-selling part."

"For having just won the game, you seem pretty down. What's wrong?"

His words were quieter now, mixing freely with the sound of anxious bubbles. "Do you ever feel like you're so busy that you're letting dreams slip by?"

"What are you talking about?"

"Did you get any painting done today, for example?"

"I finger painted with Angel—does that count?"

"I'm serious."

"I can see that. Today was my day to help out at the school. You know that."

"See what I mean? We need more time . . ."

She was relaxing. He was stewing.

"Honey," she interrupted, "I enjoy my art, but honestly, I can paint anytime. Watching my kids grow up, being there with them, with you—I'm living my dream."

He heard her assurance, but his eyes answered that he didn't completely believe her.

"Honestly, what's the matter?" she asked again.

"I just . . ." The night air seemed to reach down his throat and steal his words, tie up his thoughts. He felt so apprehensive, so unsure how to explain. "I don't know. I feel . . . well, it's like the song says, I'm running on ice. My legs are moving, but I'm not going anywhere. I feel like I'm in the dream where you run to catch the train, the last train of the day, and you run and run and run, stretching and stretching, until you're out of breath and your legs ache . . . but it's always just out of reach."

Megan splashed up straight. Her eyes brightened, as if a light had clicked on. "Wait, it's because of your birthday, isn't it?"

"What do you mean?"

"You're turning forty—you're worried! Honey, it's still three weeks away, and I'm the one getting the wrinkles. We have a terrific life. Let's enjoy it."

His head knew she was right. How could he argue? If only he could convince the anxiety punching at his chest to listen.

"Maybe it's just the schedule that's getting to me."

Megan reached for his hands and locked her eyes on his. "Life is great," she repeated. "Have a little faith in it, would you?"

"I will," he said before he hesitated. "Sometimes it just . . . it feels like I'm missing out on something, that's all."

"Like what?"

How could he explain it when even he didn't understand? He had a great job, a terrific wife, amazing children. Why the trepidation? His answer, learned from Megan, was to make light of the situation. Humor to the rescue—when you can't face the truth, you joke about it.

"You won't laugh?" he asked Megan.

"Probably. Tell me anyway."

"I've always wanted to buy a motorcycle and ride across the country."

Megan chuckled. "A motorcycle? Like a Harley?"

"Why not?"

"In your suit and tie?"

"Of course not. I'd get a black leather jacket, the kind with padding on the elbows and zippered pockets."

"Would you grow a ponytail? Just for me?"

"Sure, and perhaps a beard. I'd ride across the country, until . . . well, until I came to the Golden Gate Bridge. That's where I'd end up. Did you know my grandfather helped build that bridge? Dad said he loved it. He used to say that it was magical."

"Yes, you've mentioned that. So, you'd ride to the bridge?"

"Not just to it, I'd ride *across* it."

"Across the bridge?"

"Yep. It would be the Fourth of July. The sun would be shining. The sky would be bright and clear. A slight breeze would be blowing over the ocean and through my hair."

"Through your ponytail," she specified, evidently trying her best to tamp down a laugh.

He nodded. "And people would stare, not daring to say

anything aloud, but to themselves—to themselves they would whisper, '*That guy is so cool.*'"

It was born as a playful, fictional scene, sketched in charcoal strokes of black and grey and white, never meant to be taken seriously. But as Dave spoke the words aloud, as they stretched and breathed and filled in space of their own, the vision in his head turned to rich, descriptive color.

Megan let him silently swirl in his moment of glory before asking the obvious. "I am curious, Mr. Ponytail Man. What happens after you cross the bridge?"

Absorbed in the imagery, he let contentment linger. "It wouldn't matter," he finally concluded, satisfaction glowing in his face.

"And why not?"

"It wouldn't matter because at the very moment I crossed the bridge, I'd have experienced the best that life had to offer. I'd have lived my dream. I'd have arrived."

It was picture perfect.

"I think you've been in the hot water way too long," Megan concluded as she reached her arms around his waist and pulled herself tight, kissing him ever so lightly on the neck. "Let's get out and go to bed, and I'll give you something real to smile about."

chapter five

My father was an ironworker on the Golden Gate. It doesn't sound glamorous to the average person. Perhaps it doesn't sound glamorous to anyone. It's the kind of job that you brag about to your friends when you're in elementary school, but learn to hide as you grow older.

Ironworker. It rolls off the tongue much harsher than teacher or salesman. Everyone accepts that it's not in the same league as lawyer or dentist or fill-in-the-blank with just about any professional occupation. But what I now realize, since he's been gone, is that my father's job was worth more than all of those careers combined. You see, during his years working on the bridge, he not only raised a little girl on his own, my father also saved twenty-eight lives. He was part of an elite group of men who, in addition to maintaining one of the world's most miraculous structures, was trained to stop people from jumping off it to their deaths.

It's an odd combination, meshing the traits of a burly iron-worker with those of a compassionate psychologist. Men who work at the bridge are tough men, hard men—they have to be to handle the Gate. And yet at the same time, they can be caring, sensitive men—at least that was the case with my father. I think that's why he was so good at his job, so able to help people who had for one reason or another decided that life was too much to bear.

People will ask why ironworkers are the ones who stop the jumpers, rather than the police or paramedics. The answer is simple: when a jumper climbs over the railing and edges out onto a treacherous area of the bridge, the ironworkers are not only the first ones on the scene, they are also the only ones daring enough to follow.

It was a volunteer assignment, and I remember only one short period of time when my father gave it up and took himself off the list. It was the day I turned sixteen, the same day he took me out to breakfast to celebrate because he'd be working late that night, the same day I blew out sixteen candles that poked out of a ham and cheese omelet. It was also the same day that he watched a father jump from the bridge after first throwing his two-year-old daughter ahead of him. It tore my father apart. When he arrived home late that night, he was crying. He'd decided the stress was too much to handle for a single father trying to raise a balanced teenage daughter. Within weeks, however, he'd changed his mind and was back at work, talking people down.

When I asked him later what had caused his change of heart,

he admitted that although the job could be dreadfully painful, it
was more difficult not to do than to do.

Simply put, my dad was selfless.

Work at the office had been frenzied. No surprise. With Ellen
Brewer in charge, expectations were high. Market share was the
name of the game, and, like everyone, Dave took on more work
than he could handle. He had just finished quantifying marketing
results for Lansing Financial when Gloria buzzed his office.

"Mr. Riley, there's an Abel Lawless from the governor's office
on line three asking for you."

For just a moment, the name startled him. *Lawless?* Then he
chuckled. He and Brock had begun trading practical jokes on
April Fools' Day, shortly after Brock first hired on. He'd called
Dave on the phone, pretending to be from Google, wanting to
offer him a job in California. Dave returned the prank a week
later with the delivery of phony legal papers claiming action
against Brock in a paternity suit.

The jokes continued back and forth, usually no more than
one a month to ensure things didn't get out of hand. As the pranks
were generally harmless, Ellen winked at the fun, understanding
that it added levity to an otherwise stressful environment. Bogus
calls were Brock's specialty and had included dead-on imperson-
ations of an IRS agent, Mark Cuban, and even a birthday-gram
singer who pretended to have an appointment with Gloria. When

Dave had related the story to Brock about Axel calling from the mailroom, Brock couldn't quit laughing.

Dave picked up the line, trying to think of a clever ploy. "This is Dave, discoverer of not-so-funny pranks. Who might you be?"

Silence—then the voice on the line said, "Hello, this is Abel Lawless, the governor's policy director in Florida. A friend recommended you. I'm in town for a few days attending a diversity conference at the Javits Center. I'd like to get together to discuss using your firm for a marketing study as part of the rights initiative we'll be pushing next spring."

Dave laughed into the receiver. Brock would have to do better than that. "A diversity conference, you say?" Brock was relentless, but Dave could take it. "For diversity's sake, we need to hire someone around here who thinks Brock is funny."

"I'm sorry, I'm not sure that I follow . . ."

At that moment the door kicked open and Brock strolled in. He could see that Dave was on the phone, so he plopped down into the adjacent chair to wait.

Dave quit talking. His stomach tightened and his breathing stopped. He looked to Brock, then to the phone, then back to Brock.

"Oh, no!" he whispered, loud enough to let his anxious words spill across the floor.

Puzzled, Brock added a shrug. "What? What did I do?"

• • •

Megan ducked out of Angel's kindergarten class early and headed to the mall. She had forty-five minutes before she had to return to pick up her daughter. At the moment, she had one mission: to find a present for Dave's surprise party.

She felt bad that he was taking his birthday so hard. Could it be the commute, the pressures of work? A real midlife crisis? *As long as he doesn't get a girlfriend,* she quipped.

Traffic at the mall was unusually light. The most obvious place to start would be the sporting goods store. Dave loved to deep-sea fish, but he hadn't found much time for it as of late. There were dozens of displays sporting shiny tackle, strange hooks, and assorted water gear. How would she know what to get? And, with his busy schedule, would it just cause frustration? She wandered over to the baseball equipment. He was in his element as the batting coach of Brad's team. She scanned the aisle. As near as she could tell, he had everything.

Unsettled, she walked out into the mall and toward the department store at the opposite end. She could always get him shirts and ties. He loved to dress well. Yet that was like buying him underwear for Father's Day. This was his fortieth birthday—her gift needed to be special. It needed to be something he would love, something he'd remember.

She browsed through a few clothing racks, then checked her watch—out of time. *Another day, perhaps.* She crossed the common area and was headed for the exit when a glance toward a display window near the doors stopped her cold.

Her heart raced as she placed her hands on the glass. It was perfect, and he'd never guess it in a gazillion years. She hurried inside and checked the price tag: $795! He'd totally freak if he found out, but it was his birthday; she'd take a chance. She ran her fingers across its surface, then held it up to the mirror.

"You like it?" the clerk inquired.

"Can I bring it back after he drools all over it?" she retorted.

The clerk laughed. "As long as you have the receipt."

"I'll take it."

"That quick? You saw the price? Is the size okay?"

"Yeah, it's perfect."

Megan bounced with excitement as the girl removed a large zippered bag from beneath the counter, opened it wide, and placed the black leather motorcycle jacket inside.

• • •

When they had first married, Megan had cut Dave's hair to save money. In time, he'd grown accustomed to the arrangement and refused now to go anywhere else. She loved it because they could chat, and today there was gossip that just wouldn't wait.

"You'll never guess," Megan said, not intending to give him a chance to try. "It looks like Rob and Cindy are splitting up."

"What?"

"Yep, her phone died, and so when she borrowed his, she found a text he'd sent to a woman at his office that was . . . well, let's just say the message was unusually *descriptive.*"

"You're kidding!"

"It's true. I feel so bad for her."

"What a jerk—and he still has my leaf blower. Are they selling the house?"

"I don't think it's gone that far yet."

He was contemplative, silent.

"What are you thinking?" she asked.

"I was thinking that I better delete my text messages."

She tugged the hair on the back of his neck.

"Ouch!"

"You forget—I'm holding scissors."

"I surrender."

She checked the length in back. "Since you gave up so easily, I have a surprise for you."

"A surprise?" Dave held steady as she cut behind his ear.

"You know how your birthday is coming up?"

"No party—you promised."

"We've been over that already. I wouldn't dream of it."

"So, what is it?"

"I've made arrangements to have the kids stay at my sister's next weekend. It's spur of the moment, I know, but you seem tense lately. I thought that we could drive down to Annapolis for the weekend."

His eyes widened. "I love that place . . . oh, but I can't—there's a new account at work."

"Yeah, I thought you'd say that. I talked with Ellen yesterday. She agreed. I only had to twist her arm a little. We can leave first thing Friday morning."

Dave turned to face her. "You called my boss?"

"I asked Brock first. He agreed and backed me up." She watched the corners of his mouth slowly turn up. "Thank you, thank you," she added, offering a bow to her pretend audience.

Dave was chuckling now at the thought. "You're terrific, you know that?"

"Happy birthday," she whispered as she bent over and kissed his lips.

As Dave pulled away, he felt the need to apologize. "Listen, I'm sorry for being so down lately. I never thought the turning-forty thing would bother me—but I guess it has."

"It shouldn't."

"I know. It's just strange: one day I'm twenty, full of aspirations, excited for life's adventures that are just around the bend. Then, the very next day, I'm forty, and I'm not sure I can even see the bend anymore, and . . . well, it's exasperating. And then you surprise me with the perfect gift."

She shrugged. "What can I say? I'm just the perfect little wife."

Dave wasn't finished. "Best of all, you knew not to plan one of those lame surprise parties. Everyone giving you dopey over-the-hill gag gifts. I'd go off the deep end. I'm telling you, honey, you always know just what I need."

Megan reached for the broom and began to sweep. Seconds ticked before she answered. "What can I say to a compliment like that?" Another long moment passed. "And don't worry. I would never plan one of those silly over-the-hill parties—never in a million years."

chapter six

I accepted the assignment to research the bridge. I'll begin after I finish my current project—fourteenth-century artists— and then take a two-week vacation. I don't have anyplace to go, though I should just pick a Caribbean island and buy a ticket— the sunshine would do me good. I just find it awkward and lonely to vacation alone.

My father and I used to go on adventures together when he could get a weekend off. They weren't to exotic locations, usu- ally just up the coast. There was a little hotel near the beach in Mendocino that was his favorite. We'd ride bikes, go to movies, or just sit on the beach and people-watch. Of course, the only people that he'd ever watch were those wearing bikinis. I'd tease him and we'd both laugh; I miss his laughter.

We actually had a weekend trip planned just before he was killed. But as often happens in life, I was busy with my job at the university, and I asked him to postpone it a month. I wish so badly now that I'd taken the time.

I won't be using my vacation to head up the coast. I've only been back to the hotel in Mendocino once since his death. I cried most of the night and then drove straight home early the next morning. I'm taking two weeks off because I haven't used any vacation time in almost two and a half years, and if I don't use at least part of it by summer, I'll lose it. It's a ridiculous policy, but then again, I work for a university, a place where too many smart people are confined in too small a space—so odd policies happen.

The professor assures me that even with a couple of weeks off, I'll still have plenty of time to take on the society's assignment, the history of the bridge. Their deadline isn't until late summer. He was ecstatic that I accepted, and that alone makes me nervous. It's not that I don't trust him; he's just so meddlesome. And I've learned from sad experience that when the professor meddles, it means there's a bad date in my future.

I apologize for sounding negative. In truth, I've always been a romantic, always wanted to settle down and have a family. Currently, the notion feels so fleeting and distant.

I mentioned that I was single and twenty-six, that I lived with my father until his death. While all of that is true, and I'm still looking for someone to spend my life with, I haven't always been alone. At twenty-one, with two semesters left before graduation— my first graduation—I met Eric.

Dave turned up the volume. It was one of his favorite CDs—*American Fool*, with John Cougar Mellencamp singing his heartfelt ballad about Jack and Diane.

He'd hoped that the kids would quiet down and appreciate the music; as usual, they just talked louder to compensate.

The coastal drive was refreshing. Once they dropped the children off at Nancy's, he would really crank up the tunes. It was frustrating. Couldn't they see that this was real music—classic rock, feel-it-in-your-soul, sing-about-life, make-a-difference music?

"Hey, guys, listen up," Dave tried again. "Give John a break, will you?"

"Who's John?" Angel asked from the backseat. It was just enough to get Dave started.

"Baby, we've had this talk before," he preached. "John Mellencamp, singer of true music—ageless music."

Megan sat in the passenger's seat, deep into her novel and oblivious to life around her. In his usual sarcastic form, Brad piped in. "Please, Dad, tell us all about it one more time." Brittany rolled her eyes.

"I will," Dave replied, as he began to extol the virtues of classic rock over modern bands. "Listen to the emotion in his words—"

The boulder slammed onto the road so suddenly that Dave just caught a glimpse before it smashed into the front passenger's side tire. The van jolted to the left as the tire blew and the axle buckled. Brittany screamed as they slid sideways, the van vibrating violently as metal scraped the road. Dave jerked at the steering wheel, straining in vain to regain control. It wouldn't budge.

The air surrounding Dave felt instantly warm, hard, and impenetrable as life tore into broken pieces. Sound distorted. Time slowed. Megan's book dropped to the floor as the van rolled onto its side and then slid over the embankment. Her hand caught Dave's shoulder, grasping desperately for support, before slipping loose. The windshield shattered, bursting into thousands of tiny pieces, filling the van like particles in a kaleidoscope as it turned and bent and twisted. Dave tried to look over his shoulder—where were the kids? Brad should have been buckled in but was thrown against the ceiling, or was it the floor? And where were Brittany and Angel? A warm and dark liquid began to fill in the edges of the scene, blurring his vision. Where, he wondered again, was Angel?

Then everything went black.

I'm fascinated by circumstance—the way insignificant events catapult our lives into strange directions. It's happened to me.

I had a handful of classes left to graduate: one on European culture, and the rest electives. The required class was offered at two separate times, and, being a bit meticulous, I'd already worked out my schedule based on the Tuesday/Thursday course. When I couldn't add the class online, the registrar's office suggested I be at the school early the next morning. That's when the water pipe broke.

It was a main line—a huge, cavernous thing that runs below the busy streets, hidden from our view, silently carrying water through the city. And like so many things in our lives, no one thinks twice about it until it ruptures.

On the morning I needed to register, I awoke to a street flood in front of the house, with heavy equipment digging up the asphalt and blocking my car from leaving the garage.

Though the city's mass transit is excellent—and I'm not complaining—I hadn't planned on the extra time it would take to reach the school. When I arrived, registration was well under way, and the class I needed, the class I'd planned my life around, was completely full. I begged, I pleaded, I whined. They smiled and put me at the bottom of a waiting list thirty students long.

In addition to ending up in the Monday/Friday class, I also lost my part-time job. My boss at the time had already arranged schedules, and when my circumstances changed, he couldn't accommodate.

I was heartbroken—until I walked into European Culture and met Eric Aldridge. He was friendly and cute and we hit it off immediately. Being a bit shy, I was flattered that he'd taken an interest in me.

We started to date, and by Thanksgiving the relationship had turned serious. He was starting a job in L.A., and our plans were to marry after my graduation in April. We found a cute apartment in Long Beach, and though it wasn't the ideal situation for an engaged couple, I would come down on weekends after class to spend time with him.

As the end of the semester neared, with wedding plans under

way, I was giddy. Soon I'd be married to Eric—a man I loved, a man who lifted me up, a man who helped me forget my doubts and insecurities.

With graduation approaching, I'd planned to skip my weekend visit with Eric to finish my final project at the university. Then an odd thing happened—another water pipe ruptured near the history building, closing that portion of the campus for the weekend. It was a spur-of-the-moment decision, but I packed a few things in the car and headed to L.A.

As I reflect back now, I'm amazed how the simple bursting of a water pipe changed my life forever. If not for the flood outside my apartment the day I went to register for class, I wouldn't have met Eric.

And not just the first water pipe, but the second one as well. For had it not ruptured near the history building, the university would have remained open, I would have stayed to work on my project, and I wouldn't have surprised Eric in our apartment sleeping with another woman.

Amid my tears and heartache, my father encouraged me to not give up on love, to still keep hope alive in my heart. Since he's been gone, however, it's been difficult to believe. Yet during times of stillness, when I sit alone and ponder my life's direction, I try to remember my father's wisdom. I try to believe that if it wasn't Eric, then there still must be someone out there for me. And so I keep looking.

Mostly, though, I find myself watching out for broken water pipes.

chapter seven

Dave's head throbbed. *Was everyone okay?* He could still hear the sounds, smell the horror of the accident surrounding him. Yet, when he opened his eyes, it was gone.

The sun streamed through the room's only window. The sheets were tucked in tight, clean and sterile; the smell was clinical. He tried to sit up, but a pain shot down his left arm. A downward glance revealed a glossy translucent tube extruding from a snippet of white tape and gauze attached to his forearm.

"Megan . . . Brad . . . Brittany . . ." His voice was hoarse and raspy. No one answered. He reached over with his right arm and pressed the red button on the side rail. Nothing. He pushed it again, and then again.

The door swung open and a uniformed nurse scurried into the room. With darting eyes, she surveyed his condition.

"You're awake!" Her eyes carried a look of surprise.

"Where am I?"

"Connecticut Valley Hospital in Middletown." She moved over to the bed, held his wrist for a moment, then scribbled on the bedside chart. "Please, don't move. Stay still and let me call the doctor." Before he could mouth his next question, she whisked herself out of the room. No sooner had the door closed than it swung back open, and in stepped a familiar figure.

Dave glanced up. "Brock?"

His friend's eyes looked tired, his right cheek red with criss-crossed fabric impressions suggesting he had been sleeping against an upholstered chair. Brock approached the bed with hesitation.

"Uh, how's it going? I mean—wrong question."

"Today . . . what's today?" Dave's thoughts were clouded. It was difficult to string words together.

"You missed your birthday by a day. The doctors weren't sure at first if you were going to make it."

Both Dave's hands quivered. "Megan . . . how is she?"

Brock rocked back as he rolled in his lips. It was as if he'd been rehearsing his practiced answer for hours, but now that the question had been posed, the words had fled. All that came out was a whisper, "I'm so sorry, Dave, so very sorry."

Panic pounded at Dave's chest as he shook his head back and forth, refusing to believe the news. His movement caused the alarm to sound at the central monitoring station out in the hall.

"The kids! Where are my kids?"

Brock cast his glance downward as he continued to shake his head.

Emptiness poured in through the window and door, filling

the room and holding Dave hard against the bed. He needed to get up and find his wife and children, but he couldn't move his arms or legs—he couldn't breathe. His chest ached and heaved and a pain shot into his left shoulder, but he didn't care.

He now wished for death to snuff out his life as well.

While he continued to writhe and cry, a doctor entered the room and, with the help of a nurse, pushed a syringe of sedative into the IV tube that was taped to Dave's arm. Within seconds the room and all of its surrounding agony began to fade into a brilliant white. Dave turned his head on the pillow as his body fell limp into a drug-induced sleep.

• • •

The reporter on CNN detailed the severity of the Midwest flood. Live video of the disaster featured farmers in rowboats floating around barns. Dave witnessed the destruction from the comfort of his living-room couch.

"The president is scheduled to tour the area this afternoon," the reporter continued, "and it's widely anticipated that the governor will seek federal disaster area assistance."

The devastation didn't faze Dave—it never registered as he looked past the reporter, past the television set, past the events of the day. His gaze was distant, detached.

I enjoy my art, but honestly, I can paint anytime. Watching my kids grow up, being there with them, with you—I'm living my dream.

The picture on the set switched to the weekly forecast, where a young, smiling meteorologist predicted a continued wet year across much of the country.

Climb in bed, Angel, we'll hide here 'til Mommy catches us.

The doorbell startled him. How long had he been dreaming? He checked the tabletop for the remote—not there. He searched in between the cushions—nothing. Finally, he stepped to the set and pushed the power off. The doorbell rang again. He inched to the door, sucked in a deep breath, and pulled on the knob.

On the porch stood six members of his Red Sox baseball team. They shifted their weight uneasily, looking like they weren't sure how to properly stitch together the message they had come to deliver. Kevin, curly-haired and lanky, and the most outgoing on the team, had obviously been designated the spokesperson. "Hey, Coach Riley."

"Guys, how are you?"

"Fine, Coach. We just, uh, well, we haven't really had a chance to talk. And, well . . . we wanted to come by and tell you again how sorry we are, about the accident." Kevin's shoulders lifted, perhaps relieved to no longer carry the weight. He continued, "We've missed you at the games and stuff, but that's not why we're here."

Dave inhaled slowly. He couldn't break down in front of the team.

Kevin continued. "We didn't know if you'd heard or not, but last Friday we took the region championship."

One of the other boys pulled out a trophy he'd been concealing and handed it to Dave. The base was polished walnut; the silver statue on top depicted a player solidly hitting a ball.

"This is for you," the boy added.

"We play on Saturday for state," Kevin piped up, "and we've decided to dedicate the game to Brad. We'll understand if you can't make it . . . but we wanted to invite you anyway."

Dave bit hard into his tongue, vowing to keep his choking emotions at bay. He forced what he hoped would be considered a smile.

"I appreciate it, men. It means a lot, and it would have meant a lot to Brad." He weighed their invitation before speaking again. "I apologize for not being there for the team the last couple of months. It has been pretty rough. But plan on me for Saturday night—count me in."

The boys tossed each other affirmative glances, looking happy they'd been able to do some good. "That'd be cool, Coach. We play the Twins from East Windsor and we think we can take 'em."

"Of course you can. I have faith in you guys."

"Great, we'll see you Saturday."

Dave waved, waited, pushed the door closed, leaned back against the wood, and then slid down to the entry tile in a noiseless heap.

chapter eight

As an only daughter, I learned from my frugal father how to make simple repairs around the house. I can now afford to hire others to do this type of work, but I can't bear the thought of disappointing my father.

What this means is that I spent my two weeks of vacation painting the outside of my house. I'd been waiting for the painting fairies to take care of the project while I slept. When they didn't show by the second day, I tackled the project on my own.

The downside is coming back to the pressures of a project at the university that is behind schedule before it even starts. While most seasoned researchers would begin at the university library, I start this morning at home with my father's roll-top desk. The shelves within the desk and the wall behind it are covered with books about the bridge. Since my father's death, I haven't spent much time in his den. The desk recalls lonely memories, like barbed-wire barriers keeping me at bay. Oh, I come in and dust and vacuum and clean the windows. I've even sorted through the drawers and straightened the stacks of papers. What I haven't done is clean out its contents.

The desk is old. It was old the day my father acquired it at an estate sale up in the Mission District. But the lock and drawers still work perfectly. Today, my skin chills as I twist the key to release the catch. As the desk swallows its rickety cover, I wonder, like Pandora, if demons wait inside to be released.

But once it is opened and exposed, I am reminded that not all of the memories sheltered inside cause me grief. On the right inside panel, there is a picture I painted in the third grade of a house with a chimney and a white picket fence. I pull it toward me for a closer look.

There are smiling faces in three of the windows and a dog named Oscar in the fourth. There are cows and pigs and a pasture blended with bushes and trees and small scribbles of yellow flowers in the yard. Next to the house, tall golden and orange spires of a bridge spring forth from the ground. The cable from the bridge connects to the house, becomes a part of it—as if the Golden Gate Bridge is connected to every home.

It is a curious picture because there is no water, no deep rugged canyon, no ocean for the orange bridge to span. There is just a house, a family, a pasture with animals, and a bridge.

I remember when I presented the picture to my father. He seemed pleased, but then asked, "Katie, where's the ocean?" He meant no harm, but when he asked, I realized for the first time that I'd drawn the picture wrong. I could feel my face flush, which *he must have noticed, for he pulled me close and declared it to be the best picture of the bridge he'd ever seen. We left the house and walked together to the drugstore where he purchased a frame. At home, he waited until I was watching and then hung the picture next to the spot where he liked to sit and read. It stayed near him always from then on, and to a little girl it represented a part of me that had blended with him. And though I had no memories of my mother or the cancer that took her by my second birthday, it helped me to know that I was still part of a family. Now, many years later, I'm amazed that the desire to belong, felt by a little girl so very long ago, bubbles to the surface with such ease.*

I know that I must begin my research, so I replace my child-hood picture of the bridge and remove several volumes about the Golden Gate from the shelf—some are picture books, others are histories. As I flip their pages, I wonder what I can contribute that hasn't already been said or drawn or written. Can an obscure university researcher make a difference to anyone?

I work most of the day and late into the evening. After I've made pages of notes, my eyes begin to burn. It's past midnight, and since I have to be at work early, I return the volumes to their shelves. It is when I look for the key, which I'd dropped into the main desk drawer, that I notice the corner of a book. Only an inch or so of its spine shows from beneath stacks of old bills. I pull it out and study the cover, but there is no title. It's bound in leather, though it's flaking off in small pieces from the spine to reveal a decaying, powdery fabric beneath.

As I open the book, several pages of an old telephone

directory that had been placed loose within the cover fall to the desk. I ignore them and turn to the book's inside cover where I see the handwritten name of Patrick O'Riley. It is dated 1931. Below the date is an address in Parkside, a few miles from where I live. As I turn the pages, I see notes and hand-drawn pictures. The penmanship is hard to read, but the pages include detailed drawings and cross sections of the Golden Gate, like it could be a forgotten engineering journal of the bridge.

I search the desk and the shelves to see if I have missed other volumes, but all I see besides old bills are more directory pages. Many of the names are crossed off, and I recognize my father's handwriting in the margins.

"Not home, try later."

"Busy."

"Call back."

When I inspect the names closely, I see that every person he called, every name crossed out, every line with a notation by its side, is someone named O'Riley.

My eyes sting, but my heart races. I'm not sure, but I sense that I have just discovered something significant—either for the university or for myself.

I know I should go to bed, but instead I randomly turn the pages. What I see next causes my adrenaline to surge. There is a drawing of a cable, in particular a cross section of the thirty-six-inch cables that drape the towers. The picture is penned in ink and with intricate detail shows how the three-foot-diameter cables were wound of smaller strands, more than twenty-seven thousand in all. The drawings detail how the wire was pulled into one thick cable and then wrapped and banded to hold it intact. There are engineering calculations that note the strength of the cable, how it increases with each added strand. Below the pictures are words I've heard my father repeat often—my father's words, but written in the curious penmanship of a stranger.

"Together, we do the impossible. Like the cable that drapes from her towers, Strauss is joining men together to accomplish greatness. Indeed, we build an impossible bridge."

The words ring in my ears. "Together, we do the impossible." I can hear my father's voice as if he were speaking. I take deep breaths and reflect.

It had been difficult for my father to raise his daughter while holding down a full-time job on the bridge. Like most children and parents, we had our moments—times when each questioned if we'd make it. During those times, my father would often pause, take a similar deep breath, and say, "Sure it's hard, but, honey—together, we do the impossible." He would say it with conviction, as if he believed the words. And because he believed them, I believed them.

One time in particular, he even used an actual piece of cable from the bridge. I must have been eleven or twelve, already teenage-stubborn and making him crazy. After dinner he set the cable section on the table before me. It was tiny compared to other cables I'd seen on the bridge, but similar in design. It was about two inches in circumference, six inches long, and made up of many smaller strands twisted together in spiral fashion. When he removed the masking tape that held it together, the twisted pieces fell into a pile of corkscrew pick-up sticks. He told me it was a game, and that I needed to fit the curled pieces back together into a single cable. I tried on my own for a few minutes without much success, and then together we pieced them into one and secured the tape. He explained that the huge cable draping the bridge was no different. It was simply a bunch of smaller cables wound together to make one giant cable, capable of holding up tons of concrete, miles of steel, and hundreds of cars.

He said that people are the same as the cable. We can't make it by ourselves because we aren't strong enough, but if we unite with others, there will be enough common strength. He took my hand and said, "Katie, let's work together, let's get through this. We'll be like the cable pulling together—doing what we aren't strong enough to do on our own. Believe me, honey . . . together, we can do the impossible."

chapter nine

Dave arrived twenty minutes late for the meeting already in progress. He straightened his tie on the way to his secretary's desk.

"Gloria, sorry I'm late. Do you have the voter cross-tab study?"

"Ms. Brewer picked it up already. She's with the client."

Dave exhaled a lonely breath and headed for the conference-room door. He touched the handle, hesitated, and then pushed himself inside.

His boss was conducting the meeting. Abel Lawless sat at Ellen's right. Dave acknowledged both.

"I apologize. Traffic was heavy."

Ellen covered. "No problem. I understand there was an accident in the tunnel. Several other staff members are stuck as well."

Dave didn't mention that he'd driven the long way, over the bridge. He knew nothing about conditions in the Lincoln Tunnel.

As the lead in charge of the new account, Dave should have been directing the meeting. He let Ellen continue.

"I was just filling Abel in on the results of our focus group," she said. "So, as you can see, Abel, the majority of those who vote consistently, year after year, also attend at least one other annual community activity . . . "

The house was a mess. Was it today or tomorrow that the cleaning lady was scheduled to come? Dave tried to remember but couldn't. He'd told her to just tidy up the place—dust, vacuum, light cleaning only; *I want to save the deep cleaning for later.* By "deep cleaning," she had presumed he meant waxing floors, vacuuming drapes, jobs normally done once a year. But Dave meant something else altogether. Closets needed to be emptied, clothes needed to be boxed up, personal items needed to be stored or discarded.

"So, what is your assessment of the numbers, Dave?" Ellen repeated. Dave had let his mind drift again, didn't know how to answer, what to say. He wanted to stand up and shout that it was just another senseless study—that it didn't matter—that tomorrow, not a soul in the accursed room would care about the useless data.

"I apologize, Ellen, Abel," he addressed both, "I haven't been feeling well. Could you excuse me?" With a nod, he stood up, hurried to the door, and left the room.

• • •

Most local ball games were held at the community complex near the town center. The championship game was to be played at Barton Field, just out of Lakewood. It was slated to start at eight p.m. Dave arrived ten minutes early. The team would already be on the field stretching, practicing.

Swing level, Brad. Keep your back elbow up. Be patient. Don't swing at anything out of the zone.

He'd wanted to be there for the team, but after the accident he'd been laid up for days. He still had occasional shoulder pain, but his cuts were healing. He had promised that as soon as he felt better, as soon as he was at a hundred percent, he would be back.

When Kevin and the boys from the team stood on his porch earlier in the week, he'd decided it was time. What better occasion than the championship game?

If the pitch comes in high, Brad, let it go. Attack the ball, connect, and follow through.

Cars arrived. People laughed as they carried coolers and blankets into the stadium. Dave stayed anchored behind the wheel.

The other coaches had stepped right in and done an excellent job. The boys should be proud: they were the regional champions, after all, perhaps state champions after tonight. The team had only been together for three seasons. Who would have guessed they could pull it together so quickly? Win or lose, they should celebrate tonight.

The shortstop is playing too close, Brad, so if you pop it over his head, you're on base for sure. Keep your elbow up and swing through.

From his car Dave watched the stadium lights come on. The sun wouldn't set for another half hour, but for the big games they always turned them on early to give the halogen-filled bulbs time to reach their final temperature and offer the maximum light. At such a beautiful facility the grass would be cut short and nicely groomed. Dave hoped the hype and the allure of playing on such a large field wouldn't throw off the team's game. Soon the national anthem was echoing across the arena.

There are two outs, Brad, so Kevin will run on anything. Bring him home, son. And watch the fastball. This kid can throw.

The announcer's voice rumbled through the rolled-up windows. Latecomers scurried from hastily parked cars to awaiting bleachers.

Coach, we'd like to dedicate the game to Brad . . . the game to Brad . . . to Brad.

"Congratulations, guys, you deserve it," Dave muttered aloud. He let his wounded gaze drift away in the direction of the setting sun. "And I'm sorry, Brad."

He twisted the key, giving the engine life. Without glancing back toward the cheers rising from the stands, Dave exited the luminous stadium lot, turned right on Coast Road, and faded quietly into the welcoming shadows of the night.

A quarter of the way through the pages, amidst many scribbled notes and calculations, I find another bit of wisdom from my father—again written by Patrick O'Riley.

The words are sandwiched among engineering notes detailing the bridge's strength—interesting facts that I've heard my father recite. The bridge, he said, is designed to hold four thousand pounds of weight per linear foot, a figure derived by estimating the bridge load when packed bumper to bumper with the heaviest cars made at the time—Cadillacs, Packards, and Buicks. Of course, not everyone drove heavy cars, and there would be space, perhaps ten to twenty feet, between each as they crossed. And yet the worst-case scenario was used and then increased again by a fourth.

I can see in the notes where Mr. Patrick O'Riley summarized calculations for the towers, the trestles, and the piers. In every case, they were overengineered, designed for the worst that could possibly happen. Below his calculations, he wrote, "In life, always overengineer."

No further explanation. I've heard the lesson from my father as one of his infamous "Lessons from the Bridge."

"Quite simply, Katie," he would say, "plan for the very worst, then pray for the very best. Savor the days when the sun shines, but have your raincoat and boots ready for the storms that will always blow in from the bay."

His wisdom is sound. In the years since the bridge was completed, calamities have come—violent storms, devastating earthquakes—and through them all, the bridge has remained strong and true.

I can almost hear my father's voice. "Katie, in life, always overengineer."

I wish I had listened more closely.

Habits are born of repetition. They cause ruts in our road that either guide us for good or push us toward peril. Many habits are neither good nor bad, but simply paths worn so deep from repeated actions that our ruts become furrows, and furrows become canyons. Changing course, venturing off in new directions, finding new experience, can be arduous if not impossible.

As Dave studied his unkempt reflection in the mirror, he realized that Megan had been the only one to cut his hair for the last seventeen years. He wasn't sure where she had learned—from college roommates, perhaps. No matter . . . now that she was gone, Dave didn't know where to go, how much it should cost, or how to explain to a stranger how his hair should be cut. The simple truth was that he hadn't found the courage.

Brock was the first to say something over lunch. "Are you going for the ponytail look?"

"Something like that."

Brock pressed the issue. "Much longer and I'll have to braid it for you."

When Dave didn't answer, Brock got straight to the point. "Look, I have to tell you: Ellen mentioned it to me the other day. Thought you should know."

"Ellen complained about my hair?"

"Didn't complain, really, just wondered about it, about how you were doing."

"It's none of her damn business."

"Hey, take it easy. I don't think she meant anything by it. She's just being the boss, that's all."

"My hair is not her concern."

"Are you okay?"

They'd had the *are-you-okay* conversation before. Dave had always assured Brock that he would get through it, that he was fine. Today he couldn't keep up the façade.

"I've gotta get out of here. We'll talk later." He snatched his briefcase and stormed out the door.

• • •

The meeting in Ellen's office started at seven, early enough that Dave hadn't yet arrived. He wasn't invited.

Ellen's hands helped her words do the talking. "I don't know what to do for him, Brock. I mean, I'm truly sorry. I can't imagine what he's gone through . . . what he's still going through. But, at the same time, I have a business to run. What am I supposed to do?"

"Look, things are still rough, but I think he's improving." Brock faked optimism. Ellen didn't buy it.

"Improving? You should have seen him with Abel from the governor's office. Dave was in la-la land. When he left the room, Abel was dumbfounded. This is our most important political account and he's blowing it!"

"Let me talk to him again."

"He needs more than talk, Brock. He needs professional help. I'm telling you, we're losing him."

"I said I'd talk to him. Do you need me to take over the account?"

"Do you have the time?"

"I'll make time."

Ellen tipped her head as she considered the offer. She generally didn't take such a personal role with clients, but she'd stepped in to help cover Dave's accounts. "Thanks, Brock. You're my best lead. Just get Dave back. I can't afford to lose him."

Brock couldn't tell if Ellen was more concerned about losing a friend or an employee. Perhaps it didn't matter.

"I'll take care of it," he told her. "Just give me a few more days."

• • •

It was close to midnight when Dave heard pounding on his door. Whoever it was would know he was up—almost every light in the house was on. Before even touching the knob, he guessed who was standing on the other side.

"Hey, Brock, come in. You want a drink?"

Brock nodded. "How you doing?"

"Surviving." Dave pulled open the fridge door. "Let's see— I've got water, milk, or umm, water. Sorry, I guess I need to get to the store."

"Actually, I changed my mind. Forget the drink." Brock pulled out a chair from the kitchen table and sat down. It was clear that he hadn't come to be sociable.

Dave grabbed a glass from the cupboard and filled it half full of water from the sink—not because he was thirsty, but rather to give himself something to hold. No small talk was needed. He didn't wait for Brock. He could already see what was coming. "You want the truth?"

"We're friends. I think we both deserve it."

"I can't remember anyone but Megan cutting my hair."

If there was tension in the air, it was shamed silently away by compassion. It felt like minutes before Brock spoke. "Listen, I understand what you're saying. Let me set up an appointment with Sharon. She does mine. I realize it's a scary thought going to the same woman who cuts my hair, but you'll like her. I may even have her home number." He reached for his phone.

"I can wait. It might be a bit late to call tonight."

"You don't know Sharon." Brock quipped, before perhaps realizing Dave was right. "I'll call her tomorrow, let her know you'll be setting something up."

"Okay, thank you."

Even in the weary light, Dave hoped Brock could read his gratitude. He must have, because Brock stood and reached out his hand. The man looked downright pleased at his efforts. "Perfect! Anything else I can do to help?" Brock's tone welcomed back levity into the room.

"No, I'm good."

"Really? I had no idea it was this easy. I should have been a social worker."

It was the first time Dave had smiled since Brock had arrived. "I just need some time," he confirmed.

"Are you coming in tomorrow?" Brock asked.

"I'd better. If not, Gloria's going to move her stuff into my office."

Brock shrugged. "Women are funny about men showing up. Why is that?" He didn't let Dave answer before he continued, "So, haircut tomorrow?"

"Yeah, tomorrow for sure."

chapter ten

The more I study the journal, the more I learn about Patrick O'Riley, the man. His writing spanned a period of almost six years, from late 1931 to mid-1937, a time frame that corresponds to the bridge's construction. His early pages contain many engineering notes that seem to indicate his responsibilities on the bridge.

It is odd, though. When I search my reference books for the names of engineers who worked on the Golden Gate Bridge, I don't see the name Patrick O'Riley. A handful of fragmented comments from his journal may explain why.

"1931. Hired by McClain, a good gaffer. Odd jobs mostly 'til she begins." Later he writes, ". . . trying to keep up me skills, though most days spent welding."

The first reference to his possible work as an engineer reads, "I met a brilliant chap, Mr. Charles Ellis, and hope to soon be in his employ."

The name Ellis sounds familiar. I reference him in a book about the bridge and learn that Mr. Ellis, a senior engineer, is the man many historians credit over Joseph Strauss as the designer of the Golden Gate Bridge. I turn back to the journal and skim it further. The words are difficult to decipher, but as I do, I find another mention of the man. "I pray Mr. Ellis will see me skills as adequate. He is the most brilliant engineer I have ever known. It would be an honor to be in his employ. If God grants, I will reunite shortly with Anna and the wee ones again. 'Twill be sooner than planned."

I presume that Anna is his wife, and, with a name like O'Riley, I wonder if his family is in Ireland. As I peruse further, I find other notes that indicate his almost revered respect for Mr. Ellis.

"I met him again today, though he couldn't grant much time. He is working eighteen hours a day—but said he could hire me soon. Patience. I see Strauss bow in public, but 'tis Ellis who is the genius. The two are like chalk and cheese."

One other mention of a conversation with Ellis grabs my attention.

"I asked Ellis how he withstood the pressure of working with such brilliant men as Ammann and Moisseiff. His reply made me consider me own life—he said, 'O'Riley, excellence fosters excellence. They force me to be at my best, and the leap of excellence, once made, must be sustained.'"

I look up the names of Ammann and Moisseiff and find

they also worked as engineers on the bridge. Patrick's words ring true—I've heard them before from my father.

"Excellence fosters excellence, Katie," he would say. For this reason, he didn't object to my never-ending education. "You're surrounding yourself with good people—growing, learning, loving. Why not?"

Perhaps it was the fact that my father hadn't attended college himself. Perhaps he could read my trepidation of taking on the world. Either way, he never complained.

My curiosity about Ellis gets the better of my patience and I turn back to several history volumes. I learn that he served as the chief design engineer under Joseph Strauss but that the relationship between the two men seemed doomed from the start. While Ellis, a reserved academic, focused his energies on his work, on the soundness of the bridge design, Strauss, his boss, was overly concerned with getting credit. Most historians agree that although Ellis was unquestionably the more brilliant, Strauss was the one in charge. I shouldn't have been shocked, then, to find out that after Charles Ellis had worked tirelessly to deliver completed engineering calculations and a structural bridge design, and even before a shovelful of dirt had been turned, Joseph Strauss fired him.

I wonder how Patrick O'Riley reacted to the firing of the man he so admired, a man with whom he had hoped to work. I note the date of the firing—a few days before Christmas, 1931, amidst a deep national economic depression. In Patrick's journal I find no mention of the event, only a single, poetic notation.

"My hopes are thrown into the blustery bay wind. Vanity

is victorious over virtue. 'Twill be longer than I had expected as Anna and the young ones mire in misery."

I scan the journal thoroughly, but find no further reference to Mr. Ellis.

Seven silver hoops outlined the right ear of the female cashier chatting with Brock from behind the counter. Her nose and eyebrows hadn't been forgotten either, all heavily pierced as well. He was killing time while Sharon finished with her current customer. According to the clock on the wall, Dave was six minutes late. Brock excused himself to check his phone. No reply to the text messages he'd sent to Dave.

"Hi, handsome," Sharon purred as she approached.

"Hey, beautiful. You look astonishing," Brock replied.

Sharon laughed as she brushed away strands of black hair still sticking to her white blouse.

"Am I doing you today?" she questioned, not having checked her schedule.

"I wish," he replied, "but my buddy needs a cut worse than I do. And you have to be gentle with him."

"Is it the guy who lost his wife?"

"Same one, and I mean it—go easy on him."

"Not a problem. Where is he?"

"He'll be here." Brock dialed Dave again. Voice mail picked up.

"Hope he's not too late," she added. "I'm booked solid today, and I hate making customers wait."

"Don't worry," Brock assured. "He'll be here. I promise. Any second he'll be here."

• • •

Dave sat alone in his office. Brock didn't knock.

"Hi, bud. I missed you this morning."

Dave's eyebrows rose, his eyes widened, he glanced at his watch. "Oh, that's right . . . the haircut. I'm sorry, I forgot."

Dave's phone was sitting on the desk; Brock tapped it with his finger, hard enough to make a noticeable thud. "And you didn't hear your phone ringing? I only called thirty gazillion times."

When Brock wasn't buying, Dave's surprise turned into a shrug. He no longer cared. "Sorry. I couldn't make it. I had some things come up."

Brock pulled a chair up to the desk. He turned it around and straddled it backwards, resting his arms on the back.

"Dave, I'm going to get in trouble for what I'm about to say."

"About what?"

"Look, I'm just apologizing in advance. But if I'm going to be a true friend and not just a drinking buddy, then there are some things that need to be said." It was a side of Brock that Dave had seldom seen, and he felt his teeth clench in response. He looked first at the door, then back to Brock. "Say it, then," Dave demanded, his tone turning defensive.

"Meg, Brad, Brittany, and Angel . . . they're gone, Dave, and they aren't coming back. It's been weeks, even months, and you're not getting better. Truth is, you look like hell. You need to get some help."

"You have no idea what I've been through!"

"That's true, and I pray that I never do. But if I ever have to go through anything even half as bad, then I hope you'll be as good a friend to me."

Dave didn't answer, and Brock wasn't ready to stop. "Look, I'm not saying that you need to paste a smile on your face all the time. I'm not saying that you need to party every night. What I *am* saying is that it's time to face the situation. If you can't do it on your own, then let's find someone who can help."

Dave wanted to run—to storm out of the office. Instead, he sat like a statue, motionless and cold. After seconds had passed, his troubled eyes peered up. "Reality sucks," he said.

"Yeah, I can't argue with that, sometimes it does," Brock answered. "But even so, there are times I envy you."

"Envy me? I've lost everything! Don't be stupid!"

"I'm not saying that I envy what you've been through; nobody would suggest that. I'm talking about what you had before the accident—your wife, your children. I mean, look at me. I know I act as if life is Disneyland all the time, but the truth is that I've never had anyone close in my life, nobody who truly cared for me—maybe never will."

"You want me to feel sorry for you, then? Is that what this is about?"

"No, I just want you to realize that while you're feeling pretty lousy right now, life is a whole lot better than you're making it out to be."

It was evident that, in Brock's own way, he was trying to help.

"Look, Brock, I'm sorry I missed the appointment. I'll do better."

Brock hesitated, seeming to weigh whether he should keep going. "As long as we're having this heart-to-heart, I'll tell it to you straight. Your work is suffering—Ellen doesn't know what to do with you."

"Is she going to fire me?"

"No. Not yet, anyway. Just take a deep breath and get on with it, man. You still have a helluva life ahead of you. And hey, get a haircut, you're scaring me."

chapter eleven

I eat my lunch every day in the park next to the history build-ing because the grassy lawn and walkways there are always filled with students and teachers. It's the perfect spot to study strangers.

People-watching is a curious habit—like being a spectator in a human zoo. As strangers pass today, I wonder about fate. I wonder about the ways lives intersect. I wonder about the part that fate plays. For example, take those walking past. They don't see me; they don't even realize I exist. So, what if "Mr. Right" walks past and, just as he steps in front of me, I sneeze, and he turns and notices me and says hello, and we talk, and then get together—and so from one simple sneeze, two strangers' lives change forever. If this is how life works, then I'm terrified because what happens if he walks by and I don't sneeze?

Besides worrying about sneezes, I often make up games. Today I'm guessing people's careers. The older man with graying hair pulled back into a ponytail is no doubt an artist—a painter of modern art, to be more specific. The woman wearing too much makeup walking close behind, eyeing him, she works for . . . a cosmetic surgeon. The man with the briefcase and the tie, well, he must be the CEO of a multinational conglomerate that makes, let's see . . . tongue depressors.

Other days I'll match faces to celebrities, playing a separated-at-birth game. It's amazing how many people do look like the rich and famous. Just two days ago, for example, I swear that Paul Walker walked past. It wasn't him, of course, since he's dead. But it was still exciting.

No matter the game, I'm always curious about other people's lives. If I see a man or a woman sitting on a bench alone, and if I have a chance to study him or her closely, I often begin to interrogate the person in my mind. Are you married? Do you have children? Do you also stay up late to watch old black-and-white movies? Do you sometimes eat cold pizza for breakfast? Have you also been betrayed by someone you love? What makes you laugh, or cry? And most important, through it all, do you still hold dreams in your heart?

I also wonder about people when I visit the bridge, when I stand at the railing and peer over the side at the water, when I see the darkness of the waves rolling two hundred and twenty feet below the deck—at these times I also question how the lives of strangers intersect.

What about the people my father saved? Are they now mothers and fathers? Do they have honest jobs and are they trying to raise their children to have a better life? Are they still on drugs, or depressed, or angry? Are they even still alive, or did they find some other way to accomplish their dreadful deed? Mostly, I wonder if they've ever realized the goodness of the man who saved them. Do they understand that they ultimately took away the only person who ever mattered in my life?

I wonder if it was destiny that my father was there to save them, and if it was, then what about the man who pulled my father off the bridge? Did God play a part in that as well? I wonder if the whole thing could have been stopped. I wonder: if the man who killed my father could have been distracted, even for a second, would the outcome have been different? I wonder what would have happened if, at just the right moment, my father had sneezed.

It was dark when Dave entered the building. It was better that way. He preferred working on his projects at night, when it was easier to think, when there were no distractions.

Remnants of a cleaning crew clanked distant garbage cans, though he could see no one. They were like mice, working by night, vanishing by the light of day.

An older Hispanic woman cleaned the floor where Dave worked. He had run into her on occasion when he'd stayed late. One night she'd been humming, but stopped when Dave entered his office. She'd seemed apprehensive, even frightened. He'd tried to ease her discomfort by chatting, but it proved difficult. She wouldn't look him in the eye; she fidgeted incessantly; and she always nodded in the affirmative, no matter what question was asked.

Now he could empathize. It was so exhausting to function, to concentrate, in an office full of people who were whispering about the *guy-who-lost-his-wife-and-children.*

Dave looked over his desk at the deepening piles of work. It was always the same: he would vow to improve, promise to hit the job and life with a new attitude first thing in the morning. But, as with most silent pacts, promise proved easier than performance. Tonight was no exception.

After twenty minutes of tossing paper clips into the garbage can across the room, Dave stretched through the guilt and stood. He was self-destructing and he knew it. He just didn't know how to stop. He wanted to stay, to make an effort, but the walls were closing in and his breathing was becoming labored. He grabbed his coat and headed toward the exit. He would come in early tomorrow instead to finish his reports.

As he waited for the elevator to slide open, he noticed light peeking out from under the door of Brock's office. He walked toward it.

"Hello?"

He tapped lightly and then pushed the door open. There was no sound, no one inside. The light must have been left on by accident, or perhaps the cleaning woman wasn't finished. He checked the garbage—empty. She'd already made her rounds.

Brock had been a good friend, better than Dave might have been had the tables been turned. Dave would never have had the guts to say what Brock had said, wrong or not. As Dave reached for the light switch, he noticed a stack of mail on the chair. It was the letter on top that caught his eye. He picked it off the pile and studied it: standard business size, starched white color. What captivated Dave was the graphic on the envelope's corner, the brazen orange-and-black outline of a customized Harley-Davidson road bike.

In the protection of both silence and solitude, Dave let his finger trace the outline of the machine.

"What dreams are you missing out on?"

"You won't laugh?"

"I probably will, but tell me anyway."

"I've always wanted to buy a motorcycle and ride across the country."

"A motorcycle? Like a Harley?"

When he turned the letter over to check the postmark, he noticed that the envelope had already been sliced open. He listened again for any sounds from the office—the stillness confirmed he was alone. He pulled the folded paper from its sleeve, spread it flat, and began to read.

It was addressed to Ellen but had been copied to Brock.

Dear Ms. Brewer,

It was a pleasure speaking with you last week. As I mentioned, I've heard wonderful things about your firm. It turns out you're actually not far from our location in York.

As the nation's largest customizer of Harley-Davidson, Indian, BMW, Ducati, and other major motorcycle brands, I'd like to hear how your research can improve the impact of our ongoing national expansion.

While it's true that we take good products and make them remarkable, we'd like to better understand the demographics and purchasing habits of our clients. It's not enough to create the most sought-after customized bikes in the marketplace. We need to maximize our advertising budgets by increasing our customer understanding.

We can discuss our needs further at our meeting a week from Monday when I arrive.

> Sincerely,
> Shaun Safford
> Vice President, Marketing
> BikeHouse Custom Motorcycles

• • •

It was after one a.m. when Brock arrived home. Dave was perched on his entrance steps.

"It's about time."

"Dave? What are you doing here?"

"You dropped by my house late at night. I'm returning the favor. I'm just glad you showed. I was getting nervous that you were at a sleepover."

"Are you okay?" Brock asked.

"Do you have a second to talk?"

"Sure, let's go inside."

Dave didn't wait. "Listen, I need to know about this." He held out the envelope he'd retrieved from Brock's office.

Brock took the letter, squinted. "You've been going through my mail? Have you been drinking?"

"Just water. Why wasn't I told about this account?"

Brock plopped down on the step next to Dave. "You haven't exactly been around much lately." He let his words hang. "Where were you today, for example?"

"Point taken."

"Why do you care about this account, anyway?" Brock asked.

At the very moment I crossed the bridge, I'd have experienced the best that life had to offer. I'd have lived my dream. I'd have arrived. "I'm just interested. Do you think Ellen will let me work on it?"

Brock shook his head. "We don't even have the account yet. And when we do, it will only need one lead. Dave, you've been so . . . distant. The truth is, you'd be lucky if she let you blink on your own right now—and rightly so."

Dave knew Brock was right, but he didn't care. "If I can convince Ellen, will you let me take the account?"

Brock laughed, then moved closer. "Buddy, I'm swamped. I'd love to give it up, but honestly, I don't think you're ready."

Dave fidgeted. How could he convince him? How much should he tell him?

Brock spoke before he could decide. "I recognize that look."

"What look?" Dave asked.

"Your mind going a million miles an hour working through a problem, tracing out every possible path. I have to say, that's a look that I haven't seen in quite a while."

"I need this account, Brock."

"The only difference is that tonight you also seem a bit giddy—or desperate. Are you taking anything?"

"What?"

"You know. Drugs."

"No, of course not."

"Let me smell your breath," Brock said. It was Dave's turn to laugh. Brock leaned back. "I haven't heard you laugh like that in weeks."

Dave shrugged it off—this was working. "Brock, I'm telling you, I can handle it. I can."

Brock offered a pat on the shoulder, the kind a father might give a son. "Look, the meeting with BikeHouse isn't scheduled until a week from Monday. Clean yourself up. Get a haircut. Then talk to Ellen. What's the worst she can say?"

"Then it's okay with you?"

Brock nodded. "I'm warning you, though, there's no way you'll convince her. But if you want to give it a shot, I'll back you."

In the deep recesses of his brain, Dave began to plan his strategy. As he did, it invited questions. Why was he so intrigued? Did this client come along as a coincidence, or was there something more happening here? The possibility had crossed his mind that he might be losing it mentally, that he could be drifting over the edge. There was no reason to be so excited, so hopeful over one silly account—other than the fact that every time he thought about BikeHouse, Megan's words echoed in his head.

One problem existed—his boss still stood in the way.

chapter twelve

Desperate men take desperate measures, or so the saying goes. Dave didn't feel desperate, simply reaching—hoping to grasp something that would pull him away from the edge of the cliff, anything that would help him make sense out of the recent events in his life.

He leaned against the glass of the fourth-story office window and scanned the street. Ellen always arrived early, so it was no surprise at six-fifteen to see her green Mercedes approach the building and wait for the gate to lift open.

Dave knew it was a habit that drove her husband crazy, as the man would often voice his loud disdain at company gatherings, especially after he'd sipped a few too many drinks. "You're the boss," he'd insist to his wife. "You don't need to get there early." Ellen had confided in Dave on several occasions that her being the boss was exactly the reason she did.

Dave hurried to his own office and waited for the elevator to ring its arrival on the floor. Once it did, he gave Ellen ten more minutes to settle in before he tapped on the door.

"Dave?" Her surprise appeared genuine.

"Good morning."

Ellen stood, shook Dave's hand, and then motioned for him to sit. For the meeting Dave had chosen his best suit—a black Armani and jacquard tie, both draped effortlessly. He wished he'd had time to get the jacket professionally pressed, but he'd had to settle for an early-morning ironing at home. Despite the rush, he wore the clothes well, with power and confidence. Other than his longer-than-average hair, Dave looked . . . *normal.*

"Why so early?" she asked.

Dave had planned his words carefully. There was no bluffing on this one. From the outset he'd decided to get straight to the point.

"Brock told me about BikeHouse." Dave left out the details of filtering through Brock's mail. Ellen nodded, waiting for him to finish. "Brock is swamped with—" Not what he'd wanted to say. The truth was that Brock was swamped with the work that Dave should have been doing. "I'd like to help out by taking on the account."

Dave sat tall in his chair and tried to look confident, as if it were his first interview at the firm.

"The BikeHouse account?" Ellen leaned closer. "Your plate is already full, Dave. How's your own workload coming?"

Dave understood the real question. "I'm doing better as of late . . . much better."

She didn't seem to buy it. "Dave, where were you three days last week—yesterday, even?"

Just like her not to miss a thing. What would sway her? "I'm here today."

Her head bobbed in agreement. "I still think you ought to get your current accounts under control, and then we can get you going on other things."

Dave stood. He couldn't get emotional. It may bring sympathy, but not the account. He turned, then took a deep breath.

"Ellen, listen to me. I've been to hell and back." He paused. "Actually, I guess the jury is still out on whether I'm really back. It's been rough, and I'm sorry for the way that I've acted."

"Dave, I'm not asking for an apology."

"I know, but I owe you one. I do. I've let you down, I've let Brock down, I've let the entire company down—and then there's myself."

"I have to ask . . . what's the big deal with BikeHouse?"

How to answer? What should he tell her? The truth? "Ellen, it's a personal thing."

"Personal? What do you mean?"

What dreams have you been missing out on, honey? What dreams?

"Megan . . . well, Megan would tease me about riding a Harley. We'd joke about it. I always told her that I'd like to ride one someday."

If Ellen had been attempting to contain her flow of confusion, the dam had now burst. Dave tensed. He didn't mean it to sound so ungrounded, so sentimental.

"Dave, I appreciate your enthusiasm. And I have to tell you that I haven't seen you this excited about an account for . . . well, for months."

Dave waited.

"But my answer is still no. Not yet."

Possibilities shot through Dave's head. He could threaten to quit. Would she risk losing him? Probably. Did Dave care? Not about the job, not lately—but that was before BikeHouse had rolled into the picture. What to do? He'd already expressed his interest. Perhaps he should just back off and wait.

"You're right."

Ellen tipped her head back, seeming surprised by the retreat. Dave walked toward the door. He touched the handle.

"Listen, Dave," Ellen said.

Dave stopped, turned, waited. She opened her desk and fumbled through some cards. "I've been waiting for the right time to give this to you. I've been asking around, and I'd like you to go and visit this person, Dr. Devyn Jaspers. He comes highly recommended." She stood, stepped forward, and held out the card.

Dave took it politely and then stared at the name. "A shrink?"

"Of sorts. He's a grief counselor. He helps people who have experienced . . . you know, a loss." Dave listened. "You go see Devyn, the firm will pick up the tab. Keep improving, and you just may get the account."

"Thank you, Ellen."

"I hope that he'll do you some good, and then you can do me some good." Always a boss.

"When's the first meeting with BikeHouse?" Dave asked.

"We have our introduction a week from Monday." She paused thoughtfully. "Tell you what—why don't you plan to be there? We'll play it by ear. If you've seen Dr. Jaspers, if things go well at the meeting, if you show me that the old Dave Riley is indeed back, then BikeHouse will be yours."

Dave shook her hand, gripping it tightly. He still had a shot.

"The ol' Dave Riley will be there. I promise." He walked confidently to his office. Gloria was not yet in. He took off his jacket and hung it on a wall hook just inside. He closed the office door. He still had a chance, still had hope. After he'd checked the lock, he sank into his chair, rested his head on the desk, and with a silk handkerchief pressed tightly against his mouth to muffle the sound, he quietly began to sob.

I don't pretend to be fast in my research, but I am thorough. It's the reason the professor hired me. The trait was ingrained in me at an early age, another lesson from my father. "Katie, if you're going to do a job, do it right."

I don't find his exact words in the journal, but I see notes from Patrick that foreshadow my father's expression.

"We are spinning cable on the bridge faster than it's ever been spun in the history of bridge building—many times faster. 'Tis a tense and contradictory job. If we don't finish the cable by July,

Roebling says the firm will lose money. Yet speed must be balanced by quality. As Strauss says, it's a bridge to last 'forever.' I can't disagree, and so for the balance between speed and quality, I let me own scale tip toward the latter. We must do the job right."

It is a lesson that brims with my father's wisdom, and it makes me wonder: who was this man, and why did my father have his journal?

The receptionist flashed Dave the customary smile as she pushed the clipboard in his direction. "Please fill in the pertinent information," she said.

He carried the forms to a seat in the waiting room that greeted him with bright walls, customary magazines, and vases of fresh flowers. With the exception of an older woman asleep in a chair, it was almost homey.

Within minutes, the same receptionist stepped out and announced, "Mr. Riley, the doctor will see you now. Please come with me."

He followed her down the hall and into the doctor's office. Vibrant artwork lined two of the office walls; he realized it was all meant to cheer up depressed clients.

"Mr. Riley?" The doctor held out her hand. "I'm Devyn Jaspers. It's a pleasure to meet you."

He shook the woman's hand, trying to hide his confusion. The receptionist placed the clipboard on the doctor's desk and scurried out.

"You look perplexed."

"I'm sorry." Dave let go of her hand and stepped back. "I just thought—well, I thought Devyn Jaspers was . . . a man."

Her nod was one of understanding. "Yes, I get that a lot. It's my mother's fault, and I'll never forgive her."

She motioned to the chair opposite her desk, and they both sat. He watched intently as she scanned his information. She reminded him of a patron studying a restaurant menu, not sure what to order. He had to handle this properly, assure the outcome. The fact that she was a woman could complicate things . . . or would it help?

He studied her as she flipped the pages: perhaps early forties, though difficult to judge with her hair pulled back; organized desk—almost too organized. She sat back as she read, slightly relaxed, evident she was in no rush.

"Would you like me to call you Mr. Riley or David?" she finally asked.

As long as he could remember, everyone had called him Dave. "David will be fine."

She scribbled it into her notes. "Thank you, I appreciate that. And call me Devyn or Dr. Jaspers, whichever you prefer."

"Thank you, Doctor."

"Why don't we start with a little background. Tell me about yourself."

"Aren't I supposed to lie on a couch or something?"

"A couch? I'm sorry. All I have is the chair. Is it not comfortable?"

"Quite comfortable. I just thought—" He shrugged off the thought. "What would you like to know?"

"How long were you married?" It was a simple question with a simple answer, but in a curious way it struck him to the core. She'd asked it in the past tense, as if to imply that the marriage was over.

"I have been married for eighteen years."

"How old were your children?" She'd done it again. How could she be so cold? He looked up without answering, his hesitation obvious. "Are you uncomfortable talking about the accident?" she asked.

"Shouldn't I be?"

"I want to start by saying that I'm very sorry."

"Yeah, so am I."

"David, you've had a loss that most people can't even imagine. My job is to help you get through the grieving process in the most manageable way possible. It won't be easy. It never is, but if you'll try, you will get through this." He shifted in his chair as she continued. "Have you talked much about the accident with family or friends?"

Megan had been his confidante—they had discussed everything. Now she was gone. Who could have replaced her?

Dr. Jaspers tipped her head to the side, as if anticipating Dave's response before he had even moved his lips. "So you don't have family? No support at all?"

"I'm an only child."

"Friends?"

"I have associates—Brock is my friend."

"Have you talked with Brock about the accident, about your grief?"

"Briefly. He's never lost anyone. In fact, he's never been with anyone long enough—well, he could never understand."

"You should give him a chance. It will help if you talk with others about your loss, share your feelings."

This was their first meeting—what did she know about his friends or his feelings? He had lost his wife and family, and she had the nerve to sit across from him in a padded chair and suggest that all he needed to do was talk. He studied her face more carefully. Younger than forty—thirty-five, perhaps. How much experience could she have?

"I'm just curious—are you married?" he asked coldly. He wanted to control the flow of the meeting, manipulate its outcome. He could feel his emotions taking charge.

"No, I'm not."

"Divorced?"

"No, I've never been married."

"I should hook you up with Brock." His tone mocked.

"David, I'm here to help you. I'd like to be your friend."

Friend—the word irritated. He'd barely met the woman. They certainly weren't friends. "Can I be brutally honest?" Dave asked.

"If you don't mind."

"I see grief as something I need to deal with on my own, not pawn off on friends—or worse, strangers. If you want the honest truth, Doctor, I'm here so that Ellen, my boss, will give me an account at work, an account I need to move forward with my life. Grief is my responsibility—not yours, not my friends'—mine."

After the words had spilled out, he was angry at himself for having betrayed his motives. He'd wanted to remain in control and he'd blown it.

"Forced into it?"

"No gun, but essentially, yes."

"I take it that your work is suffering?"

"What do you think?"

She ignored the question. "In what ways, exactly?"

He wished that he could stand up and walk out, even slam the door on his exit, but his boss would certainly find out. Instead, he took a deep breath and closed his eyes.

"Tired. I feel tired. I drive around late at night. I oversleep, show up late. I find my thoughts constantly wandering. I can't concentrate. I watch people bickering at the office about petty things that don't matter and it makes me want to scream."

"Grieving can be exhausting." She made a note on her pad, then put down her pen. "I can help you get through what you're feeling right now, David. I can't take it away or make it disappear, but if you'll work with me, I can soften, perhaps even shorten, your grieving process. I need your help . . . if you'll let me."

One minute she was so clinical, so cold—now instantly sincere. Sincere? He pondered the word. It was her job to be sincere; it was her job to pretend.

She waited to speak again until he looked directly at her. "You said earlier that your friend Brock has never truly loved someone, and so he doesn't know what it means to experience true loss. Then you asked if I'd ever been married. I understand your meaning, what you were implying. You need to know, David, that I *do* know what it feels like to lose someone."

Her directness caught him off guard, and he regretted his harshness. She continued. "I can never know exactly what you are feeling—no one can—and in that aspect, you are indeed standing all alone. But don't you dare think for a moment that I don't care or that I can't empathize."

"I didn't mean it to come out that way."

After a long, almost painful moment, she spoke words that seemed to carry extra sadness. "David, I'd like you to take as much time as you need, but tell me all about Megan—why you loved her, why you miss her. Then, when you're finished, I'll tell you a little about Jonathan and my loss as well."

chapter thirteen

I should be working on the society's report, but instead spend hours studying the journal. Before bed, I continue to read Patrick O'Riley's words.

"I'm working with a team of lads, hard and calloused men, on the Marin tower. Today a fierce storm far out at sea caused tremendous swells to roll into the bay, swells that caused the tower to pitch and sway.

"As the tower shifted, I grabbed a beam for support, then glanced at me men to see if I'd been betrayed by me terror as a coward. 'Twas odd, but I noticed the fear of death in their eyes as well. Later, in the pub, I asked Bull Myers about it, the most hardened of men. He grunted and said, 'A man without fear is a fool.' He is right. Men who deny fear, they take chances, do stupid things to prove valor.

"I no longer try to mask me fear. I see no shame to admit that the bridge scares the life from me. But what is even more frightful

is the thought of not holding Anna and the young ones in me arms again. And so as it grows heavenward, and I climb the tower day by day, me fear grows into courage and keeps me safe.

"Courageous men are not fearless men, but those who climb despite fear. Everyone has a bridge to climb. At the end of the day, fear and I shake hands and part knowing we'll meet again when we climb our bridge together."

As I read Patrick's words, I imagine the panic my own father must have felt working on the bridge. And yet, I don't remember ever seeing his fear. Oh, he'd tell me that work was forbidding, even terrifying, but I didn't notice it in his eyes—only in mine.

Since my father's death I have avoided towers, preferring to stay huddled on the ground. I wonder about uncertainties, my own swells and storms. Will I ever be as courageous as Patrick O'Riley, or as brave as my own father?

While the lesson is significant, it is Patrick's affection I find most stirring. Below his wisdom, in the margins of the page, Patrick often wrote thoughts of Anna. They are always apart from the engineering calculations, as if he didn't want their significance to be lost or confused. I don't pretend to understand their meaning, but two phrases cause reflection. They are haunting expressions, but words that carry strength.

"With this crown, I give my loyalty."

"With these hands, I promise to serve."

Ellen was reviewing financial charts on her computer when Dave tapped lightly on the door.

"Dave, come in. Listen, I just spoke with Abel at the governor's office. They said your conclusions on voter trends were right on the money. They've calculated a projected six percent increase in turnout next election cycle with limited resource outlays. They're talking about expanding the study."

"That's great." Dave tried to sound excited.

"You're not thrilled?" she asked.

"Of course I am. It's fabulous. Listen, I've been seeing Dr. Jaspers."

"Already?"

"Three times since we talked, counting this morning."

"Well, that's great. So, he's competent?"

"Of course. Our meetings are going well. I'm scheduled twice a week now for the next eight weeks. I just thought you should know."

Ellen nodded her approval. "Thanks, Dave—and have him bill the firm directly if insurance doesn't cover it."

Dave paused at the door. "You've never met the doctor, have you?"

"No. A friend gave me the card and said he was terrific. Why do you ask?"

"The *he* is actually a *she*."

"He's a woman?"

As his boss shrugged with surprise, Dave reiterated the

message he had come to deliver. "She's helping me. I'm doing much better. I just wanted you to know."

When Dave arrived back at his desk, he stopped just long enough to gather up some papers and his jacket.

"Gloria, I'll be out the rest of the day."

• • •

Dave hoped that his suit and tie wouldn't make him stand out like a tourist. As he approached the building, he regretted not having taken time to go home first and change. He knew, however, that if he was going to convince Ellen to let him handle the BikeHouse account, he'd need to learn everything he could about the company.

Long ago, he'd discovered that the most useful information about an organization always came from the people in the trenches, those working directly with the customer on the front line. The front line was exactly where he was headed.

He expected to find a rundown shop with a greasy mechanic or two milling about working on their hogs, something out of an *Easy Rider* movie. Instead, the showroom at the Lakeshore BikeHouse location was breathtaking.

It was more reminiscent of Las Vegas than of any biker movie scene. Rows of gleaming customized motorcycles stood in perfect symmetry, each basking in its own halogen spotlight. There were dozens of bikes, various makes and models, all immaculate and begging admiration. It wasn't a motorcycle shop, it was an art gallery—Michelangelo would have been in awe.

But there was more. Behind the bikes was a store within a store, an area brimming with black leather jackets, shirts, pullovers, sweaters, gloves, socks, and every other imaginable fashion accessory—all branded with popular motorcycle logos. Not only dazzling, it was bustling.

Dave slid quietly around the machines, hoping to not attract attention. His plan was to blend into the background and study the place before asking his questions.

"Hi, can I help you?"

The voice startled him. He'd been so involved in taking in the scene that he hadn't noticed the salesperson approaching from behind.

"Thanks, but right now I'm just looking."

"They are okay to touch."

"I beg your pardon?"

"The bikes. They're okay to touch. I mean, look at them. Have you ever seen anything more beautiful?"

Dave scanned the room. The guy had a point—the polished machines were waving for attention.

"I need to be honest with you . . ." Dave leaned over to read the salesman's tag.

"The name's Redd. Pleasure to meet you." He held out his hand and Dave shook it. Redd was a large, older man with a round face that matched fat fingers, but he shook hands with authority, or at least enthusiasm. He smiled behind a grey handlebar mustache turned up just enough on the ends to make him look like a circus ringmaster.

"Redd, I'm Dave Riley. It's nice to meet you, but actually, I'm not here to buy a bike. I'm here to do some market research. I don't want to waste your time."

Dave expected a look of disappointment or puzzlement. As near as he could tell, Redd showed neither.

"No waste of my time. I normally work in the shop or at the parts counter. I come out to the sales floor when the regular sales guys are busy." As if Dave's comments were just now registering, Redd paused. "Market research . . . what does that mean?"

Though his company technically hadn't landed the account, Dave decided that for the sake of easy explanation, he would pretend they had. "I work for Strategy Data; we're a marketing research and opinion firm. We've been hired by BikeHouse corporate, and, well . . . I'm here to learn more about the product."

"Corporate sent you?"

"Not exactly. I picked the closest location and came in on my own."

Redd seemed intrigued. "What do they want to research?"

The question was a fair one that Dave couldn't answer. He would be truthful. "I don't know yet; we haven't gone that far."

"Well, if they want to know about the bikes or the people who buy 'em, they can call me. I'll tell 'em what they need to know for a tenth of what they're paying you. No offense."

"None taken. So, you've ridden a road bike for a while?"

"As long as I can remember."

"Do you mind if I ask you some questions?"

"Not at all—I'm paid by the hour." When he flashed Dave a smile, a silver tooth glistened.

Dave began with a list of questions he'd been forming in his head on the way over. "Tell me about your customers. What type of person buys a customized motorcycle?"

Redd took the question seriously, carefully considering his explanation. "When you look at a person, you can't tell so much who's a longtime rider as who's *not*."

"What do you mean?"

"Well, take you, for example. I'd venture to say you've seldom been on a bike, customized or otherwise."

"Am I that obvious?"

"Well, look at you—you're scared to death." Redd swung his leg over the machine next to where they were standing and grabbed the handlebars. He looked more comfortable *on* the bike than *off.* "Now take a look at the guy there in the suit." Redd gestured to an older gentleman Dave had noticed earlier. "What would you guess about him?"

Dave shrugged. "He looks to me like a businessman killing time on his lunch hour."

Redd half-nodded. "He's a businessman all right, but don't let the suit fool you. That's Mason Weller; he's ridden in a club for years. He comes in from time to time just to check out the new inventory. Not all riders sport tattoos and leather, you know."

"Fair enough," Dave conceded. "Why do *you* ride?"

"Now, that's a different question altogether." Redd swung off the bike and motioned for Dave to follow him. They walked past the browsing customers and through a door marked *Employees Only*. In the back of the open warehouse, next to a partially opened garage door, sat a maroon and silver machine, polished like it was parade day.

"That's my baby." Redd talked like a proud father. "It's an '83, FXSB Wide Glide, Shovelhead engine, Girling rear disc brake, twin discs up front."

The words could have been Greek. Dave shrugged, half pretending to understand. However, it was Redd's next instruction that startled him.

"Get on."

"What?"

"You asked why I ride. I'm gonna show you."

Dave stepped back. "How about you just tell me?"

The remark caused Redd to laugh aloud. It was a jolly laugh, and had his clothes been red with a white beard attached, Dave could have imagined Redd working the mall in December.

"Look, I'd just hate to get grease on my pants," Dave added, attempting to save face.

Without uttering a word, Redd snatched a white rag from the adjacent counter. He spread it over his thick fingers and wiped it down one side of the shiny bike. Without looking at it, he held it up for Dave to see that there wasn't so much as a smudge.

Redd tossed the rag back onto the counter and turned back to Dave.

"Look, I'm not asking you to ride it; I just want you to feel the power of the engine." In a fluid motion Redd swept his leg over the bike, turned the key, and pressed the start button. The engine rumbled to life.

Dave raised his voice to make sure Redd could hear over the machine. "So you don't have to kick-start it?"

"Electric start." Redd stepped off, then motioned for Dave to swing onto the echoing bike. Dave climbed on, then settled down into the leather seat. It was more comfortable than he'd expected. He grabbed the handlebars and pulled the weight off the stand. As he did, Redd kicked the stand up into place against the frame.

"How does she feel?"

"Good." He couldn't deny it—the power that sat beneath him, at his command, was exhilarating, even intimidating. "So, is the clutch in the handle?" Dave posed the question more to make conversation than to suggest any intent to actually ride the machine.

Redd nodded. "You want to inch it forward, just to get the feel?"

"I'm all right, really."

"Come on, inch it forward."

It was either peer pressure or salesmanship at its finest. Dave hated to look foolish, so he nodded in the affirmative. Redd explained how to pull in the clutch and drop the bike into first gear.

"Just let it out slowly. Let it roll forward a few feet and then pull her back and apply the brake. It's simple."

When Dave eased off the clutch, he released the handle too quickly. The bike lurched forward, and Redd had to grab the machine to keep it from falling. Dave's cheeks flushed. He looked to

Redd expecting to see concern; instead, only excitement stared back—Redd had a new pupil.

"Did you feel that power? And this bike's nothing compared to a customized Dyna Wide Glide. That one will really get your legs excited, if you know what I mean."

Redd reached over, switched the key to off, and dropped down the kickstand. He was almost bouncing. Dave stepped off, happy to not embarrass himself further.

"So, you're saying it's the power of the bike that attracts people?" Dave asked, picking up the conversation where they'd left off in the showroom.

Redd's tone hushed. "Oh, these machines certainly have power, Dave, no question about it. But to answer honestly—no."

"Okay, then what?"

Redd glanced around the garage, as if he were about to reveal the wisdom of ages. "It's the freedom, Dave," he answered in a tone so reverently whispered he could have been in church.

"Freedom?"

"Sure."

"What do you mean?"

"We'll go riding together sometime and I'll show you."

"Can't you just explain it?"

"It's kinda hard to explain, really."

"Give it a try."

"Well, it would go something like this." Redd leaned against his bike. "When you head out into this great country on your bike, and you watch the stripes of the pavement fly past, and you get to suck in the fresh air and marvel at the expanse of the sky and feel the warmth of the earth and realize there are forces bigger than you . . . well, it gives you a chance to clear your head, to find a place that's peaceful—that's meaningful. That's what I mean by freedom. Isn't that what everyone is looking for?"

Dave's intuition had been right. If you want to know about a company or a product, go to the people on the front line.

"You're not a mechanic," Dave stated emphatically.

Redd seemed confused, not sure what to make of the remark. "I'm not?"

"No. Not at all." Dave added, "You're the best damn salesman I've ever met."

chapter fourteen

Patrick O'Riley was more than an engineer, he was an artist. His drawings are stunning. Beside each one I find meticulous calculations. Most I do not pretend to understand. Instead, what I find intriguing is the personality of the man that shines through his work. His anecdotal wisdom is everywhere, sometimes hidden in a phrase, other times highlighted in notes that span pages. With each discovery, my questions about him grow.

"I calculated the cable's dead-load stress under normal temperatures, then presumed fully loaded side spans and recomputed the live-load stress for the hottest of days. I was astonished. Stress is less with a live load than with no load at all! The cable is more stressed when the bridge is empty than when it is crowded with autos. I presumed a mistake but checked me figures, and the calculations remain. I was bothered for several days until Mr. Moisseiff explained that the stiffening truss should be a limbering

truss and that, in our bridge, the truss literally shirks the load, handing it over to the cables. It is marvelous indeed.

"With Anna and the wee ones distant, I too carry a greater load when empty. At times me emptiness seems unbearable. I miss Anna so and wish I had the means to reunite sooner. At times she is but a distant memory, and I imagine she is not real at all, but the desperate vision of a wanting man. During those times, I stare at her picture, remember her smile, and know that each day I spend working on the bridge is a day closer to our reunion—a day closer to the time our family will be together. Must go now. Have been assigned to an evening crew. But I go with a smile. I go to work on the bridge for Anna."

Another note is written in the margin.

"With this heart, I give you mine."

I sense these expressions hold a deeper meaning. When all three are strung together, they sound almost like a wedding vow. Could it be so simple? Below the last phrase is a final plea, a mystery that confuses me further. "I pray, Anna, that your crown be left and out—that is me heart's deepest desire."

I'm curious by nature, and while I do find the words comforting, I also find myself wondering. Crown? Left and out? What in the world could this possibly mean?

• • •

Professor Winston calls our meetings "employee evaluations." Our conversations, however, feel more like father-daughter talks. He said that he's been thrilled with my attitude as of late, though

I hadn't realized I was any different. He accused me of secretly dating, and when I told him I hadn't, he promised he'd arrange something for me. I almost slapped him on the spot. Let me explain why.

Four months ago I asked the professor to recommend an accountant. With a gleam in his eye, he set me up with his own accountant, a man who'd recently been divorced. When I say "set me up," I don't mean for a tax consultation. At first I refused, but the professor often gets his way. He's a man who loves to get in the last word.

As it turned out, his accountant was a good ten years older than me, and certainly not my type—neither for dating nor for accounting. To be polite, I forged ahead with the evening. He took me first to a movie and then to dinner, both nice enough, but afterward we drove to his apartment, where I was under the impression we would meet the professor and his wife for drinks. It turned out the professor wasn't coming, and I was alone with Napoleon Dynamite.

He was nervous and trying way too hard, which in turn made me uneasy. He put on some soft mood music, poured each of us a drink, then pointed me toward the couch to sit and talk. He began by relating details of his divorce, but then clued in from my manner that he was making a huge mistake. He fumbled for a bit; then, as a last resort, he reverted to a subject he knew well: "Tax Law Changes and the Middle Class." When I couldn't endure another moment, I excused myself and headed to the bathroom.

Looking back, I'll admit that I was nervous and thus

irrational. But while in the bathroom, I noticed his toilet was running. When I say running, I mean that the float inside the tank that shuts off the water desperately needed an adjustment. Even after I'd flushed and waited, it still sounded like a river flowing down into the drain—and in a city where water conservation is pounded into the head of every child from birth, it grated on my nerves.

I returned to the couch where my date hadn't missed a beat, but all I could hear was the toilet in the background. I couldn't decide which was worse: water torture or tax law.

I can't pin down the exact moment when I snapped, but I believe it was between "Depreciating Assets for Maximum Tax Benefit" and "Increasing the Effective Yield on After-Tax Earnings." I raised my hand, as if in school, and when he paused, I asked for a screwdriver.

In my defense, I was raised by an ironworker, a man who spent his days maintaining the bridge, and he'd taught me well— leaky toilets were my specialty. I'm sure my date was shocked at my request, but he obliged and then followed me into the bathroom, where I removed the lid on the toilet tank and adjusted the float. When I looked up, he mumbled something about the kitchen sink, and when I followed him there, sure enough, his faucet was dripping. I asked for a crescent wrench; he gave me pliers. I made do, and fifteen minutes later that drip was also fixed. My hands were now greasy, and I don't know if it was shock or intimidation, but as he watched, he was unable to form any words—totally stumped as to where to pick up the conversation.

His romantic background music now stood out like hip-hop at a bar mitzvah, so he hurried into the living room to shut it off. I followed and extended my hand in preparation for my polite departure. He shook it and then checked his own to see if the grease had rubbed off. I turned, expecting him to open the door for me, but he stood frozen, with his eyes locked on my hands. I shrugged, opened the door myself, and escaped into the sanity of the hall. As I walked toward the street to grab a cab, I wasn't sure whether to laugh or scream, until I realized the reason for his stare—I was still holding his rusty pliers. I chose to laugh.

The next day, as I protested to the professor while describing the evening's events, he chuckled so hard he snorted. I threatened him with bodily harm if he ever set me up again, but I must not have been convincing—he's been trying ever since. As a reminder to just say no, I still have those rusty pliers.

Before I left the professor's office, he said something that I can't get out of my head.

Next weekend the Golden Gate Commemorative Society will hold a banquet that I'll need to attend. I dread the thought. The finicky old society ladies remind me of fancy house cats, but since they are paying for the study, I understand.

That's not what has me curious and nervous. As I stood to leave, the smiling professor added, "Don't be late! I will have a surprise for you that evening, Katie. Trust me when I tell you, it's something you'll remember for the rest of your life."

Just in case, I'm going to take my pliers.

chapter fifteen

"David, good morning." Dr. Jaspers reached out and shook Dave's hand.

"Good morning to you," Dave replied as he settled in. He hated the small talk. She seemed to enjoy it. Today he stepped around it. "So, what do we talk about?"

"Let's start with the things that frustrate you." The doctor's question was a fair one.

"I go crazy when people say to my face that I'm still young, that I'll get married again. Like age matters, like some other woman could replace Megan, like the act of being married was the thing that was most important—not the person."

She nodded her agreement. "What else?"

"I hate it when people tell me that they know how I feel. No one knows how I feel. They don't understand the moments that I shared with Megan and the children. They haven't a clue what my family meant to me—they simply can't. They shouldn't say they know what I'm going through—they don't."

Although Dave often felt the doctor was controlling, and he still despised being forced into the sessions, he couldn't deny that their conversations were helpful, even soothing. He continued, "I suppose you're going to tell me to cut them some slack, that the people who say those things are only trying to help."

"Aren't they?"

"I guess so. It's just confusing. How do you control yourself when you're feeling two opposite emotions—disdain and gratitude—both at the same time?"

"Don't be too hard on yourself, David, or on others. It's a painful process, so try to be patient."

Her answer was indirect, not really an answer at all. Perhaps there was no answer.

"David, during our last visit you said that you were going to clean out some of Megan's personal things from the house. Have you done that yet?"

"No. I've been busy at work."

"I want to prepare you for the experience. When you do find the time, it can be difficult." She stood and adjusted the thermostat, then added, "You said that work has been busy—I'm glad to see you're getting involved again. I am concerned, however, that you're using it to hide your feelings, to smooth them over rather than face them."

He leaned forward in his chair. "I'm facing them . . . little by little." His words were paced and steady.

"David, if you feel that working hard will assist in easing the pain, then I don't see a problem with it. I'm just saying that you need to be careful that you don't let it get in the way of healing."

"That sounds just like something my mother would have said." His tone mocked, but she accepted the comparison.

The alarm on his watch sounded. He used it to limit the length of their conversations—an excuse to get back to the office.

"The fact that you are able to reason through these feelings, David, that you are able to talk about them now—I think you're making progress."

He nodded his satisfaction, stood, and shook her hand. He thanked her again for her help and insight. On his way out, but before the door had closed, he confirmed what both already knew.

"See you on Friday?"

• • •

The game had been fabulous. With the Mets behind by one in the bottom of the ninth, and a runner on second base, their third baseman nailed a line drive to the shortstop. The ball bounced off his glove, and the runner on second rounded third to head for home. It was close, but the umpire yelled safe and the game was tied. At a two-and-two count, the next batter connected solidly, hammering the ball toward right field. It seemed to hang in the air, as if hesitating, but perhaps encouraged by the roaring crowd dropped just out of reach over the fence for one of the most memorable walk-off home runs Mets fans had ever witnessed.

It was nearly eleven before Brock's car stopped in front of Dave's house in Jamesburg. "What a game," Brock announced for the umpteenth time.

Dave agreed, the mood celebratory. "I'm gonna run in and see if they show highlights on the news. I still can't believe Westman's play at the plate."

The evening had been refreshing: no sentimentality, no discussions about pain or loss or anger—just an evening of hot dogs, beer, and baseball.

"What's your plan for tomorrow?" Brock asked. "Do you wanna pick up some women?"

Dave laughed. "Thanks, but I'll pass. Believe it or not, I made a haircut appointment for tomorrow morning—and on my own, I might add. After that, I've got some yard work to do."

"A haircut? Way to go! But don't strain yourself mowing. Your big meeting's on Monday."

"Nine a.m. in the conference room."

"See you then."

The friends slapped hands, then Dave stepped out and closed the car door. The night was gorgeous. He stood in the street and watched Brock drive away, and as the purr of the engine faded into the darkness, Dave wondered if there could be a more exhilarating sound in all the world. He grabbed the mail out of the box and wandered toward the house. The neighborhood was quiet, and he considered sitting on the porch for a bit to drag out the moment, until he checked the time—just after eleven. News would run for another ten minutes; then he could catch the sports recap.

He pushed his key into the lock, opened the door, and switched on the inside entry light. A flash startled him as the fixture's last bulb blew. He'd been meaning to replace the two that were already burned out. "Nothing like darkness to force a guy into action," he mumbled.

He felt his way into the kitchen, clicked on the light, and opened the pantry door. Where were the extra bulbs? None there. He stepped to the island and pulled open the junk drawer. Every home had one, a place for odd tools and one-of-a-kind parts that fit nothing (until after they were thrown away). He rifled through the junk, but no bulbs.

He glanced at his watch. He still had time to check the hall closet where Megan kept the cleaning solutions. Nothing. Thinking maybe she kept the bulbs up high where the kids wouldn't break them, he pulled aside a black plastic bag that took up most of the top shelf. If he didn't hurry, he would miss the replay of Westman's slide.

And then an unexpected smell caught his attention.

He pulled out the bag and tore it open. It had been such a good day, a needed day, that it took a minute for the demons he'd unleashed from inside to escape and then assault.

The leather jacket was thick and soft, the construction solid. The smell seemed to rise and circle before constricting around his neck and chest. When he turned the jacket over, he noticed the subtle Harley-Davidson logo embossed in black on the left sleeve. An envelope slid out that Dave managed to catch before it hit the floor. The flap was tucked inside; Megan hated the taste of the glue. He pulled out the card and stared—a funny card, she always bought a funny card.

There was a dog on the front and words that read, "Howl old are you again?"

Another day, another time, perhaps he'd have read the punch line and laughed. Not today. The only place his eyes focused was on Megan's handwritten message.

Hey, Ponytail Man,

Don't be sad, honey, about turning forty. You have your whole life ahead of you. I'm just grateful you chose me to share it with you.

Enjoy the jacket, but don't get any ideas! Have a wonderful birthday! You are the love of my life, a life that would be incomplete without you!

Forever,

Meg

P.S. Remember, no matter what, I'll always be younger!

It should have been a special gift—it *could* have been. Why did he think the pain wouldn't return, cutting his heart like a razor? He dropped to the floor, the jacket clutched in his fingers. Heaving sobs rushed in to replace the space abandoned by the day's happiness.

On hands and knees, Dave crawled to the cherrywood cabinet and grappled for the closest bottle—it didn't matter what. Then, whiskey in hand, he cowered along the wall to the waiting darkness of the hall, where he began to drink . . . drink and forget.

chapter sixteen

"He's not here yet?" Ellen questioned. Gloria shook her head. Shaun Safford from BikeHouse had been waiting in the conference room for almost ten minutes. Not a good way to impress a client.

"I just tried his cell. He's running late. He said to get started."

"Late? Are you kidding?" Disappointment spread across Ellen's face like an afternoon shadow. She turned to Gloria. "We're going to start without him. If he arrives within ten minutes, send him in. Otherwise, tell him I have the account covered."

"Yes, ma'am, I understand."

Dave walked through the door twenty-two minutes later. Gloria glanced up in horror at his appearance. In place of his Armani suit and slacks, he wore jeans, a T-shirt, and a black leather jacket. Stubble showed on his face. His hair was tousled.

"Mr. Riley? Are you all right? You look like . . ." She stopped herself before the word slipped out.

Despite being late, Dave didn't rush. He seemed to be in no hurry to get to the meeting. "Honestly, I've had better weekends," he replied.

"Is there anything that I can do?" She pitied his condition, hated to see him this way. It was tragic—no, heartbreaking—to watch someone with such potential waste away.

He shook his head. "Thanks, I'm fine."

"The meeting has started. Ms. Brewer asked me to tell you she has it covered."

"Thanks, but I'm supposed to be in charge."

"Yes, but she—"

He ignored her words and walked to the door. He could hear Ellen's voice inside. He looked back at Gloria and mumbled. She couldn't tell if he was speaking to her or to himself. Either way, it was an unfolding disaster.

"Just doing the best that I can," he repeated.

Dave glanced down, as if noticing his appearance for the first time. Then, wiping all emotion from his face, he twisted the handle and pushed himself inside.

At eleven a.m., I grab my jacket and head out the door. The drive to the bridge is short, and I park at the south end, near Lincoln Boulevard. I enter the maintenance offices and walk past the receptionist as if I belong. She looks familiar, but I can't remember her name. She looks like she is thinking the same about me.

Though it has been two years since my father's death, many of the same people still work on the bridge. I am looking for one man in particular, Tom Woods.

Tom was promoted to fill the position of team supervisor after my father's death. The two were close, and though he's a roughened man, it was especially hard for him to accept Dad's passing.

I find Tom sitting in the office that was once my father's. He seems genuinely surprised by my visit. "Katie Connelly? Wait, let me guess, you're engaged!"

I can't tell if he is joking, but that is his nature. His subtle wit causes me to relax—to feel at home in a place that now feels foreign.

"Not yet! I'm waiting until you're available."

I know he's amused, but he doesn't smile—not at his own jokes, and certainly not at mine.

"I just need to check with Millie." He doesn't give me time to think of a comeback before he continues, "So, to what do I owe the pleasure?"

Two men are sitting close, and my reluctance must be apparent.

"Tell you what," he says, "I need some fresh air. What do you say we take a walk?"

I nod and we step out to stroll across the bridge. After a moment, I begin. "I appreciate your time." I'm not sure how much to tell him, but I know that I must start somewhere.

"Katie, the pleasure is always mine."

I continue, "I'm wondering, does the name Patrick O'Riley mean anything to you?"

He stops and tips his head, as if that will help him think. Seconds pass as he processes the name. "No, not that I recall, but at my age, I can barely remember what I ate for breakfast."

I add more information, hoping it will help. "I found a journal in some of my dad's things. It's an old journal, Patrick's journal. He was an engineer or a worker on the bridge."

"You're trying to find him?"

"I presume he's dead. I'd just like to know more about him, about where the journal came from. I was hoping that you'd know."

"I'm sorry, Katie. I wish I could help, but your father never spoke about a journal—at least not one that this old brain can recall."

He can read my disappointment, but we continue to walk and reminisce. We talk about my father, the good man that he was, and as we do, I see the slightest sign of sadness in Tom's face.

"Every day!" he finally whispers, though it's almost a mumble.

"Every day what?" I ask.

"Your father," he concedes. "I think about him every single day."

I reach out and squeeze the man's hand, hoping to comfort, but he wears a halo of hesitation, like the words he needs to say are lodged in his throat.

He turns to face me directly. "Katie, if I had just—"

"Tom!" I demand, stomping on the cement. "There's nothing you could have done!"

He takes a heavy breath. "That's hard to say," he replies as he rocks backwards. "Katie, I don't believe I ever told you, but I was supposed to be out on the girder with the jumper that day. It was my turn to take the next one, and I would have, except . . ."

It's news that he shares with such sorrow, my chest tightens. "Except what?" I ask.

"Except that I forgot my gloves. We were just beginning our shift, and so I went back for them. But by the time I'd caught up to your father, he was already out on the beam across from where the boy was standing. He was just talking to the kid like they were friends in the park on a Sunday afternoon."

"Kid? He was eighteen, right?"

"Yes, and so I guess he should be called a man, though he looked like a scared boy to me."

"They said it was an accident. Was it?"

Tom nods as he answers. "The kid was out on the far girder and was threatening to jump. I guess he was having family problems. It took just a minute or two for your dad to talk the boy into coming back. Your father was good at that, so approachable—but then the boy lost his footing. As he slipped sideways, he grabbed onto the top of the beam with one hand, screaming and barely hanging on. The only way your dad could get close enough to help him in time was to undo his own harness."

"I wish he hadn't done that," I whisper.

"Katie, not all the workers would have—but your dad was

different that way. You see, some of the guys here look down on the jumpers as if they're . . . I don't know . . . delusional, or damaged—but not your father. People's problems didn't keep him from seeing them as . . . equals . . . struggling with their own issues, certainly, but, as he would say, aren't we all?"

"Yes, I remember that."

"It was hard because I couldn't get there in time to help. He'd reached for the boy and had managed to grab one of his arms, except the kid was stronger than he looked. He was terrified that he was going to fall. Your dad had him, and it would have been fine, but as he swung the kid close, the boy somehow reached out with his free hand and grabbed your father's boot, and, well . . ."

Tom's eyes shimmer with guilt, mine with sorrow.

"It wasn't your fault, Tom," I reassure.

"As I said, that's sometimes hard to say. I guess I just wanted you to know that your dad was brave—but you knew that already."

We stand quietly for a long moment, and then I thank him. When I extend my hand to say good-bye, he surprises me by leaning forward for an unexpected embrace. Then, as I walk away, he calls after me.

"Wait, Katie. Do you remember Ben Bryant? He worked with your dad for several years before I came on board. You may want to give him a try . . . about the journal. He may know something."

I remember Mr. Bryant as a bald and cantankerous old man, though it has been at least ten years since I've seen him. I'm not even sure that I would recognize him, let alone hope that he'd remember me. "Does he still live in the city?" I ask.

"No, as I recall, he retired to Palm Springs."

"I hope Palm Springs, California, and not Palm Springs, Florida."

"California, all right. I think he bought a condo there with his wife—don't remember her name. I can check with Human Resources and see if they have his number."

I tell him how much I appreciate his help and friendship. For the second time I see a glimmer of emotion—this time, gratitude. We talk for a minute longer, then I say good-bye and head toward home.

On the drive, I am already planning. Palm Springs is eight hours away in good traffic. I have the silly banquet this weekend, but I consider driving down to see Ben the following weekend. Of course, the simpler alternative would be to look up his number and call. And yet, if he doesn't remember me on the phone, I could blow my only chance. As I weigh the alternatives, I find words from the journal rushing into my head.

" . . . and so for the balance between speed and quality—I let me own scale tip toward the latter."

I decide not to rush it. At the moment, Ben Bryant is my only lead.

chapter seventeen

When Dave entered the room, all conversation stopped.

It was called the *Brain Room,* the place in a growing company where, every Monday morning, meetings were held with key executives to discuss strategy. Until the accident, Dave had attended every one. This morning he studied the ornate woodwork as if seeing it for the first time. A large Blackwood table filled the center of the room. Two dozen chairs outlined the perimeter; only three were currently filled.

Dave's attention turned to those seated at the table: Ellen, Brock, and Mr. Shaun R. Safford from BikeHouse. Any one of them could have adorned the cover of a fashion catalog—anyone but Dave.

Ellen's eyes grew noticeably wide. Shaun shifted in his chair. Brock stood, breaking the silence in an obvious rescue attempt. "Dave, glad you could make it. We've barely started."

It was group hesitation before Dave stepped forward and

held out his hand to the only person in the room he didn't know. He tried to sound confident. "Dave Riley. You must be from BikeHouse . . . very nice to meet you. Your company is expanding like crazy. Very impressive." He offered no excuse for his appearance or for being late.

Shaun stood. Hands were shaken. Ellen made the formal introduction.

"Dave, this is Shaun Safford, Vice President of Marketing for BikeHouse. Mr. Safford, this is Dave Riley, he's . . . well, he's one of the members of our team." Dave moved to the nearest vacant seat on the other side of Brock. As he sat, he caught Ellen's glare.

She addressed Dave with disdain dripping noticeably from her words. "We've been reviewing their image, Dave, explaining how with our research and marketing studies, we can enhance the effectiveness of their advertising dollars. I was just discussing the fact that our agility as a smaller research and marketing company is actually to their advantage, compared with our bureaucratic competition."

Dave nodded, didn't utter a word as Ellen continued to spout on about the benefits of their company. Shaun listened politely but twice glanced noticeably at the newcomer.

"Mr. Safford, do you have any questions at this point?" Ellen had been doing most of the talking. Safford now appeared anxious to have a turn.

"I'm sold on your abilities as a company. If I wasn't, I wouldn't be here in the first place. It's obvious that you have the manpower and the smarts. I've heard from a couple of good sources that your ability to sift through and discern marketing data is second to none. What I want to find out from this meeting is if you have the *soul* necessary to work with a company like BikeHouse."

The words caught Ellen off guard. "The *soul?*" she mumbled aloud.

Safford continued, "Sure, you know . . . the emotion, the empathy. Can you relate enough to our audience to ascertain answers from your gut, rather than just regurgitate little dots of meaningless data plotted out on a marketing research chart?"

Seasoned company president Ellen Brewer was ready to respond to any analytical concern that Safford—or any advertising director, for that matter—could throw at her . . . every question but one about *soul.* "I think that as a firm we have more than enough experience to both provide and understand the answers that come in."

Ellen waited, but Safford was not about to let her off that easily.

"You have the experience to collect good data, no question about it. I agree there. What I'm asking here is, do you have the ability to understand our customers as equals? Will your data really point us in the right direction?"

"Well, we have the know-how, the expertise to draw the most accurate conclusions possible." Ellen was stumbling, and everyone could see it.

"You're not understanding my point," Safford repeated.

Dave watched a smile cross Brock's face. It was no doubt refreshing to watch the boss struggle. The question was, how long would Brock let her burn before getting out the extinguisher? After a protracted moment of silence, Brock interrupted.

"Shaun, I drive a sports car. I have friends who drive Harleys, others who prefer Triumphs. I even have clients out of New York City who own lifted four-wheel-drive trucks. All these people are seemingly different breeds, yet as a company we can relate to them all, because we're professionals. We realize that market research doesn't lie and it doesn't discriminate. In fact, we've just been asked by the governor's office to complete a second research project for them. They came back after just weeks because we were so effective at analyzing their data trends."

He waited for Safford's response. "The governor's office?"

From his tone, Dave sensed immediately that it was a mistake for Brock to have included a public-sector study into a private-sector marketing pitch. Ellen hadn't yet picked up on that fact; she was still nodding up and down like a bobble-head toy.

Safford continued, "Do you think hot-button policy wonks know anything about custom motorcycle riders?"

Brock was silent. Safford wasn't. "If you can't answer that question, try this one." The man was relentless. "What direction would you recommend our ad agency take when developing this year's campaign? Do you all follow me? What do you all think is the most important message to portray in our advertising—the one that will motivate Mr. or Ms. Average-Joe-American to discover the beauty of, say, a customized Harley, Triumph, or Indian motorcycle?"

He turned and waited.

A sinking Ellen continued to take on water. "We assumed this meeting would be geared to just the research aspects of our business, you know, an introduction. Give us a day or two and we can certainly give you some terrific recommendations."

Safford ignored the floundering response and turned back to Brock, who had tried to regroup and reload. "As Ellen mentioned, we have the ability to research that exact question. Give us a chance to prove ourselves, and trust me when I say you'll be impressed."

"That's a great canned answer, but sports car drivers and customized Harley riders are . . . well, *oil and water* is the worn-out expression that comes to mind."

Brock looked surprised by his curtness, and when he glanced over at his boss, he could see her squirming. It was evident they were about to lose the pitch. Brock tried again, "If you want bikers, we can find bikers."

Safford responded by asking a question. "It's Brock, correct?"

"Yes, sir."

"Brock, have you ever ridden a customized Harley—or any Harley, for that matter?" The silence was smothering.

When no answer came, Safford turned to Dave.

"What about you? Any ideas? You've been pretty quiet."

Dave's first reaction was to walk out and keep going. He would be fired after the meeting anyway. But although Safford was certainly abrasive, his questions were fair. And while Dave weighed his request, the only answer that kept echoing in his head was a simple one-word reply spoken by Redd, a motorcycle mechanic, just a few days earlier.

"Freedom."

Other than the introduction, it was the first word Dave had spoken during the meeting.

"I beg your pardon . . . it was Dave, wasn't it?"

"Yes, sir, Dave Riley, and the message you need to portray in your advertising is *freedom.*"

Ellen sat silent. Brock waited for the guy to rip into Dave's answer. He didn't.

"What do you mean by that?"

"I mean when a person walks into your showroom and sees a customized Harley or Triumph for the first time, when they smell the leather, when they feel the magic, they do so because they seek freedom." Safford leaned back in his chair as Dave continued. "It's what we're all searching for, in one way or another."

Safford's eyebrows arched. His head tilted to one side. During his pause, Ellen shifted forward, ready to add her reinforcement. Brock reached out and touched her arm, signaled her to hold off.

Safford questioned Dave further. "Can you expound?"

Dave recalled Redd's comments about providing his own market research for a tenth of the price Strategy Data International was going to charge. Turns out the old guy may have been right. Dave tried to remember the mechanic's words, to repeat them exactly. He would offer it straight from the source. The only concern in Dave's mind was if he could do it with the same conviction.

"When they hit the road, Mr. Safford, when they see the stripes of the pavement zip past for the first time, when they smell the air and see the sky, at that moment they know they're riding off to a place where they'll find answers—where they'll find peace—where they'll find freedom and hope. That's the reason that your customers will buy a BikeHouse customized motorcycle. But, of course, you know that already, don't you?"

Safford grinned. Dave continued, "If you hire us, that's the message we'll help your ad agency get across to your customers. We do understand your customer, just like Ellen said. It's the reason that Strategy Data has such a sterling reputation. When we say that we can glean information from the data that others can't, we mean it. Look, if you are in the market for a bike and you want the best damn motorcycle in the world, buy a customized machine at BikeHouse Custom Motorcycles. If you don't care about reputation and results, then I guess a moped will do. Same holds true in market research. If you're looking for a moped, you're in the wrong room."

Brock looked ready to stand and cheer; Ellen was poised to jump up in unison beside him. Safford leaned forward for a better look. "You're the only one in here dressed like you know the back end of a Harley from a horse's behind. How long have you owned your jacket?"

Dave didn't hesitate. After the weekend he had just been through, he had no reason to care. "I just got it. It was a late birthday present. I put it on Saturday night for the first time—and in all honesty, I haven't taken it off since."

"When's the last time you were out on a bike?"

Dave glanced down, considered his answer. It was a short ride, two feet perhaps, but it was still a ride. "Last Wednesday." Dave tried to remember the model. "A Springer Softail." He knew he would blow it if he tried to recite the rest.

It was enough. Safford was hooked. "Nice bike."

"Yeah, it is." He would tell the truth if the guy asked him about owning the bike. Safford didn't.

Instead, he turned to Brock and Ellen. "How about you two? Have either of you ever been for a ride on a customized machine?" Brock shook his head. Ellen followed. It didn't matter—Safford had turned back to Dave.

"Freedom, you say?"

Dave nodded. "Absolutely, Mr. Safford."

"Please, call me Shaun. I'll set up a meeting with our ad people so we can discuss the scope of the study, but I have to tell you, I'm impressed. I just love throwing that *soul* question in first thing. It always throws the die-hard marketing people for a loop. The fact is, it gets 'em every single time. Dave here was ready. I like that."

Hands were shaken, cards were exchanged. Ellen walked Safford to the elevator door and then out to his car. When she returned, she couldn't contain her excitement.

"Genius, Dave. You're a freakin' genius! I'm telling you, when you walked in with no shave and a leather jacket, I thought you'd lost it. I should have given you more credit." She laughed now at her reaction. "Boy, I'm getting slow in my old age. I mean it. I should've caught on. I should have known." She turned to Dave and slapped him again on the shoulder. "Welcome back, Dave. Welcome back. And your hair fit perfectly. I can't believe I was worried about you. You should've just told me. And don't you dare cut your hair until this baby's through. I mean, did you see his reaction? I'm telling you, you're a market-stealing, deal-making, jacket-wearing genius."

chapter eighteen

The banquet hall is bursting with more well-intentioned overachievers than the gym after New Year's. These are society's capable meddlers. The conscientious. The punctilious. The doers. They have assembled today to hear about the bridge.

The woman on the front row two seats from the end, with the wire-rimmed glasses and straight brown hair, looks surprisingly like Diane Keaton. It's hard to tell from a distance, but the man standing in the back beside the lady in the purple dress vaguely resembles Justin Timberlake. The only other obvious match in my celebrity game is a man sitting a dozen rows from the front—the spitting image of a young Tom Hanks. The rest are mostly gray-haired society women wearing fancy dresses and too much lipstick.

I don't like large groups of people; they make me nervous. If I'd known I was going to be seated on the stand next to Professor Winston and his wife, perched in front like produce at the super-market, I surely would have found an excuse to stay home.

After scanning the crowd, I am utterly relieved that I wore my longer floral dress instead of the short green one. Even though I'm wearing nylons, everyone knows that raised platforms, short skirts, and crowds are a scandalous mix.

I do my best to pretend I am listening to the man on stage, the man wearing a badly fitted tuxedo, yammering on about heritage and posterity. Finally, unable to take any more torture, I invent a new game to pass the time—a perfect game for a crowd of old ladies. I call it, "Guess the Price of the Walmart Skirt." Soon my mental fun has evolved into a full-fledged game show in which contestants pair up audience members wearing similar outfits. It is the best game I've invented yet, and I half expect a booming voice to announce the many fine prizes in the studio for those on today's show.

My fun is interrupted by the professor, who glances in my direction. Perhaps I am getting a bit too involved, my excitement a bit too obvious—and then the speaker announces my name.

When he turns toward me, the professor leans over and whispers in my ear. "Told you that you'd be surprised. Sorry for the lack of warning. Talk for about two minutes and tell them about the research you're doing. Give them a little flavor of what's to come. You'll do fine."

I don't move. I feel like killing him right here, in front of all these people. Sure, there are plenty of witnesses, but I can plead insanity.

The professor pats me on the knee, as if that will speed me up or give me the strength to stand. My face is flushed and my hands are trembling. I don't have any idea what to say, and so I sit there, not moving from my chair.

The room is growing silent as the clapping subsides. The people in the crowd who were dozing begin to stir. The professor is now physically lifting me gently out of my chair, and so, seeing no other choice, I stand and trudge to the podium. As I do, I can feel him breathe a sigh of relief. I can see people in the audience breathe too, but I can't catch my own breath.

I look out over the expectant faces and long for my cubicle at the university, for my solitude. From the podium I have a perfect view of the woman who looks like Diane Keaton. She stares at me. Justin Timberlake stares at me. Young Tom Hanks stares at me. The gray-haired ladies stare at me. I stand in silence. I have nothing prepared, nothing to say.

"Just talk about the research that you're doing," I hear the professor whisper. He doesn't know that I haven't started the research, that I've been too caught up in the journal.

I glance back at him and then again at the crowd.

I apologize—never a good way to begin. I stumble through a few basic facts about the bridge that pop into my head, then stammer about how important the structure is to the community. I mumble. I pause. I stutter. I recite meaningless drivel. I sound like the professor.

I realize I am repeating phrases. It is a disaster, and it occurs to me that I should end my misery and theirs, but I can't find a way to close. I stop again and try to collect my thoughts, to salvage what little is left of my credibility as a researcher. The crowd waits patiently.

As I grope for words of substance, for some way to conclude, for any thought that will tie my rambling together, my father's words come to mind. I remember my childhood and the game of pick-up sticks that I played at the table with the piece of cable. I remember the words my father taught me as I played that lesson from the bridge. Mostly, I remember the man who was always there for me.

The surprise of being called on to speak and my fear of crowds, coupled with memories of my father that flood my mind, have made me a nervous wreck. I feel emotions taking complete control of the helm. Next, in front of so many strangers, I do something I absolutely dread. I begin to cry like a child.

The professor steps to the podium to hand me a tissue, and for the first time he seems concerned that he has stepped over the line, that he has pushed me too far beyond my capacity. I take the tissue and nod. I know I should sit, but instead I turn back to the audience and try to explain my behavior.

I apologize again, but then tell them why I am crying. I tell them about my father bringing the cable home from the bridge. I tell them about matching the strands together. I tell them about the lesson he taught me, about working together, and about how much I have missed him since his death. I echo his words and then say, "Together, we also can do the impossible." Then, with mascara running rampant down my face, I stumble to my seat and sit down.

The room is silent, until one of the gray-haired women on the front row stands up and begins to clap. Soon, many people are on their feet, applauding. They don't stop. The professor smiles and nods as if the accolades are for him. He pats my knee again and continues to bow to the crowd. I clutch the tissue and dab at my smudged eyes. I keep dabbing, the black keeps coming, and the crowd continues clapping. And all that I can think of is how grateful I am that I didn't wear my green dress.

At the reception afterward, strangers congratulate me on an outstanding job. I find out that Diane Keaton's twin is actually the vice president of the Society, that the Justin Timberlake look-alike owns a chain of furniture stores and is one of the larger financial contributors to the group, and that young Tom Hanks is the principal at a high school in Crescent City, where my information will début. They all tell me that they are excited to see the final product and add that if it is anything like my presentation, it will be outstanding.

Then the principal steps right up beside me. "Miss Katie!" he exclaims, as he reaches out with both his smile and his hand to again enthusiastically grip mine. "Your words were inspirational, even sensational. This entire evening has been . . ." He pauses, laughs, and then concludes, " . . . educational!"

His eyes don't turn, and while I smile back, my research brain has automatically started to scour for other closely rhyming words. Oddly, the only one that spits out is available.

Others continue to draw near to applaud me, and though I should be happy to receive their praise, it all causes a knot in my stomach. *I haven't begun the research, haven't even put together an outline. I've been too consumed by an odd journal penned by a man I don't know.*

As the crowd thins, the professor and his wife offer me a ride home. I politely accept, deciding to hold my rebuke until the next day at work.

The professor congratulates himself again as he pulls up in front of my house. "You were the hit of the evening, Katie . . . the hit of the evening. I'm so glad I trusted my instincts."

I mumble my thanks, though I am not sure for what, and then I get out of the car. Before I can close the car door, he says, "And one more thing . . ."

"Yes?"

He speaks the words quickly, laughs, and speeds off, causing the open door to slam shut on its own. It takes a minute for his remark to register, and when it does, I can only swing my purse in the direction of his car. But his words also make me smile as I unlock my door and step inside.

"Katie, you look beautiful without mascara."

Dave slipped out of the office just before three. This time no one questioned his absence. He found Redd at the Lakeshore BikeHouse showroom, standing in front of a stainless-steel table strewn with parts.

"Dave, what's up? How are the suits treating you?"

"Very well. I gave Shaun Safford your line about freedom—he went nuts."

"It's 'cause it's true, man. Like I told you, they should hire me."

"That's why I'm here. I'd like to."

Redd's mustache curled along with his confused lips. "Say what?" His eyes grew wider when Dave took out his wallet and started counting bills.

"Whoa, wait a second. I was joking. I ain't taking your money." Redd motioned him close, lowered his voice. "I'll tell you all you want to know—no charge."

Dave nodded his acceptance. "Fair enough. I'll take you up on that offer. You tell me everything that I need to know about BikeHouse and their customized motorcycles—no charge."

Still, he continued to lay bills on the table next to the pieces of a carburetor.

Redd stared in confusion. "I told you, no charge."

Dave nodded. "Then we're in agreement. But this money isn't for your knowledge about the machines."

"What's it for, then?" Redd questioned.

"I landed the account because of you. Now I truly need to learn everything possible about the company, the people, the product."

"So?"

"So, before Shaun Safford asks again and I'm forced to either lie or embarrass myself, I need you to teach me how to ride a Harley."

chapter nineteen

First thing Monday, I stretch on my running clothes and take my biweekly jog through the streets of the city. I end, as always, at my father's favorite deli, several blocks east of the house, to sip my morning herbal tea and cool down—a choice my father could never understand. I'd tell him that herbal tea is an acquired taste; he'd answer that "acquired" means it tastes nasty. Although I love coming to this deli to reminisce, I never know if I'll leave with a chuckle or a tear. It turns out that a woman's feelings are a lot like herbal tea—hard to explain.

I am so caught up in my thoughts that, at first glance, I don't notice the man who has stepped into the line to order. He is wearing a suit and a tie and reading an order scribbled on a yellow sticky note. His hair is trimmed, his shoes are shined, and he flirts with the girl behind the counter.

I wear no makeup, I am dripping in sweat, my T-shirt smells, and I feel bloated in these tight shorts. As he walks past, I shield my face with my hand and lower my eyes. He pays no mind—doesn't notice me at all.

Artfully balancing several cups of coffee, he opens the door and treks across the street. I watch from the window and consider following him to discover where he works. It soon becomes apparent there is no need. He approaches the entrance to a large, glass-covered office building nearby, waits as a suit-clad woman politely opens the door, and then follows her inside.

I've been so caught up in the life of Patrick O'Riley lately—so enthralled by his romance with Anna and so intrigued by the mystery of the journal—that for many days I've forgotten there is misery still hiding in my heart.

It is best that I didn't force an encounter with the man who ordered the coffee . . . not because of how I look today, but because of how I may react when we eventually speak. You see, that man the one who came into my father's favorite deli, who is apparently working at an office a mere handful of blocks away from where I live—is Eric Aldridge.

Betrayal is a damning sin. Not only does hatred often spawn in the heart of the one betrayed, but guilt begins to grow like mold as well. I've learned that it was easy, when the offense first occurred, to douse the offending party with blame. I've also discovered since that some of that blame, in the form of guilt, can slosh out to dampen the one holding the bucket.

It's an emotion I have yet to fully understand. If it was Eric who made the decision to cheat with another woman in our *apartment, why do I always find myself looking inward for answers?*

I don't shed tears on my walk home—I've shed too many over Eric. And yet at the same time, I feel my wound begin to pull open again and bleed. This time, however, something inside is different. I can't say what compels me, what suddenly drives me forward, but as I arrive home and sit down to work on my report, I resolve to find closure.

I decide to talk once more with Eric.

If Redd was going to get paid to teach Dave how to ride, he'd vowed to do it right. They would start in the classroom. The anxious teacher had set up two chairs in the back warehouse against a spotless stainless-steel table that only days before had been strewn with parts.

It was time to begin.

Using his own bike as the main prop, Redd taught Dave in two and a half hours more than he could have learned in two and a half months on his own. The man explained the design, the disc brakes, the V-twin, air-cooled engine. He showed Dave how the fuel mix is precisely injected to maximize the thrust.

He taught him the history, how in 1894, Hildebrand & Wolfmüller became the first production motorized bikes in the world to be called motorcycles. He described how others followed: George Hendee with the Indian in 1901, Bill Harley and the Davidson brothers with the first Harley-Davidson in 1903.

He expounded on the notion that while production bikes were fine for the average schmo, in truth, nobody wants to be average. He preached that no two riders have the same tastes, and so every serious bike rider should have a customized machine to match those tastes.

He moved on to talk about the accessories, the maintenance, the nostalgia, the image. And after all was said and done, he even taught Dave how to properly inflate the tires.

Dave sucked in every word. He made observations, asked questions, pondered, and listened. He put to memory all he could and wrote notes for everything else.

Indeed, the bikes were sleek and overwhelming. However, after a little education, once you were formally introduced, once you shook their hands and looked them in the eyes, it was easy to see past their shapely exterior—there was power in those pistons.

On his first visit to the showroom, Dave had been intimidated. Now, after an evening of instruction and illumination, the bikes were approachable, even congenial. While they may have started out as cheerleaders, beauty queens, and supermodels, they were quickly becoming the girl next door—more Mary Ann than Ginger. As Redd watched Dave's perception shift, he knew it was time for the man and the bike to hold hands.

"That's all I have, Dave. If there are no more questions, it's time."

"We're done for the day?"

"Not at all. It's time to take a ride."

• • •

Of the three BikeHouse focus groups slated for phase one of the study, the first was scheduled to begin at eight a.m. at the Marriott hotel near Brock's apartment. Staff in other cities would be conducting similar clinics simultaneously. Dave, Brock, and half a dozen Strategy Data employees arrived to set up a few minutes before seven. Dave was directing the show.

It was the usual drill, one he'd orchestrated countless times; today would be no different. At a few minutes before the hour, the first survey participants began to filter in to the grand ballroom. Before letting a soul even think about picking up a pencil, they fed them all a hot and hearty breakfast. It was the first rule of market surveys—keep the people happy, keep them involved. If they get hungry, angry, tired, or irritable, especially before the questioning phase begins, then emotions can take over, causing what the researcher fears most—skewed data.

As people finished eating, Brock and Dave used a computer to divide them into separate survey groups, an exercise they hoped would create a cross-section of America—a tidy slice of the world that would expose opinions, habits, prejudices, perceptions, likes, and dislikes. The game was to figure out, through a series of questions, observations, and algorithms, just what made people tick. More important, the job of Strategy Data International was to divine the data, sift through the answers, and analyze every response—collectively and individually—to discover, through it all, who was most likely to purchase a BikeHouse customized motorcycle and why.

After all the people were surveyed and all the questions had been answered, resulting data was tallied into a laptop and then transferred to the office, where more in-depth analysis could begin. It had gone smoothly—just like old times when Dave and Brock had worked together on the same account. Now, with the last of the equipment loaded, Brock jumped into Dave's car, and they headed to the office.

The conversation was light—golf, women, the survey, and, in particular, Brock's concerns with Jeanine. It was amusing conversation, normal conversation, and Brock couldn't help but notice the improvement, especially as Dave chuckled over the radio announcer's sports jokes.

Others at the office had also mentioned Dave's demeanor, his dramatic turnaround since the doctor visits—and since the BikeHouse account had materialized. Ellen had especially taken note.

Dave's mood today certainly confirmed his place on the road to recovery. He seemed so sure-footed and *back to normal* that Brock was caught off guard by Dave's final question as they approached the office parking structure. It was asked with a laugh, but seeping with serious undertones.

"Do you ever get the urge to keep on going?"

"Say what?"

"When you drive to work: do you ever want to pass up the parking lot and—you know—just keep on driving?"

"To where?"

"I don't know. I don't think that's the point. I just wonder if it wouldn't be an adventure to keep on going to wherever the road leads."

Brock, at first puzzled, turned agreeable. "Yeah, good idea, let's do it right now. We could go across the country—soup kitchen to soup kitchen—begging money for gas. It would be fun."

"I'm serious."

"I know, I can see that. That's why you're scaring me." Brock tried to read his friend's eyes. "Look, buddy, you've got a decent six-figure income and stock options that will make you a millionaire. Be patient. Make your fortune first, then buy your Winnebago."

Dave shrugged lightly. "You're probably right."

"Besides, you can't just take off," Brock added.

"Why not?"

"I have Mets tickets again next week. If you don't go, then I'll have to take Jeanine from accounting, and she's smothering me."

When Dave laughed aloud, it was such an instant and complete change in demeanor that it was Brock's turn to stare and wonder.

"What?" Dave questioned.

Brock reached over and slapped him on the shoulder. "I won't be able to let you drive alone to work anymore, will I?"

Dave shrugged, signaled, braked, and then turned methodically into the company parking garage.

chapter twenty

In a vain attempt to harness my swirling thoughts and emotions, I pull half a dozen books from the shelf and haul them to the kitchen table. I have to at least start on the Society's report, and I decide that if I stay away from the den, where I've placed the journal, the temptation won't be so overwhelming. I'm also trying to avoid the windows. If I can't see the city, perhaps I'll forget about Eric.

But I wonder, with so many unanswered questions in my life, with no certainty of closure, will I be able to focus enough to create a compelling report for others?

I scan through several volumes for nearly an hour and then methodically rework my outline, tossing attempt after attempt into the garbage. I am ready to try again when I get a call from Tom at the bridge with an address and phone number for Ben Bryant in Palm Springs.

For the next thirty minutes I hold a staring contest with

myself, my books, and Bryant's address. I blink, and the address wins.

My phone call to the professor is short. When I tell him that I need two days off to visit a friend in Palm Springs, he's hesitant. When I add that the friend is a man, he wishes me well.

I tell myself that I'll be quick. I'll find out what I can about the journal, return straight home the following day, and finish my first draft by the weekend. Then, on Monday, after I turn it in to a waiting and anxious boss, I'll gather my courage and confront Eric.

• • •

Traffic swinging past L.A. is worse than I anticipate. By the time I arrive in Palm Springs and check into my hotel, it is nine-thirty at night. I question whether it's too late to visit Mr. Bryant, but decide to drive by and see if a light is on.

The sheer number of new developments is shocking, but I soon locate the Dumuth Park neighborhood where Mr. Bryant lives—cookie-cutter, but clean and well kept. I find his house number on the mailbox and am relieved to see through the windows that the lights are on inside.

I don't know if he'll remember me, so I have brought a picture of my father. I push the doorbell, wait, and then hear shuffling. When the door opens, I am greeted by the confused stare of an old man—late eighties, bald head, with weathered, shriveled skin. At first I am not sure it is Mr. Bryant. His features are even more sullen and brooding than I expect.

"Yeah?" His voice is coarse.

"Mr. Bryant?"

"What?"

"Mr. Bryant, I don't know if you remember me. I'm the daughter of Kade Connelly." I hold out the picture of my father, and with unexpected swiftness he reaches out and snatches it from my hand. He pushes up his glasses and then lowers his head to study the huge frame of a man standing in my photo on the edge of the bridge. Ben's eyes soften as his focus seems to drift. I give him time, waiting to see if I can detect any recognition. I see none.

"Do you remember him?" I question, hoping for anything as he hands the photo back.

"Your father was a man's man, Katie," he answers, his voice still gravelly but more kind.

"You remember me?"

"Remember you? Hell, I remember that as a baby you used to spit up all over me. Does that count?"

He's a craggy, rough-hewn man, but I remind myself that with men on the bridge, their façade is often misleading. He invites me in, offers me some coffee, and we sit on his couch to visit.

"I hope I'm not keeping you up," I say.

"Don't sleep much lately. Not since Frances died."

"I'm sorry."

"It's okay. It will happen to the best of us."

"Yes, I know that firsthand." I don't mean to sound pitiful in

my answer. I am just trying to make conversation, but immediately I regret my words.

He leans forward, understanding that I refer to my father. "I'm sorry I didn't make it to your dad's funeral. I lost Frances a few weeks before—they wouldn't let me drive anymore, and . . ."

"It's okay. I understand."

We sit without speaking until the silence becomes uncomfortable and I decide that I should get to the reason for my visit. "Mr. Bryant . . ."

"Please, call me Ben."

"Ben, I'm here to ask you about a book that I found in my father's things. It's a journal written by a man named Patrick O'Riley."

"Patrick O'Riley." He repeats the name as if he's heard it before.

"So you know about it?" I ask.

He seems hesitant. "Officially? No. Don't know a thing about it. You aren't a reporter, are you?"

I smirk at the thought. "I'm too shy for that. I found the journal in Dad's desk. Judging from his notes, he seemed anxious to find its owner. I need to know more about it."

Ben takes another long stare, probably trying to decide if I am harmless.

"What am I worried about?" he finally says. "They can't fire me, and I doubt they can take away my pension. Just in case, though, you didn't hear it from me."

"I understand."

"We found it," he replies matter-of-factly.

"Found it? What do you mean? Where? How? When?" As my questions rattle out, it dawns on me that I sound exactly like a reporter. I stop and try again. "Why don't you start at the beginning and tell me all about it."

"Can I get you some more coffee?" he asks, in no apparent hurry.

"No, thank you. I'm fine."

"So, you want to hear about the journal?"

He pats my knee as if I were still a little girl—and perhaps, to an old man, I am.

"I was working with your father that day under the trellis, replacing some of the older rivets with new, high-strength bolts. It was your father who spotted the metal box tacked to the inside of the beam. I don't know how he noticed it, the way it was hidden, but he did. It was built to look like a beam extension and then tacked on at the corners. We broke the spot welds and pulled it off, not really understanding what we'd found. He presumed it had been placed there by the original crew to cover a poor seam. It wasn't until we ground off the corners and it popped open that we realized what we had. Best way to describe it is a homemade time capsule. Some of the original bridge crews were known to do things like that."

"There were other boxes?"

"Not like ours. I'm talking about men leaving their marks on the bridge: their initials, coins with messages scrawled onto them dropped into the cement pours, that sort of thing."

"So there was more in the box than just the journal?"

"Sure. It was full of stuff."

"What kind of stuff?"

"Notes from the crew, pictures of the construction, jewelry, housing receipts, couple of pin-up postcards, letters, lots of things. It was all wrapped in a pouch that tied in the middle. I still remember the words they'd burnt into the leather. It said, 'Built Forever.'"

"Was it an official time capsule?"

"Doubt it. There'd be records of that. This stuff looked like something an iron crew might toss together. Our bet was they did it on their own, that nobody else knew."

"What happened to the rest of it—the notes and papers? Do you have them?"

"Me? No. I'd have been fired for keeping stuff like that."

"So, where are they?"

"We should have turned it all in and told everyone what we'd found."

"But you didn't."

"No, we didn't. Our boss at the time was a real . . . well, in the presence of a lady, I'll just call him *challenged*. We didn't know what he'd do with the stuff, so we emptied the contents into our lunch pails and then tossed the steel box off the bridge into the bay. It was stupid, I know, but sometimes people do stupid things."

"Do you know where everything is now?"

"I thought we should sell it. Your dad kept saying that we

needed to give it to a museum. He took the journal home to look it over. I kept everything else. All we knew was that we couldn't turn it in or tell people where it had come from—not after so many days had passed, not without the risk of losing our jobs."

"So, what happened?"

"You're an impatient little thing, aren't you?"

"Sorry. Go ahead."

"There wasn't a bridge museum, so I dropped most everything off with an anonymous note to one of the universities."

"But not the journal?"

"No, your dad kept the journal. He decided it was like a family Bible—that it didn't belong to a museum or a university or anyone but the family of the guy who wrote it. He figured whoever wrote it was probably dead, but he took it upon himself to find out, and if the author was dead, then your dad planned to give it to his family."

"But he never did."

"No. Not that I know of. He tried—oh, how he tried. Honestly, I think he felt guilty for keeping it, and then when he couldn't find the owner or his family, well, it bothered him."

"Mr. Bryant, I noticed you said that you dropped off 'most' everything. Did you keep anything at all?"

He pauses. "You sure act like a reporter."

"I'm sorry; I didn't mean it to sound that way."

He studies me for another long minute before he stands and shuffles out of the room. He's gone for only a minute.

"The stuff wasn't ours, but since your dad kept the journal,

I figured it wouldn't hurt to keep something as well. There was a ring that my wife took a liking to, so I gave it to her. She loved it and wore it for years. But since she's gone, and since your dad found the box to begin with, Katie, I think you should take it."

He places his wrinkled fingers in mine and passes along an intricately carved silver ring. It's beautiful. I am stunned, unable to offer any better response than a mumbled thanks. We visit a little longer, until I sense it is time to leave.

"Mr. Bryant, one last thing, and then I'll let you go."

"What is it?"

"The rest of the items that you said you dropped off at the university. Do you remember which one?"

"It was the one on the west side, near the lake—let's see, what's it called?"

I smile at the thought. It's the university where I work. "SFSU, San Francisco State University?"

"Yeah, that's the one. Check with them. Who knows, they may still have everything."

• • •

On the drive home I can't get the journal out of my head. My father was right. It doesn't belong in a museum where people will glance at the cover under glass as they stroll past. There are too many dreams, fears, and hopes embedded in its pages. It's a personal story of a life that needs to be cherished by his family. It belongs to his children, and their children, and then their children.

My father desperately wanted to find them. He'd tried every

O'Riley in San Francisco, probably every O'Riley in California, and, knowing Dad, every O'Riley across the country. But my father was an ironworker, not a researcher. I, on the other hand, am paid to dig up obscure facts and information. I know the ropes; I have people I can call, places I can look. And now, with the Internet, surely I can track down his family. I owe that much to my father; I owe that much to Patrick O'Riley.

The more I contemplate the task, the more energized I become. It's right down my alley, a job on my own turf. And not just for Patrick, or for my father. Deep down, I know this is a job that I need to do for me.

My breathing quickens, my thoughts jump around with waving hands. Instinctively, I map out the paths I'll take, the places I'll start. As I do, one obstacle keeps flashing a warning in my head. I've promised the professor that in just a few days I'll submit a comprehensive outline.

I can't do both.

• • •

I drop the ring on the table. The design is unlike any I've ever seen. The band is formed by what look to be two connecting arms, each reaching around until they meet. The hands at the ends of the arms are intricate, with every detail of the fingers and nails showing. In the center, where the fingers touch, they hold a small silver heart. And below the heart—in fact, connected to it—extends a small crown.

I consider what might possess an ironworker to include a ring in the box. I've known many men who worked on the bridge, but most refused to wear jewelry, afraid they would catch it on a rivet and cause injury. Intrigued, I push the ring onto each of my fingers until it slides safely around the third finger of my left hand. I twirl the ring around and again study the design sculpted into the surface. There is something familiar. I'm sure I have seen these shapes before.

I sit perplexed until my mind makes the connection. When it does, I jump from my chair. As I hold it close, words from the journal flow from my lips.

"With this crown, I give my loyalty. With these hands, I promise to serve. With this heart, I give you mine."

The crown, the hands, the heart—they are all there. In an instant, I know. On my finger I wear Anna's ring.

chapter twenty-one

He didn't need to keep his appointment with the doctor, not after landing BikeHouse. His boss would never ask about the visits again. Dave had come today because, for the first time since their conversations had started, he had something he needed to discuss.

She started first. "Let's talk about baseball," she said.

"Baseball?"

"Sure, why not? On your first visit you mentioned that you once coached a youth team. I'm just wondering, why baseball?"

"Well, because it's a fabulous sport."

He would often anticipate her questions. Not this time. "But why is it so great?" she persisted. "Don't grown men just smack a white ball with a stick and then run around?"

Dave perked up. "You're confusing it with golf. Baseball isn't just *smacking* a ball—it's much more than that. It's skill, it's discipline, but it's also planning and strategy. It's watching your opponent's move and then deciding how best to react. Baseball is symmetry and grace and beauty and power, all woven into a single fabric. Simply put, Doctor, it's a perfect game."

While her question appeared to be idle chat, he realized afterward that it was meant to probe his emotion, to gage intensity.

"Okay, I believe you. Do you still coach?"

"Coach? No, I gave it up after the accident," Dave said.

"Why?"

He paused. She let the silence drag.

"I couldn't go back. It brought back too many memories."

"But aren't they good memories?"

"Sure, but . . ."

"I hope you see, David, that it's okay to remember. It won't always cause pain. In time, you'll create new memories, good memories that will blend with the old. Your life will continue. You'll still have hopes, dreams, passions. In short, you still have a full life to live."

The idea felt so distant, so unreachable. Instead of accepting her words, pretending to agree, and moving forward, Dave raised a topic of his own. "Before we go on, I'd like to talk about my jacket."

"The one from Megan?"

"Yeah. I told you how I found it, but I didn't tell you the whole story."

"I'd like to hear it."

"I didn't tell you that I wore it to work—that I hadn't shaved or showered. I'd been drinking. I was a mess."

"I'm not sure I follow."

"I got the account—I got BikeHouse because of the Harley jacket. Do you see any significance in that?"

"I wouldn't try to read too much into it. Life is full of coincidence—it just has a way of helping us out sometimes."

"Nothing more than chance? You don't see it as a sign or something?"

"A sign?"

"That's why I'm asking."

"David, it's normal to want to believe that life is ruled by fate. But be careful about giving away control. If you turn your life over to destiny, then it takes responsibility away from your actions. We'd all like answers as to why awful things happen in life, but the answers are not always there. Sometimes life is awful—just because. Does that make sense?"

"I guess so."

"You're grieving over the loss of your wife and family. That's the reason we're talking. But understand that life will keep right on going around you. Be careful about stepping off. Be careful about chasing dreams that are only wispy puffs of hope not based in reality. Be careful about giving up. If getting this account is indeed a sign, as you imply, then it's to tell you to move on with your life. Let go of the pain and move forward. You deserve happiness."

His eyes narrowed; his head flinched slightly back. When he finally spoke, his words caught her by surprise. "You mention hopes, passions, and dreams. But how far should I go in search of answers?"

"Answers to what, David?"

"To questions like, where do I find the hope you talk about? Where do I find the will to get up each morning and live my life? Where do I find out if there's more to life than just sitting here asking you questions? No offense."

"I want to understand you completely, David. Can you expound a bit further?"

His intensity was turning into frustration. "I'll narrow it down. Where do I look to make my life meaningful again?"

It was her turn to pause, to ponder. She picked her words carefully. "Many places—I think that you have to look in many places, David. You mentioned that keeping busy at work has helped. Isn't your job meaningful, for one?"

"At times, sure, but if that's the only reason I can find to get up each morning, then smother me with a pillow now. Don't get me wrong, my job can be challenging, but there has to be more to life than Strategy Data. Look, here's what I'm getting at—just a couple of months ago, I'd have answered that my family was the place to look, but now I don't have a family. So with no family, with no wife, and no children—where do I look for meaning?"

"We've already discussed the fact that nobody can replace what you've lost. But, David, whether you want to hear it yet or not, you will most certainly love again."

She waited for his reaction.

"I don't think you answered my question," he said, "so let

me ask it this way. At our first meeting, you told me about losing your fiancé, Jonathan."

"Yes."

"You may have mentioned it, but how long ago did he pass?"

"Nine years."

"And have you found someone else in those nine years?"

"Shouldn't I be the one asking the questions?"

"Please, I'd like to know."

"No, not yet," she said. "But I'm certain that with time, I will."

"Certain? How do you know?"

"Know? I guess I don't know. I simply hope."

"That's exactly my question, Doctor—that's what I want to know. How far do I go to find hope?"

chapter twenty-two

Every major university library has a Special Collections Department. I've used them often. The books and material are old, frequently historic, generally priceless. None of it can be checked out, but it can be held, read, and studied, if done so with gloved hands, appreciation, and care.

I am embarrassed that it hasn't occurred to me before now to search there for items relating to the bridge. I recognize Gwen, the librarian in charge, and she recognizes me. She is a pleasant older woman, and if I was playing my separated-at-birth game, I'd say she reminds me of a modern Mary Poppins.

"Professor Winston's assistant, right?"

"Yes, that's correct."

"What project are we working on today?"

"It's an assignment about the history of the Golden Gate Bridge."

"There's a fun way to spend your weekend."

"Tell me about it." I chitchat until the timing is right, then I get to my point. *"Listen, I'm looking for old books or letters from men who may have worked on the bridge during its initial construction. Do you have anything like that?"*

"Honey, we're in San Francisco. We have shelf loads: notes, letters, pictures, drawings. You name it."

It turns out that she is not exaggerating. There are several drawers of letters, minutes from government meetings, photos, even plans and drawings of the bridge. I ask specifically about items that may have been dropped off anonymously years earlier, but she has no way of checking. Anything so acquired would have simply been cataloged eons ago. I take a pile of the material and spread it over one end of a table. The information is fabulous— and I mean fabulous—and I quickly get lost in my work.

I'm transported back to a harder, lonelier time. I am reminded of the climate and conditions, of the fact that the country was in the throes of a debilitating depression.

"August 1934. It is late summer, a time carpenters normally cherish—a time of abundant light and warm weather. That is not the case at this forsaken place. The Gate is plunged in cold, wet gloom. During normal times one would never consider working in such a place—but these are not normal times."

Another reads, *"1933—times are tough with the Depression going on. There are always men looking for work, and so if you mess up, they let you go quicker than the bay fog. Take time for a smoke and they replace you. And we only get paid for time put in, no matter how long we've been waiting for work to begin.*

Even guys out on the steel, where it's cold and miserable as hell, they all just feel damn lucky to have jobs."

I leaf through the various notes and letters, pondering the conditions, wondering what role Patrick O'Riley played.

"May 4th, 1934—Never seen a completely calm day at the Gate, always windy, a gale that seeks men out. It blows up our sleeves and pant legs, no matter how many layers we wear. When this hellhole ain't windy, we're shrouded in fog. There are days we stand in sunshine on top of the tower, but we never see the water because of the fog. Sometimes it's all around and you wonder what the hell you're doing out here—fog, cold, wind in your face. But you stay, and despite the weather, the tower continues to rise—and it is a beautiful sight."

As I read, I am surprised to find that an earthquake struck the bridge while it was being built. The event was recorded by a bridge worker, Frenchy Gales.

"It was early June. I was on the tower when the quake hit. It was so limber that it swayed sixteen feet in each direction. There were twelve or thirteen guys on top with no way down. The whole thing would sway toward the ocean and the guys would say, 'Here we go!' thinking the tower was going to collapse into the water. Then it would sway back toward the bay. Men were throwing up. I figured if it collapsed into the water, we'd hit the iron first. It never did."

As I continue to peruse their words, one fact becomes obvious. Through the insurmountable hardship of bridging the Gate, a comradeship developed among the men—a feeling that all were taking part in something historic.

A note left by a tower worker makes me chuckle.

"We had toilets on the tower where the waste collected in a trap. It was always a temptation to open the trap on one of the passing ships, like dropping a live bomb. Nobody did, 'course, till we heard that the Shensu Maru, a Japanese freighter, would be steaming through the Gate. It wasn't long before the war, and the Japs had already invaded Manchuria. A lot of the guys on the crew weren't fond of 'em. I guess the temptation became too great for one of them. I can't say who, 'course, other than to say I heard he figured his precise timing the day before. The next morning when the ship appeared right on schedule, steaming toward the bridge in the outbound shipping lane, there was a sudden waiting line to use the toilet. Funny how all the guys had to go at once. Well, whoever the culprit was, he missed the smokestacks but still managed a direct hit all over the deck. You could hear the men's hoots 'n hollers all the way to the shore. The Japanese filed a protest and inspectors came around asking questions—'course, nobody knew nothing, nothing at all."

There are also letters documenting the tremendous amount of concrete and steel consumed by the bridge during its construction.

"Two separate concrete plants have been erected, one on each shore. Cement is poured day and night, a huge river of aggregate that never ceases to flow. I would not have believed the scale of

the project had I not been here to see it with my own eyes, to touch it with my own hands."

And then another note from Frenchy Gales. *"There were guys down in the cement who would level it off. At the end of a pour we took count, and we were one guy short. The pours were deep. Everybody started stabbing around in the cement trying to find the guy, but we couldn't. The timekeeper asked if I would go with him to notify his family. It was one-thirty in the morning when we knocked on their door. The timekeeper nearly fainted when the missing guy answered the door in his pajamas. He explained that he got tired, slipped out, and went home to bed. That was the last time he ever worked on the bridge."*

The name *Frenchy Gales* appears often. He apparently worked in many areas of the bridge, and I can't help but wonder if he knew Patrick. Were they friends? Did they work together, laugh together, drink together?

I continue to sift. There were times when the construction moved along at surprising speed, but other times when the Gate refused to be bridled. I find notes from Russell Cone, a man who headed one of the major construction companies.

"On October 31, an unexpected storm rolled huge waves into the Gate. They struck the steel forms with tremendous force, breaking over the deck of the access trestle. They kept buffeting until the fifty-ton tower began to shudder six feet forward and back. The oscillation worked the foundation pipes loose. The trestle groaned and creaked and then a mountainous wave, higher than any of the others, hit the forms like a cyclone. Before our

eyes it swept a tangled mass of wreckage into the Golden Gate. All we could do was stand and watch. It didn't just tear out the trestle that day, it also tore out my heart. It was ten months of the hardest kind of work imaginable, and in just one swallow, it was gulped up unmercifully by an angry sea."

I am struck by their persistence, amazed by their determination to overcome all obstacles. Just six months after the storm had devastated his company's work, Cone notes, "May 4, 1934. I was heartbroken when the storms washed the trestle out into the bay, but we have found the will to move forward. The work continues, and the bridge is now taking on an almost living quality. Today, we rode the elevator some seven hundred feet up from the tower's concrete base. It was a raw, windy day—perhaps fitting—when we placed the American flag on the top of the bridge tower for all to see. For a certainty, the men now know, we will succeed!"

They were asked to tame one of the most treacherous pieces of water meeting land known to man—and they did.

They found a way.

chapter twenty-three

Dave plucked the yellow sticky note from his phone. Gloria's scribbles said it all. "Four more days!"

"And two of those are the weekend," Dave added, to no one.

In ninety-six hours, Shaun R. Safford, one of BikeHouse's top executives, would be sitting in the adjacent conference room with a close circle of highly paid staff. Four creative types from the company's ad agency would also attend, as well as three support staff from Strategy Data.

Dave would lead. Brock would assist. Ellen would stand at the door and play boss. She'd shake hands, carry on about *new partnerships* and *working together for the mutual good*—PR propaganda.

The room would be packed with capable executives watching Dave's every move, listening to his every word. All eyes would be on him—he was the man in charge. It would be dog-and-pony at its finest.

He shouldn't be nervous. Speaking in front of business groups was second nature to him. He'd done it hundreds of times, in groups larger than this one. Why, then, was his stomach knotting?

He needed someone to talk with, someone to calm him down. Dave paged through the contacts in his phone, weighed his options. When he dialed a number, a familiar voice answered.

"This is Redd."

"Redd, it's Dave."

"Dave? I was just trying to call you on the other line. You must be psychic."

"Or psycho. What's up?"

"Can you come down here right away?"

"Is there a problem?"

"There's someone here that I'd like you to meet."

"Who is it?"

"A friend. I think you two have a lot in common. I told her you'd be right down, so don't make the woman wait. I have to run. I'll look for you soon. 'Bye."

Click—and Redd was gone.

• • •

Dave's first real ride on a customized bike, besides his initial two-foot lunge, had come at the end of his first lesson. "A couple of loops around the parking lot," Redd had said, "just to get the feel of the machine." By the end of lesson two, Dave had graduated to the public streets in the vicinity of the Lakeshore location. By number three, he was testing short stretches of the Garden

State Parkway. Dave hoped it would soon be time to hit the open road.

"You look a bit tense today," Redd said when Dave walked through the door.

"Tell me about it. I'm meeting with Safford and crew next week. Not sure why, but I'm oddly nervous." Dave glanced around, but he could see no one waiting. "You said you had someone I should meet?"

"I do." Redd's eyes twinkled like stars at midnight. "Dave, have you ever bumped into a person and known from the first moment that they were perfect for a friend?"

"No. I haven't."

"Well, that's what happened."

"Redd, I appreciate it, but . . . I'm not looking for . . . companionship right now."

Redd was only encouraged. "True, my friend, but sometimes it comes looking for you. She's waiting in the back, so please be a gentleman and at least say hello."

Dave was tense and tired; he needed to talk, not engage in some social hour. He protested again as he followed Redd through the door into the shop.

"Redd, I'd rather not . . ."

The place was empty except for Redd's smile and a gleaming black and red Harley Sturgis.

"She came in this morning. She's mint. She not only has a belt-driven final drive, but her primary drive is belt-driven as well. I've checked her over, inside and out, and I've never had a bike traded in better condition. I've made a few modifications, but she's mint—and she keeps calling your name."

Dave reached down and let his fingers drift over the curves of the tank. He had not expected this.

"She's beautiful, Redd," Dave said.

"That she is. And the leather's original. Seems the guy spent more time giving her polish than riding her. Here's the thing. I have to ride down to Frederick, in Maryland, tomorrow to pick up some papers from my sister. I was thinking that you and your new friend could tag along. I've already made arrangements with the boss—we're calling it a test drive."

"I'd love to, but my presentation is in four days."

"What's your point? You seem wired. Nothing better to settle you down, to get you ready, than a good old-fashioned ride into the caring arms of Mother Nature."

Dave pondered while Redd pushed.

"I'm telling you, it'll do you good."

"What time are you leaving?"

"First thing in the morning, 'bout six—before traffic gets heavy."

Dave touched the bike again and then climbed on. He let out a breath, couldn't help but grin. "Let me make some calls, but . . . yeah, let's do it."

chapter twenty-four

Soaring across the open road, leather jacket deflecting the wind, rumbling bike between your legs—it was like a sports car on steroids, an adrenaline cocktail shaken *and* stirred. Yet, it wasn't the power available at the simple twist of a wrist that intrigued Dave. It was the solitude, the peacefulness that came with the ride.

It was such a contradiction, such an irony—intensity and energy, and yet serenity. It was watching trees and fields and open sky, understanding that a bigger picture surrounds, a picture that can't be seen from a high-rise office. It was discovering a larger world, and therein finding yourself.

More important, it offered Dave time to think.

Rather than take I-95, Redd opted for the scenic route—I-78 over to I-81, then down to I-70 and straight into Frederick. It was twice the distance, but that was exactly the point.

Just out of Chambersburg, Redd pulled off the interstate and onto a frontage road. When he passed Parker's Drive-In, a home-town burger joint, he pulled in and stopped alongside a picnic table in the back. It was badly in need of new paint. Yet, despite the place's dilapidated state, or perhaps because of it, it managed to emanate country charm. Dave parked alongside and shut off his bike.

"Now that you've had a few hours in the saddle, what do you think?" Redd asked.

"She's amazing!" Dave replied. "And did you see the look from those kids in the school bus? That alone was worth the trip."

"It's about to get better. They have a pastrami burger here that will cut a month off of your life. You want one?"

"Works for me."

"Watch the bikes. I'll be right back. Treat's on me."

Dave relaxed at the table. The surroundings were quaint, serene—and he couldn't help but think that Meg would have adored the place. This trip had been a good idea after all.

When Redd returned, the burgers were all he'd described—pounds of artery-clogging pastrami piled with enough condi-ments to feed a small town. Eating as they soaked in the sur-roundings, Dave posed the question to Redd that had been perplexing him—a question he'd been pondering for the last two hundred miles.

"Redd, do you mind if I ask you something?"

"No, what's up?"

"It's a question I asked my shrink the other day and, well, I'd like a second opinion."

"I'm competing against a shrink?"

"Don't worry, I won't sue for malpractice."

"Okay, lay it on me."

"I'm wondering how far one should go in search of hope?"

"Sounds philosophical."

"I was actually hoping for practical."

"What did your shrink say?"

"She said I'm *emotionally vulnerable*—that I need to be rational, to think with my head. Otherwise, she suggested, I might end up doing something, well, *irrational.*"

"Like learning to ride a Harley?"

"No, like taking off on my bike and never coming back. Would that be stupid?"

"I suppose it depends on where you're going and what you'd be leaving behind. Have you thought about it—just taking off, I mean?"

Dave shrugged first with his eyes. "I guess I have. The problem is that the doctor's right. I have been a bit unstable lately. I mean, at times I feel like my life is getting back to normal, whatever normal may be. But at other times, I just feel empty, like the answers are out there somewhere, waiting, and it's up to me to find them. I guess that sounds a bit bizarre."

"Sounds to me like you had a little more motivation to ride a road bike than just market research."

"Perhaps. I just keep thinking about Meg—about a conversation we had about life and dreams and jackets and motorcycles."

Redd took another bite of burger and another swallow of

Coke, as if that might help him formulate a profound answer. "Not sure what to tell you, Dave. Never been too good with questions like that. I work on motorcycles. It does seem to me, though, that you may be asking others to decide something only you can answer."

"I suppose you're right."

Redd hesitated, as if he had more to say, as if he wanted to expound but wasn't sure he should.

"What is it?" Dave asked.

"I guess you just remind me of someone."

"Who?"

"Me."

Dave laughed. Other than his recently acquired affection for customized Harleys, he hadn't figured they had much in common. "And how's that?" he asked.

"I took off once, just like you describe."

Dave set his burger on the table. The man had his attention. "You're serious?"

Redd nodded.

"Can you tell me about it?"

When Redd rolled his lips inward, his mustache completely concealed his mouth. It was a moment before he spoke.

"I don't mind telling you, Dave. You're my friend. It's just that you need to understand this is *my* story. I don't want to suggest it applies to anyone else. You understand what I'm saying?"

Dave nodded. "I think so."

"I took off one day on my bike. Just dropped everything and rode away—it was right after the war."

"The war?"

"As a young man, I spent some time in Vietnam."

"I didn't know."

Redd shrugged. "There's a lot we don't know about the people who surround us."

"What happened?"

"I was drafted in April of '69. I was supposed to ship out six weeks later. I didn't believe in the war, Dave." His eyes narrowed as he spoke. "I wasn't about to go fight in some hellhole halfway around the world, killing people for reasons nobody could explain."

"You bailed?"

"That was the plan. I was gonna ride my bike to Canada with some buddies. A lot of my friends were doing it."

"So you dropped everything and took off?"

"No. It didn't work out that way. I got home late that night—too late. I was gonna leave early the next morning, but I'd been drinking. I overslept. My dad was up by the time I got downstairs. The first thing he asked was where I was going. I tried to be funny, told him I was going down to sign up. He knew I hated the war; I thought it would make him laugh. Only thing was, he didn't get that it was a joke. He got all teary-eyed and started to go on about how proud he was of me, how proud my mother would be if she were still alive. It was the first time I ever remember my dad saying he was proud of anybody. The first time . . . "

"What'd you do?"

"I packed up my bike and rode out of the driveway. The only problem was, I rode down to the recruiting office. Three months later I was sitting in a dirty foxhole near the Mekong Delta, wondering what the hell I'd done. I was just a scared, lonely, stupid kid. I shouldn't have been halfway round the world killing nobody—not at that age."

Redd paused, contemplated his burger as if deciding how to attack his next bite, then chewed slowly. They were in no hurry.

"I made a friend there. His last name was Harris; first name was Leslie. What kind of parent would name their son Leslie?" It was a question that expected no answer. "We called him Les—Les Harris. He was a bit older than I was—actually, he was a lot older, had a wife and a kid at home. Guess he felt sorry for me, 'cause he always watched out for me. He was just a damn fine person.

"We were going out on patrol. It was my turn to take the point. It wasn't dangerous. We hadn't run into any VC for weeks. I'd been sick, puking the night before—hadn't slept hardly at all. I felt like hell and I must've looked it, 'cause Les took one glance at me and said he'd swap me turns at point. He said that I could hang near the back.

"The route was the same. We would wade across the river and then hike six miles, running a perimeter check through the jungle." Redd's muscles tensed. "I was dragging at the back when the gunfire started. It took me a minute to register what was happening. Three men went down in our patrol before we realized where the shots were coming from. Turned out there were two

VC hiding in the jungle. By the time we took care of them—"
he paused, then turned to Dave. "*Took care of them* . . . what a
bizarre expression." He didn't wait for a response. "By the time we
killed 'em, several minutes had passed."

His words slowed. "When I got to Les, he was bleeding from
his mouth. He was trying to whisper something, but I couldn't
tell what he was saying. I tried, Dave, but with all the blood he
was coughing up, I just couldn't make out his words. After a few
minutes of trying, he just quit talking, and then, a few minutes
later, he quit breathing. He died in my arms. I couldn't help him;
I couldn't even tell what he was trying to say."

Redd stopped as if he needed a moment to compose himself.
He took a long drink of his Coke before he was ready.

"I was so screwed up after that—I can't even tell you how
screwed up I was. I came home from the war angry—angry at
the Vietcong, angry at our country for sending me there, angry
at life. The whole damn mess just didn't seem fair, not right at
all. It should've been me, a young, stupid kid, to take a bullet to
the chest, not a good man with a wife and kid waiting for him to
come back home.

"After I got back, I went to see his wife. Hanna was her name.
She looked so empty—so lost and lonely. I told her how Les had
saved me, how I should've been at the front of the line that day.
She didn't say it, but I could tell that she was also wishing it. She
asked if Les had said anything before he died. I didn't know how
to answer. All I could do was shake my head no.

"It was a bad war, Dave. Afterwards I had no direction, no

faith in life, no hope for mankind. Frankly, it was hell just to be alive when I should've been the one to die. I drifted for a long time, taking odd jobs to get by—the whole time letting the anger build inside.

"Then in '82 I noticed on the news that in Washington they were dedicating a memorial to the war. I went nuts, completely snapped—they were building a memorial to a damn mistake of a war! Can you imagine that? I decided by then that I'd had enough living in hell and I was gonna do something about it. I stuck a .45 in my saddlebag and headed out on my bike to this so-called memorial.

"It was somewhere along the ride that I decided when I got there I was gonna climb to the top of whatever monstrosity they'd built, and I was gonna blow my brains out in front of everyone—a statement to the world about the injustice that had occurred."

"You don't have to tell me all this, Redd."

"I'd like to, if you don't mind. It was strange what happened next, and you may not believe what I'm about to tell you. Have you ever been there, to the Vietnam Memorial—to the wall?" Redd asked.

Though Dave had lived on the East Coast for most of his life, he was embarrassed to admit that he'd never visited the site. He shook his head.

"You should," Redd chided.

"I will."

"I got there, Dave, on a Wednesday morning. It was raining,

and there weren't many people around—a good thing, considering my state of mind. I took my gun and shoved it into my belt, underneath my shirt. Then I turned and headed toward the wall to make my statement.

"The walls are made of thick black granite from India. They're about ten feet high, and each slab is inscribed with the names of thousands of guys like Les, guys who didn't come home. Well, I walked to the wall with a heart full of hate and disgust, but when I touched it, Dave, something went all wrong with my plan.

"It's hard to explain, but touching the wall—being there, seeing it—a reverence came over me that to this day I don't understand. In an instant, I realized the place wasn't there to celebrate the atrocities of war—that's not why it was built at all. It's there to remember the lives of the guys who died for us, the guys who served. You see what I'm telling you? It ain't about us, Dave, it's about them—the sacrifice that they made.

"Call it a vision, call it a gift, call it crazy, but in an instant after I touched the wall, the whole place . . . well, it felt like hallowed ground. I just couldn't desecrate it by killing myself there. I searched until I found his name: Leslie Harris. I touched his name and I started crying, a big ol' burly man in a black leather jacket, touching the wall and bawling like a baby. Couldn't help myself. I ran my finger over every letter. And while I was standing there, thinking about Les, I . . ."

Redd choked up, unable to continue. Dave waited until Redd was ready.

"After I touched his name, Dave, he spoke to me. I know it sounds nuts, and at the time I was. But I swear, I heard him as clear as I can hear you today—and there was no question it was the voice of Les. There was no mistaking Les."

"What did he say, Redd?"

"He said that life was gonna be okay. He said that it was worth living. He said to keep hope alive and stay strong for others. And the peculiar part is that, at that moment, I knew he was just repeating the same thing he'd been trying to tell me in the Mekong jungle years before. It sounds crazy, but Les saved me in 'Nam and then he saved me again at the wall."

"What happened next?"

"Nothing. I just kept living. I kept getting up every day, doing the best that I could do. Couple of years later I met Sherry, got married, had two kids. Life ain't always been easy, but I've been getting by okay since that day. I've just been trying to do what Les said."

"Did you ever go back and find his wife, tell her what happened?"

"I tried. I looked her up, but she'd moved on. Years later, I heard through a buddy that she'd married again, had a family, that she was happy. I don't know, but I'm guessing that somehow Les spoke to her as well."

Redd set his empty Coke cup on the table.

Dave leaned forward, closer to where his friend sat. "At times, Redd, I feel a bit crazy as well, not sure if I can handle it all— moments when I'm not sure what to do."

"Just do what I did—what I still do. Keep living, keep moving forward, even if it's just a bit at a time." Redd stood. "I need a refill. Do you want something else?"

"No, I'm good."

"I wish I had something better to tell you, Dave. I mean, if I had all the answers, I sure wouldn't be a motorcycle mechanic." He turned and walked to the entrance of the drive-in.

Dave's reply was low, too low for Redd to hear.

"Maybe that's why you are."

chapter twenty-five

Dave arrived at the office early. It was becoming a habit. He couldn't sleep at home, and at least this way he would get a parking space. He moved behind the receptionist's counter and flipped a few switches. Lights flickered on with a buzz, interrupting the morning's silence.

He tossed his jacket over a chair and headed to the conference room. It was immaculate, every chair in place. Gloria was worth every dime Ellen paid her. He picked up the bound packet from the table. The art department had come through again—color embossed cover with a gleaming BikeHouse logo, perfect-bound—and the information the book contained was the finest Dave had ever assembled. The data had been analyzed, quantified, charted, and copied. Graphs and pictures had been prepared. It was all there, brightly bundled and easy to follow.

A PowerPoint presentation was already loaded on the laptop for projection onto a screen that would roll down from the ceiling at just the right moment. The slides were concise, color-ful, and enlightening. It would be the showcase of his career. *The showcase*—it was odd, really, that he'd wanted the account so badly. Now that it was here, now that the work was done and the presentation would soon begin, he found himself wishing it was over.

Brock entered the room at seven. Dave had moved to a conference-room chair and was resting his head on the table.

"Are you dead or just practicing yoga?" Brock quipped.

"Good morning," Dave said, sitting up straight.

"You want some coffee?" Brock asked.

"Not yet. I don't want the caffeine kicking in too early."

"Did you bring your jacket?"

"It's in my office."

"Ellen asked about it yesterday. I told her you'd have it. She thinks it's mystical."

"Maybe it is."

"Sure, or maybe you don't give yourself enough credit. I'm telling you—you're going to kill it today. I can feel it. Just make sure you throw in plenty of *soul.*"

The first hint of a smile crossed Dave's face.

Brock took a seat beside his friend, then turned quizzical. "Look, I know that you wanted this account pretty badly. Has it been everything you expected?"

It was casual conversation, words to kill time until the meeting started. It was also the very question Dave had been pondering for the last twenty minutes. He hesitated in his answer. "I don't know, really—I'm . . . I'm not sure."

Brock shrugged. "If not, it will be. Hey, I'm going to grab coffee," he said, standing up. "Then I'll be in my office until it's time to start. Are there any changes in my introduction?"

"No. Do it just like we discussed—just like old times."

Brock nodded and pulled the door closed with a click, leaving the room's solitude to surround and envelop Dave as if it were still waiting to hear his answer.

Has it been everything you expected?

• • •

At nine sharp the elevator doors pinged opened and Mr. Shaun Safford, Vice President of Marketing for BikeHouse Customized Motorcycles, stepped out. Five protégés followed, one more than Dave had expected. Ellen waited with her hand extended. The show was about to begin.

"Mr. Safford. Gentlemen. It's great to have you here. I trust you had a good flight." Dave let Ellen handle the formal greeting, the small talk, the useless chatter about the weather.

"I just wish we'd have had time to ride over instead of fly," Safford added.

Ellen chuckled, perhaps not understanding the man was serious. "Yes, well, of course. Um . . . we have some coffee, pastries, and such. We can wait in the conference room for the others to arrive."

Dave and Brock shook hands with the entourage. Safford

grabbed a pastry and then returned. Not wanting to miss a thing, Ellen stepped into the circle as well.

"Dave, have you been out riding lately?" Safford asked.

"I took a ride over the weekend down to Frederick." He spoke matter-of-factly, as if he spent every weekend on the road.

"What'd you ride?" Safford continued.

"A '91 Sturgis, mint." Ellen nodded to Dave's answer, as if the words meant something to her. Safford didn't notice her; his focus was locked on Dave.

"How was it? The ride, I mean."

"Best ride of my life—enlightening."

"Long rides usually are."

As the conversation continued, a second group of suit-clad executives stepped into the room—advertising folks. There were more introductions, more handshakes, more business cards exchanged. Four employees of Strategy Data followed: three support staff and one intern assigned to the project.

By quarter past the hour, everyone had filled a plate, and Ellen piped up, "Well, I know you all have busy schedules, so let's get started." She waited another few minutes as people staked their claims to the various chairs arranged throughout the room.

When all appeared ready, she began. "I think you all know I'm Ellen Brewer, President of Strategy Data International. And let me begin by telling you how excited and pleased we are to have such a distinguished group here today . . ."

Dave couldn't argue that Ellen was a good boss, despite her sometimes callous behavior. He'd certainly had worse. And everyone at the firm would agree that her leadership and strategic decisions had been critical in moving the company forward and making it a success.

"We're also glad to have you gentlemen from AdCore here today. There's no question that you do a fine job filling the advertising needs of such a stellar company as BikeHouse Customized Motorcycles . . ."

The woman was smart enough to surround herself with competent people. She believed in hiring the best and then paying them well. Not that the money came without a price. Ellen gave her all to the firm, and she expected everyone else to do the same.

"And I'd like to thank the people from our own staff in attendance today who have helped us put this information together . . ."

While she was more than competent, the one trait that Dave found irritating—at times even exasperating—was the fact that she didn't understand when to sit down and shut up.

" . . . and as you know, the scope of the study was broad. Who buys a customized bike and why? Our research may surprise you . . ."

While Ellen droned on, Dave began to consider Brock's question once again. *Has it been everything you expected?* He knew the answer—it was simple, obvious. He just couldn't bring himself to admit it or to verbalize it.

It begged a follow-up question. If not, then does any of this really matter?

Dave let his fingers drift across the surface of his leather jacket. The aroma, the newness, still lingered. It was a pleasing smell, but it also let memories tag along—memories of Megan, of the children, of better times. Dr. Jaspers had been right. They should be happy memories, joyful memories. Yet, so often when they surfaced, they brought only loneliness and guilt.

Guilt? Strange, but that had never been discussed with the doctor. Why should he feel guilty? It was an accident, after all. And yet, wasn't he the one driving?

What if I'd swerved at just the right moment? What if I'd been paying closer attention or just waited ten more minutes to leave? What if . . .

Brock stood—Ellen had finished. Brock would give a quick introduction, discuss the basis and scope of the study, explain the reasons for their approach—in short, he'd give validity to the conclusions that Dave would present. It was a great format. They'd used it countless times.

Dave knew from experience that Brock would take exactly five minutes, hitting his mark within ten seconds either way. It was a speech Dave had heard often, though adapted to each particular situation.

Brock had been a good friend, helpful in his own myopic way. He certainly did not understand Dave's loss, but at least he pretended to—perhaps even wanted to. And Brock's question had been a fair one. *Has it been everything you expected?* He had expected more, hoped for more. Finding the jacket had been painful, but then to land the BikeHouse account because of it . . . it seemed like too much of a coincidence.

And yet, in just over an hour, the pastries would be gone, the reports would be distributed, the research presented, and conclusions drawn. There would be pats on the back for everyone, whether they deserved them or not, and the men in their tailored suits and women in their designer outfits would wander back to their self-important jobs in their self-serving world—and in the end, Dave wondered, would he have made any difference at all? Would anyone walk out the door a better person?

In the end, people would still buy motorcycles, Ellen would continue to fret about next year's growth rate, and Brock would persist in putting the moves on every woman entering his life. But what about himself? Dave questioned. He would continue to drive home each night alone to find a cold and empty house full of nothing but aching memories, a house of misery.

"I'll now turn the time over to Dave to explain our conclusions and recommendations."

Brock's question had been simple—*Has it been everything you expected?* He would be lying if he pretended it had. BikeHouse was just Novocain, anesthesia numbing the wound without ever healing it. Inside, Dave was still bleeding.

"Dave, you're up." Brock's voice hardened, his volume increased. "If you'd like to explain our conclusions and recommendations, the time is now yours."

Dave stood slowly—all eyes focused on him, tracking his every move.

His voice flowed with emotion. "I'm sorry. I apologize. I let my mind wander a minute there. That's easy to do when you're thinking about a BikeHouse customized ride. I'm convinced they're the most amazing custom bikes produced anywhere." He paused to collect his thoughts, looking like he didn't know where to start.

Ellen gazed around the room, seemingly fascinated by the attention Dave had instantly commanded. By pretending to drift, by acting as if he weren't paying attention, he now had every person in the room staring intently.

She hadn't been shy about voicing her support. She'd already told Dave that as far as she was concerned, he was nothing short of brilliant. Now, with simple, unadulterated drama, the crowd was eating out of his hand. Her smile said it all: give the man an academy award.

Dave continued, "I was thinking about motorcycles because of my jacket—and because of the amazing circumstance in landing this account. You see, I've been in search of something that I've lost—something that I've been missing for quite a while now. And the funny part is, I somehow got it into my head that I would find my answers here—with this account."

Ellen may have been buying into the change of plan, but Brock wasn't. One look at him said he understood that something was terribly wrong.

Dave continued, "I took a ride this past weekend with a friend of mine. I asked him about my search, and he told me that I'd been looking in the wrong places—that I had to look inside. I've been sitting here this morning pondering that, but with an inside so hollow and empty that it's hard to say what I expect to find. And then Brock asked me if working on this account had been worth it. It's a simple question, but I realized—and no offense to Mr. Safford—the answer is *no*. There's something still missing, I'm not sure what, and that's what has me a bit perplexed."

His words dripped with despair. Safford cast a glance toward Ellen, who sat forward in her chair for the first time since Dave had stood. If calculated, the combined gross payroll of the assembled executives would be staggering. All now stared shellshocked at the man in front of the room, the man in charge, the man wearing the black leather jacket.

Brock leaned forward, looking ready to lead Dave out of the room to have a quick talk. Instead, he took a breath and waited.

Dave glanced down at the floor and then again over the crowd. His odd monologue, his peculiar demeanor, was finally causing his boss to shift and fidget.

"The thing is, though—I can't continue this way . . . without knowing . . . with nothing changing. I just can't."

Dave's shoulders slumped, as if the weight of his words was becoming too much to carry.

"I had another good friend who I could tell all of my problems to, all of my concerns. And the thing is, she was always able to find me an answer."

I've always wanted to grow a ponytail, buy a Harley, and ride across the country.

A Harley? Like a motorcycle? In your suit and tie?

No, of course not. I'd get a black leather jacket and I'd ride across the country, until—well, until I came to the Golden Gate Bridge, and not just to it, I'd ride across it.

Across the bridge?

Yep. It would be the Fourth of July. The sun would be shining; the sky would be bright and clear. A slight breeze would be blowing over the ocean and through my hair.

"Dave, are you okay?" Brock was standing now beside him. Ellen had jumped up as well.

Dave gazed at Brock and then out across the room before focusing on his jacket. Worry rolled across his lips. "What's today?" he asked.

"What?" Brock replied.

"Is today the twenty-sixth?" Dave turned to the crowd as if asking a school class. The intern, a guy who had come to watch a *master* at work, spoke up first.

"It's the twenty-sixth, Mr. Riley."

"Twenty-sixth," Dave repeated, doing the math in his head.

Brock touched his shoulder and pushed him toward his empty chair. "Dave, why don't you take a seat and let me take over here?"

Dave's tone shifted, quickened. "There's still time. I can make it."

"Still make what?" Ellen called out.

If Dave heard his boss's question, he didn't respond. Instead he turned to Shaun Safford. "I'm sorry, Mr. Safford. Brock will explain the study. I have to go." With that, he sidestepped around Brock and bolted through the conference-room door.

chapter twenty-six

Dave followed Redd through the back doors at Lakeshore until both men stood beside the '91 Sturgis that Dave had ridden to Frederick. It was polished and ready. As they looked the bike over, Redd spoke first. "She's all fueled up and clean as a new-diapered baby."

"Thanks, Redd."

"The boss will want you to sign this." Redd picked up a sales contract that waited on the counter and handed it to Dave. "I'll take care of the rest of the paperwork."

Dave scribbled his name on the dotted line without reading a word.

"You know where you're heading?" Redd asked.

"I've known for a while—it's a bridge my grandfather helped build. I visited once as a boy, when I was seven or eight. I barely remember it. We went out as a family for my grandfather's funeral. It's funny because I don't really remember him—my grandfather—yet I have a curious recollection of staring up at these massive orange spires on the bridge, as if they were enormous fingers that reached up to touch the clouds."

There was a long pause before Dave spoke again. "I also remember my father telling me, very distinctly, that my grandfather found answers at the bridge." Dave took another breath. "I don't know if I ever told you, Redd, but Megan bought me this jacket before she died. It's hard to explain why I need to go, I just do."

"Dave, I'm the one guy you don't need to explain that to. Just be prepared. You need to realize that the answers you find may not be those you expect."

"I'll keep that in mind. And thanks for teaching me to ride, being my friend, everything."

"No problem. Listen, you've got my number if anything comes up?"

"I do."

Redd pressed a green button on the wall, and the metal overhead door clanked into action. Dave pushed the bike outside, threw his leg over the seat, and engaged the engine. He raised his hand toward Redd, a mixed gesture of thank you and good-bye; he couldn't hear Redd's reply over the rumble, but he could read his lips.

"Godspeed."

Dave twisted the handle, released the clutch, and rolled smoothly out of the parking lot while Redd watched the bike and his newfound friend disappear.

• • •

On his way home from BikeHouse, Dave stopped at REI and purchased a sleeping bag that he stuffed into his bike's leather saddlebag. He didn't plan on using it—it was only for emergencies. He'd been a camper as a teenager, but that felt like a lifetime ago. Camping to Megan, after all, meant a weekend at the Marriott.

At home, Dave gathered up the rest of his essentials—clothes, toothbrush, toothpaste, a handful of power bars, two bottles of water, a cell phone, and his printed maps, just in case.

That morning he'd spent more than an hour on the computer calculating the mileage, the days, the stops along the way. He had plenty of time. Even with stops for food, gas, laundry, and sleep, he would still make the Golden Gate with at least two days to spare before the Fourth of July.

Two lights were left on, the front and back porch. It wouldn't matter—he lived in a secure neighborhood. He glanced around one last time, wondering if he'd forgotten anything. The newspaper had been stopped; he'd put a hold on the mail. He'd called two boys on the baseball team to keep up the yard; they were more than happy to oblige. The security patrols had been notified that he would be on an "extended vacation."

It was time.

Once in the garage, Dave locked the door leading to the house, then wheeled the bike out into the driveway. He checked the latches on the saddlebags for the third time—they were fine—then entered the garage code. He watched the door drop until the bottom rubber edge pushed tight against the pavement. It felt symbolic, a door being sealed behind, uncertainty opening ahead.

He took a breath, swung his leg over the bike, and pressed the ignition. It roared to life. With the clutch engaged, he clicked the machine into gear and twisted the handle. His action was still not as fluid as Redd's, still not as certain—but it was adequate.

Though he'd vowed not to look back, he couldn't resist a final glance as he rolled toward the street. At the mailbox he squeezed the brake to bring the bike to a stop and check traffic. The sun was just beginning to set, causing a glare from the west. He wouldn't get far tonight, but he was leaving anyway. He couldn't stay another night in the emptiness alone.

With the sun in his eyes, it was difficult to make out the shape of the car coming down the street toward him. The sound, however, was unmistakable. He waited for Brock to pull in front of the mailbox, shut off his ignition, and step from his car. Dave turned off his engine as well, then watched Brock study him—first the bike, and then the scene before him.

"Looking good. Looking very good," Brock finally said.

"Thanks."

"I mean the bike, of course. The real question is, are you okay?"

"I think so." Dave kept his answers short. He waited for Brock to get to his point.

"You sure you want to leave like this?"

Dave responded with the slightest of shrugs.

Brock continued. "You're kissing off a six-figure-a-year job. I'm sure that's filled with some terrific irony or hidden meaning, but I sure as hell don't know what it might be."

"Look, I know it doesn't make sense. I just need some time off, that's all."

"Time off, huh?" Brock questioned.

"Yeah."

"Are you sure? 'Cause it sounds like a bit more than that."

"No, I'm not sure at all. It just . . . feels right."

"Feels right?"

"Weird, I realize, but yeah."

Brock accepted the answer, seemed to understand that nothing he could say would dissuade the man. "It's not going to be the same at the office without you."

"I appreciate that. How did Ellen take it?"

Brock's eyes rolled heavenward. "She went ballistic—threw the reports across the conference room, swore up a storm. Not in front of Safford, but before the elevator doors had finished closing. Yes, I'd say you did a fine job of burning that bridge to a crisp. Even if you changed your mind, the truth is, it's probably too late for you to come back."

"She'll get over it."

"Perhaps," Brock said. "And I also talked to Dr. Jaspers today. She said you weren't answering or returning her calls."

"She means well."

"She asked if I'd have you call her."

"In time."

"So, where you heading?"

"West. There's a bridge my grandfather help build."

"The Golden Gate?"

191

"Same one."

"You're not going there to jump off, I hope?"

The remark caused Dave's first smile. "I hadn't looked at it that way."

"Well, don't. I'm sorry I brought it up."

Dave exhaled, sucked in a fresh breath, tried his best to explain. "I remember hearing a lot of family stories about the bridge, mostly concerning my grandfather. They say he found answers there. I just thought I'd go have a look."

"That sounds . . . *quaint.*" Brock's tone reeked of ridicule.

Dave ignored it. "It's what he believed."

"When will you get there?"

"By the Fourth—I have a stop to make first, but I'll still make it by then."

Each out of words, the silence settled around them, then nudged. Brock extended his hand. Dave reached out and clasped it to pull his friend close.

"For the record," Brock added, "I think you're crazy as hell, but at the same time—good luck."

"Thanks."

"And I am going to try to smooth things over with Ellen. So, if you get to the bridge and it's closed or something, call me."

Dave nodded, pulled on his helmet, started the bike, and then reached for the clutch. Before squeezing it tight, he raised his hand in a stationary wave. Brock reciprocated.

A quick shift, a gentle rumble. Brock turned left; Dave turned right. Brock toward home and Dave toward the lingering glare of the setting sun.

chapter twenty-seven

Upon my return to the library, I find a note by a man named Alfred Finnila. "I was walking on the catwalk and I slipped my watch into my pocket. It was a gold pocket watch. I missed my pocket, and the watch went down my pants leg and kept going all the way down into the water. It gave me a funny feeling."

I understand how he felt.

Another man, Peanuts Coble, noted, "Ed Reed was a full-blooded Indian who boxed professionally on weekends. I was boarding with him at an old widow lady's place in Sausalito. Ed was sometimes a bit short on manners. We were eating with the widow and her kids at the table, when she said to Ed, 'Don't you feel proud that someday your son or daughter will look up at that bridge from a cruise ship and say, "My father helped build that"?' With a mouthful of food and without missing a beat, Ed responded, 'Just so the little bastards don't say I fell off of it.'"

When I laugh aloud, Gwen, the librarian, wanders over to

find out what is so funny. She reads the account and her smile lingers. "I hope you find what you're looking for."

"Thank you," I say, but my frustration must show, because no sooner have the words come out than she continues to probe.

"Are you sure I can't help you find something?"

I'll take all the help I can get. "Gwen," I say, "I'm looking for information about a man named Patrick O'Riley who worked on the bridge. I was hoping to find something here, but no luck. Any ideas?"

"Did you check the electronic index?"

"Yes—nothing."

"And you've checked some of the better histories written about the bridge?"

"Yes, and again nothing."

She lists a few more ideas, but none that I haven't tried.

"We do have some material out on loan to two or three other universities. I can check the log to see what turns up. Did you say the name was O'Riley?"

"Patrick O'Riley."

I thank her kindly, but my chances are slim. Thousands of men worked on the bridge, thousands made their contribution, put in their years, and then filtered out into the vastness of America. I am hoping for the impossible.

As Gwen wanders away, I continue to read stories of struggle, lessons of triumph. I find words of sorrow in the histories, but also words of accomplishment. I read about the men's lives and I wonder about their families and how their wives and children *left at home must have worried. Did these men have their own Annas?*

The information is captivating, but the lights dim and the library will soon close for the day—and I have yet to see the name of Patrick O'Riley. It appears he arrived out of nowhere, dedicated a good five years or more of his life to the bridge, and then dropped off the face of the earth.

• • •

I call the professor early and tell him that I'll be at home working on the project. I don't dare tell him that means I'm obsessed with learning more about Patrick and Anna.

I came up empty at the library, but bumps in the road are expected. I begin today by calling the Golden Gate Bridge Highway and Transportation District, the agency that was formed to finance and construct the bridge. They were slated to disband once the bridge was complete and the construction bonds were repaid, but, like most government agencies, they proved harder to dispatch than to organize. While they once managed construction of the bridge, today they oversee all transit in the Golden Gate corridor. I talk with three people before confirming what I already suspect—there are no employee records that cover the building of the bridge. I'm reminded that they only oversaw the work of hired private companies.

Next, I attempt to track down records from the contractors themselves. There were ten prime contractors and various subcontractors selected to work on the structure. To my dismay, none are still in business.

The room's air is beginning to smother me—it's time to take a walk. I open the journal and scribble down the address Patrick has written on the inside cover. It is in Parkside, a good five miles from where I live. I change into my jogging shorts, lace up my running shoes, and head out the door.

I picture finding an old apartment building, historic but well kept, a place where a friendly elderly gentleman in the office talks about the workers they once housed during the construction of the bridge. He'll speak of being but a small boy, perhaps five or six, when his father or grandfather owned the building, and he'll still remember the men. He'll confirm that of course they have all their records from over eighty years ago—that they are kept in an old wooden filing cabinet upstairs in the attic. He'll tell me to help myself, and to lock the door on my way out. Or even better, he'll tell me that though he was just a lad, he recalls a charming Irish gentleman in particular.

It's a good vision that keeps me running. But when I arrive at the address, I find a supermarket. I contemplate jogging back home, but I flag down a cab instead.

My wall is getting taller, wider, and deeper. In research, you climb over, you dig under, you find a hole. It's a matter of time, persistence, and patience.

Where is the weakness in my wall?

Ellen reclined in her deep leather chair, her feet squarely on the desk. It was a position she seldom took. Her stare was at unseen objects out the window, past the city skyline.

"Damn him!" she mumbled to herself. "How could he just get up and walk out like that?" With no one by Ellen's side to bob their head along with hers and agree that she was right, she cursed again for good measure, just to feel better. The woman wasn't through ranting. "Dave knew how important this account was. How could he do it?"

It wasn't easy being the boss, especially of a company where her father had once been in charge. Ellen wished she could be sympathetic, but she had a business to run. Dozens of people depended on her for their paychecks, not just Dave Riley.

"And to not wait until the meeting was over," she continued, "to leave right in the middle with the client sitting there in shock." It was unacceptable. There was a line of common sense, of decency, of professional demeanor. Dave Riley hadn't just stepped over it, he'd taken a running long jump.

The familiar beep of the intercom startled her. She pulled her feet in and sat up straight in her chair.

"Ms. Brewer?" It was her secretary, Kathy.

"Yes, Kathy?"

"There is a call for you on line seven. It's Mr. Jim Wiesenberger."

"Wiesenberger . . . Wiesenberger." Ellen repeated the name. It sounded familiar, but she couldn't place it. "Kathy, do you know who he's with?"

Kathy's tone echoed surprise, since usually her astute boss recognized the names of such important men. "Yes, ma'am. It's Mr. Jim Wiesenberger, the CEO of BikeHouse Customized Motorcycles. He's calling from Wisconsin. He needs to speak with you right away. He says it's urgent."

chapter twenty-eight

My first call of the morning is to Janet Metcalfe, a friend in Salt Lake City. After getting a history degree from SFSU, she moved to Utah to work for an insurance agency. I call her first because she's an avid genealogy nut, and I use the term in the nicest sense of the word. The Mormon church operates a Family History Library there that is one of the best in the world. I know that Janet uses it regularly to research her own ancestors, and I'm hoping that she'll know the ropes and use it to help me.

"Good morning, this is Janet."

"Janet, it's Katie Connelly."

"Katie? It's about time you called. How are you?"

We chat for several minutes, catching up on old acquaintances and gossip. I find out that she is engaged; she finds out that I am hardly dating. She loves her new job and is surprised to hear that I am still working at the university. She and her fiancé are planning a trip to Hawaii for their honeymoon; I tell her that for my vacation, I painted my house. Before I get too depressed, I cut short the small talk and get to the reason for my call.

"Listen, Janet, I'm calling to ask a favor."

"Sure, what is it?"

"I'm looking for a man . . ." I pause at the wrong moment, and she jumps in before I have a chance to finish.

"Well, it's about time. You came to the right person. I know several who are available."

"Let me rephrase that—I'm looking for information about a man. He lived in San Francisco from about 1931 to at least 1937. His name was Patrick O'Riley. I was thinking that, since you are so good at genealogy research, you could check the Family History Library for me."

"I'd be happy to. Do you know when he was born?"

"I don't."

"You don't know how old he was?"

"No, not exactly."

"He was from San Francisco, though?"

"No, I don't think so."

"A U.S. citizen?"

"I doubt it, but I don't know."

"So, all you really know is his name?"

"Pretty much. I do know that he had a wife whose name was Anna; at least, I think they were married. I know they loved each other. She was living somewhere far away, perhaps Ireland. I was hoping that you could look for him in both San Francisco and Ireland."

"Let me get this straight. You want to find a man named O'Riley from Ireland, and that's all you know about him?"

"I guess."

"Should I look for a Smith from the United States while I'm at it?"

If she is trying to make me feel stupid, it's working.

"I know it's not much, but it's all I have right now," I admit.

"It'd be easier to just find you a man."

"I called because you're the best researcher I've ever known."

"You know me, Katie, flattery will get you everywhere. You say his first name is Patrick?"

"You'll give it a shot?"

"Sure, but no promises. Now, is there anything else you can tell me about him? Anything else at all?"

"He may have been an engineer or attended engineering school. Does that help?"

"About as much as knowing his favorite color, but it's something."

"I appreciate this."

"Just promise you'll come to my wedding."

"It's a promise."

I confirm my address and say my good-byes. I hate to admit it, but Janet is right. I need more information. Before I make any other calls, I pick up the journal, open the cover, and carefully turn page after page.

There must be something I've missed.

The steel and concrete buildings blurred as Dave headed south, away from the city, away from the job, away from Brock and Dr. Jaspers and Ellen Brewer, away from his empty home in Jamesburg—away from the memories.

There was one visit he needed to make before his journey to the bridge could begin—one place he felt compelled to see. Traffic in Washington, D.C., was heavy when Dave arrived, just as it had been every other time he'd ever been to D.C. Once, three years earlier, feeling guilty for not providing enough "culture" for the children, he and Megan had piled the family into the van for a long weekend in the nation's capital. They'd made plans to see all the historic sites—the Washington Monument, the Jefferson Memorial, the Constitution Gardens, and, yes, the Vietnam Veterans Memorial—the "wall" that Redd so deeply revered.

Unknowingly, however, they'd picked the same weekend as the annual Cherry Blossom Festival, the time each spring when the trees blossom and the crowds throng in hordes to see. By the time they'd hit Constitution Avenue, traffic had come to a standstill. After moving only two blocks in forty-five minutes, the family voted to bail. They would get historic another time. Instead, they opted for Annapolis, one of Dave's favorite getaway spots. They rented rooms at the Prince George Bed and Breakfast and spent the weekend going to movies, restaurants, and even a wax museum. Those were good memories, but also reminders that the city's historic sites remained on the *someday* list.

Today was the day.

Dave found a parking spot along Henry Bacon Drive and locked up his bike. It was a short walk to the monument nestled in the grassy park of Constitution Gardens. His pace slowed as he neared the structure. It was exactly as Redd had described: black granite panels, arranged into two arms that extended to form an angle. The area sloped gently toward the center of each so that for a person entering at ground level, the descent toward the middle would reveal more and more of the wall. At the highest point, Dave guessed the wall extended about ten feet.

He studied the design. It was striking but unimposing, less grand than he'd imagined, and yet certainly profound. Each of the long black granite slabs sunk down into the earth—obviously symbolic of the men and women who had died and were buried. And it was indeed a place of calmness and serenity.

Dave stepped back to record mentally what he was seeing, feeling—if not for himself, then for Redd. Most staggering were the sheer numbers of names cut into the stone's surface—thousands upon thousands of names, each holding a story of lost life, love, and legacy.

An older, olive-skinned man and woman shuffled past Dave toward the wall. They were speaking Spanish; as they neared the granite, their tones hushed. The old man bowed his head and looked down while the woman raised her hand, extended her wrinkled finger, and touched a name.

Farther down the wall Dave watched three teenage girls, one writing in a notebook while the other two strolled silently back and forth. It was more hallowed behavior than one might have expected from teenage friends on a beautiful summer day.

Dave stepped up to the granite slab, picked a name at random, and let his fingers trace the letters. *Clifford Paxton.* Who was he? Who had he left behind? Dave's fingers moved to the name adjacent: *Simon Ellison.* Did he leave a wife? Did loved ones still visit and trace outlines of his name? Was he still remembered?

Books had been placed at each end of the wall that listed the soldiers alphabetically, making it easy for friends and family to find their loved ones. Dave walked to a book, flipped through its pages, searched for Leslie Harris, and then located the panel where his name was engraved. Dave let his fingers trace the furrowed letters, as Redd had done so many years earlier and no doubt many times since. But what about the soldier's name below Leslie's, or the one above? Every single one, like Leslie, had given his or her life, had left grieving family behind. While he was grateful for the chance to touch Leslie's name, to remember Redd's story, to offer a silent moment of gratitude for the man's sacrifice, Dave also realized that each and every name would do.

He had read about the war in school, recalled the history. Countless books and movies had been written and made, and he had read and seen many of them—yet it had never felt like his war.

An elderly woman approached and placed a flower at the base of the wall. Dave could see no tears, and yet she touched the wall with reflection. What was her story? Had she lost a friend, an uncle, a father? He thought about approaching her, asking, but didn't. Instead, he bowed his head, closed his eyes, and offered a tribute to those whose names stretched out before him—to Les Harris, to thousands of faceless others, and to Redd.

He was thankful he had taken the time. It was a hallowed place, a sacred place—Redd would be proud. And yet, although he knew he would never take the war for granted again, he also realized this was not where he would find closure. Without looking back at the woman, the teenage girls, the couple, or the many others who had come to pay their respects, Dave turned and walked back across the grass and down the street to where his bike was parked. Many came to the wall to shed tears; Dave did not.

Instead, he strapped on his helmet, climbed on his bike, and rode—away from Redd's answers and toward a search for his own.

chapter twenty-nine

As I study the journal again, combing for clues, I find something new.

Patrick wrote, "When Russell Cone came to inspect me work on the cable, we discussed how the bridge moves and deflects as the cable length changes. 'Tis this giving of the bridge that gives strength to the structure and absorbs strain. Me bridge is almost a living, breathing thing."

I find his comment intriguing, for as a child I also imagined the bridge to be alive. With the wisdom of years that adulthood brings, I understand that she is just a bridge. Yet there are times, even today, when she takes on a life of her own.

I also notice that Patrick references God, and if he was a religious man from Ireland, it means that there are two choices—Catholic or Protestant. Thankfully, both are notorious record keepers. If he had attended a local congregation, there still might be a record.

When I explain my plight to Father Muldowney, my own priest, he is happy to help. He promises to check surrounding cathedrals as well as fax me a list of additional churches worth investigating.

Next I head out to see the city clerk. If Anna and the children moved to San Francisco, there's a possibility that the family purchased a home. My chances are slim, but I am getting desperate.

The woman at the desk smiles a friendly hello, but if I expect her cheeriness to make my work pleasant, I am soon disappointed. The job is drudgery. Two hours in, I discover a P. O'Riley who owned property in Stonestown, but my hopes are dashed when further digging reveals he was Mr. Pierce O'Riley, not Patrick, and dates on the documents preclude him from being my O'Riley at all.

After six more hours, I head home for a hot bath and bed, flush with frustration, needing to extinguish the feelings of failure building in my chest. On my way, a haunting comment from the journal keeps flashing into my head. It is a simple, almost reflective statement Patrick made in the journal's final pages.

"It is interesting," he said, "that bridges, the most permanent of structures, are so often built by the most transient of men."

Is he speaking of himself? If bridge builders are migratory, if they follow the work, then did Patrick also move on to another bridge? If so, where? Once home, I find a government website that lists all the bridges in the United States. My chest aches when I notice the number—six hundred thousand!

I narrow my search by filtering for large, historic bridges. The

Tacoma Narrows Bridge pops up first. It was a suspension bridge, the first to cross the Puget Sound, and construction began shortly after completion of the Golden Gate. Within minutes, however, I have dozens of possibilities. I see bridges in Connecticut, Pennsylvania, New York; I find bridges along the East Coast, the West Coast, and in between. They are everywhere.

It doesn't take long for hopelessness to roll and boil, for the bleakness to bubble. I am looking down another impossible road. Even if he moved on to work another bridge, the never-ending list on my monitor flickers a truth that bounces about the room—Patrick could have gone anywhere.

• • •

Visiting churches should be soothing—today, not so much. While some of the priests and ministers are pleasant, the rest must moonlight at the DMV. Several insist that I make an appointment—not a problem, except it's for weeks down the road, and I can't wait weeks.

At the churches friendly enough to let me peruse their records, I find the work grueling. It isn't like typing words into a search engine. Instead the places are stuffy, the smell of must and mildew is overwhelming, and the rooms are miserably hot. Honestly, I envision hell to be quite like the back rooms of a church. Each page must be scrutinized individually, and the writing is nearly impossible to read. I start my quest with excitement, with a vision of success, but my enthusiasm ages into despair.

I take a deep breath and remember that I need to be elastic and flexible like the bridge. But I don't feel elastic, I feel tense and rigid. I understand that this search is a self-imposed burden, one that I opted to carry the day I vowed to find the family of Patrick O'Riley. And if it is self-imposed, then I should be able to cast it aside—but I can't. It has taken hold of me and won't let go. It has grown into an obligation that wraps its fingers around my heart. With each beat I keep asking: what if, after all my searching, I can't find him? What if I never learn more about Patrick and Anna?

I should go home. I haven't eaten since breakfast, and I can feel my blood sugar is at an all-time low. Instead, with stress clouding my logic, I commit a cardinal sin. I pass Chang's Chinese Buffet with its "all-you-can-eat" neon sign flashing like a hypnotist's trap. I wander inside, hand the plump Chinese woman my money, and then for the next forty minutes I perpetrate diet suicide. I eat like it's my last supper. I chow down on sesame chicken, sweet and sour pork, and orange beef. It's like popcorn: once you start eating, it's almost impossible to stop. With everything fried in oil, I can eat through my entire monthly allowance of saturated fat in one sitting.

I've always had the willpower to resist, but tonight I gorge like a screaming pig. By the time I can't pop another piece of fortune cookie into my mouth, all I desire is to crawl home and throw up—not because I feel sick to my stomach, but because I feel sick in my heart. It's a deep-down sickness that I'm feeling because, soon, I'll be forced to admit that I have failed to find Patrick O'Riley.

• • •

In the safety of my home, I get angry—more than angry, I am livid. I scream at the computer. I crumple up papers and hurl them into the wastebasket. I move into the kitchen and swear at the stacks of books piled high, uttering words that I never say in public. All the while my unfinished outline mocks from the table. I utterly detest that ridiculous assignment—busywork from the Society of Ladies with Too Much Time on Their Hands!

I have been home for all of five minutes and my pity party is in full swing. In my frustration, I move close to the table and dump the remaining pages of my report into the garbage can. As I do, I interrogate myself.

"Why is it, Katie, that you can't finish the report, can't find Patrick, can't accomplish anything you set out to do? Why is it that you're still alone? Why are you still stuck at a university unable to move forward, too nervous to even face the man who betrayed you? Why, Katie?"

I ask as if I expect a different Katie to answer. But there is only one Katie at home, and her life is unraveling. As I wait for answers that don't come, I realize for the first time since walking through the door that I smell atrocious. I've worked up a sweat in the hot and stuffy church rooms, and the ensuing stench coming from my shirt is disgusting. I don't just stink with body odor, I reek of failure.

In disgust, I tear off my shirt, head to the shower, and pull on the hot water. I'm usually one to conserve, to do my share for the community, but tonight I don't care. I plop down in the middle of the shower's tile floor and let the water cascade over me in torrents, watching it pool, mix, and swirl with my guilt and then flow down the drain. I vow to leave the water on until the pipes in the city run dry, until the conservation police kick down my door and haul me off naked and screaming to jail.

After thirty minutes, however, my skin begins to shrivel. I renege on my vow to run the city dry and decide instead that using up all the hot water in the house will be revenge enough. Ten minutes later, I am a prune, but the hot water keeps blasting.

We have a deep, old-fashioned bathtub in the bathroom upstairs. Dad loved to soak in it after a hard day at the bridge. With an active teenage girl in the house, he would often run out of hot water. It drove him crazy until one Saturday, he brought home a new water heater, a huge, seventy-five-gallon model. Together, we connected it to our existing unit so that one feeds into the other. As my skin now starts to itch, it dawns on me that since that time, I don't remember running out of hot water—ever. I could be here all night. I could drown. After five more minutes, I wave the white flag and push the valve closed in disgust. I am a failure at everything.

My hands are white and wrinkled. I look like an old, dead, white woman. As I pat myself dry, my skin begins to scream for lotion, and there is none left in the bathroom. I want to simply crawl into bed naked to begin the cry of my life—and I will, just as soon as I get more lotion from the kitchen. I find the other bottle on the counter, but when I discover that it too is almost empty, I am about to start my tantrum over—when something catches my attention.

The notification light on my phone is blinking.

Someone called while I was staging my shower sit-in. I tap the screen to hear the voice of Gwen from the library. She must have called just before closing. I want to believe that this is the break I've been praying for. I need to hope, but as I consider my actions of the previous hour, caution seems my best ally. If I raise my expectations, I'll set myself up for a drop off the emotional edge that I just can't handle.

But her words cause hope to rise in my chest.

"Hi, it's Gwen at the library. I think I may have found something."

chapter thirty

From Washington, D.C., Dave headed northwest on I-70 across Maryland and into Pennsylvania—past the steel mills of Pittsburgh, past factories, past apartments. I-70 soon meshed into I-76 toward Cleveland, then into I-80 past Lake Erie, Toledo, and Gary, Indiana.

When Dave was hungry, he would stop and eat—burgers and sandwiches, mostly, at drive-ins, cafés, fast-food diners, whatever was convenient. When he was tired, he'd find a motel and sleep— usually in the smaller towns, away from the big city, far from the memories he was trying to distance. Sometimes, when the monotony of the freeway began to grind, he'd exit to the back roads and traverse at a slower, less frenzied pace. Other times, when anxiety would take hold, when he worried about making it on time, he'd jump back onto the interstate and push it to the limit.

Just missing Chicago, then across Illinois and into Iowa, familiar city names—Davenport, Iowa City, Des Moines—but names that mixed and mingled, never letting him be sure, as he traced the route in his head, if they were places he'd just passed or those still to come. He drove by farms, endless fields of crops, scattered tractors and cows. He passed small, blurring towns— Guthrie, Oakfield, Hancock—almost nameless, each looking like the one before.

Through them all, he kept a close eye on the weather, and it had generally cooperated. He'd detoured only once near Newton to avoid rain that was predicted to blow across the plain from the northeast. It was a detour that proved unnecessary. The guarded storm stayed distant, as if it understood that the determined man on the motorcycle needed to get past and be on his way.

It was a solitary ride, a reflective ride, a lonely ride—and yet it provided time to think, to wonder.

With Megan things had been easy. Life's road had been busy, at times a veritable eight-lane freeway, but she had always been there providing a direction and a destination. Without her, it felt as though he'd lost his orientation. The once-solid path was now more like gravel, and sometimes it led off into so many diverse directions that it was impossible to know which to choose. Or worse, at times the road ended, leaving only weeds, brush, and craggy rocks.

Dave had hinted more than once to Dr. Jaspers that a change of scenery might do him some good. Her answer was always the same: "I wish it were that easy to run away from the pain, David. If it were, I'd open up a travel agency. But it follows you. It chases you. The pain needs to be dealt with from inside, David, not from the outside."

Was she right? Was this journey helping the inside? With each mile, the nagging questions remained. Was he avoiding his problems—or running toward the only place he could find answers? He had no idea; he simply knew that it was time he ran toward something.

Past the state line and into Nebraska. More fast food, more cheap motels. Omaha, Lincoln, Aurora—into the heartland— Kearney, Lexington, North Platte. Chased by demons, perhaps chasing solace, but moving. If the constant riding was merely deadening the pain, one thing was certain. As soon as he stopped, as soon as the numbness wore thin, the returning ache would be devastating.

I arrive at the library just before eight a.m. and wait by the entrance to the area that houses the Special Collections documents. Gwen doesn't arrive until almost eight minutes after the hour. "Hi, Katie. I had a feeling you'd be waiting. Sorry to be late. I couldn't find my keys, and without my keys, nobody gets in."

"That's okay. In your message you said that you found something?"

Gwen nods as she fiddles with her large silver key ring. She locates the key and slips it into the lock to open the door. I follow like a puppy.

"I checked the electronic index of the documents on loan to

three universities. *They didn't show a Patrick O'Riley. I was about to call you and tell you the bad news when I remembered the interdepartment log sheets. From time to time, department heads can request that material be transferred to their care, as long as they're using it on campus for an approved project. The problem is that those items on request don't show up on our loan sheets or in the electronic index until we get the confirmation logs back from the department heads."*

I remind myself that this is a university, so to someone obviously much smarter than I, the system must make perfect sense.

Gwen continues, *"Of course, it sometimes takes weeks; heavens, I've seen them take months to be returned. So, when I checked the log sheets, I could see that the chemistry lab had a bundle of letters that they've been using for date testing—items relating to the bridge. They are listed in the index as a bundle, rather than by author. That's why nothing showed up. Anyway, I called Dr. Stanton, and apparently they did have a bundle of letters from the early to mid-1900s."*

"Did have? They don't still have them?" I question, getting impatient at the depth of her explanation.

"Not exactly. They were sent down to the extension in Los Angeles to Dr. Markus, still technically part of the campus. I called his assistant and she checked through the material. Sure enough, there was a letter that's signed by . . . are you ready?"

She pauses, as if expecting a drumroll to materialize from nowhere. When it doesn't, she finishes on her own. *"Patrick O'Riley.*

Now, I don't know if it's the same Mr. O'Riley you're looking for, but I thought you'd like to know."

It was the best news I'd heard in weeks. "How long will they have the letter?"

"They're scheduled for another two months, longer if they request an extension."

"Can I drive down and see it?"

"You can, but you don't need to. I had a copy sent over to me yesterday."

I feel my neck chill as she turns to her desk and picks up three sheets of paper. I see the top piece has a sticky note attached with my name written on it. I glance at the first page and instantly recognize the handwriting. It is the same as in the journal. It is indeed a letter written by Patrick O'Riley—my Patrick!

"This is amazing, Gwen. I owe you."

"Just doing my job. I do hope it helps."

I thank her again profusely and then, as politely as possible, excuse myself to one of the nearby cubicles. It's not that I care if anyone else reads the letter—obviously many people have. I want to study the letter alone because it feels personal. Perhaps I'm also afraid of how I might react.

February 11, 1937

Dearest Anna,

The bridge is almost finished and she is a wonder! I can't wait for you and the young ones to see her. She spans a deep canyon, a channel filled with treacherous currents and a perpetually frenzied sea, like the Atlantic that beats upon the shores of Ireland. The two great cables that drape from her towers contain enough strands of wire to encircle the equator thrice, and the concrete poured into her pylons and anchorages could pave a four-foot-wide sidewalk from me to Dublin. The structure is indeed a wonder, and she will open to the public in just over three months.

I could not help but feel a little pride today, Anna, as I walked her span. The wind was blowing, as it always does, and the gale caused me to remember the many days I had spent on her girders. At times the wind would gust so hard the bridge would sway back and forth nearly five times a man's height. I would think of you, even in those conditions. I would picture your smiling eyes, the warmth of your touch, your laughter. I would think of the children and I would pray silently to God and the saints to sustain me.

Only now, Anna, with me work almost complete, will I admit to you that it has been dangerous. 'Tis a job that loses one man for every million dollars spent. And yet, by God's good grace, only one had perished—until February.

The safety net had saved nineteen men from plunging to their deaths into the cold, swirling sea. We called 'em members of the "Halfway to Hell" club. Thank the saints I was not among 'em. Perhaps we took the net for granted—until the day it failed.

Twelve lads were standing on the scaffolding when she collapsed. Eleven fell into the net, and for but a moment the men cheered. Then the web began to tear, and screams of joy turned to terror. I watched in horror, Anna, as the web gave way and all of me friends plunged into the open jaws of the ocean below. 'Twas a tragic and painful day.

The wonder is that, only minutes before, I had stood on the same scaffolding! I do not tell you this to cause alarm—me intentions are just the opposite. I want you to know, Anna, that it was God who spared me life.

I have devoted five years to build her—five years of longing for you and the children. And though this bridge has robbed me of sacred years of fatherhood, she is also me savior. Without the endless days spent welding her frames together, I could never have saved the money needed to snatch you and the young ones out of the slums of Dublin that hold you captive.

It is true, Anna. You will all soon be free. I have booked you all passage on the <u>Virginia May</u>, which sails from Cork on the 29th.

I am enclosing $60 for the journey. Take only what you can carry. Leave quietly. Bid farewells carefully. I will spend me days waiting your arrival. And when you and the children come, there is something that I want all of us to do. We will take a boat across the bay to the north end of the bridge. We will hold hands, and with gratitude we will walk as a family across her length—across our bridge to freedom.

You will soon see that I don't exaggerate her greatness. I want you and the children to see her majesty, feel her power. I want our young ones to understand that she is more than just a bridge—she is our liberty, our life, our hope for the future. And not just for our family, but for all those who cross her span in search of better times.

'Tis true. God is good and merciful and so when we reach the other side, I know a place on the south shore where we can kneel together as a family and say a prayer thanking Almighty God and all the saints for our reunion and our future.

Anna, I hope you will not think it strange, but when we rise from our knees on that opposite shore, we will no longer be the O'Riley family from the sully side of Dublin. At the moment we stand, as a symbol of our new life, we will be the Rileys—and we will be from America!

Please, dear wife, do not think that the sea air has rusted me brain. I am not forsaking our heritage. We both know I'll be Irish 'til the day I die, but the children, Anna, the children will have a new life in America, and a new hope! And not just our children, but their children, and then their children, and the chain will continue because of our courage and because of God's goodness.

We have lived in poverty and misery, but soon it ends. The bridge is spectacular, enchanting, even magical. As we cross over the sea and to her opposite shore, we will be a family once again.

I count the days.

Your loving husband,
Patrick O'Riley

He changed his last name! No wonder my father couldn't find him. No wonder the man appeared to vanish. With tears clouding my eyes, I mouth my thanks to Gwen and hurry toward home. On my way out, I pass Professor Winston.

I've always had a hard time hiding my emotions. I can't mask my joy when I'm happy or my gloom when I'm sad. Right away, he sees tears streaming down my face, but he also recognizes that I am beaming. He's a man, so he is immediately confused.

"Katie, are you okay?"

"Good morning, Professor. Yes, I'm fabulous. It's been such a productive morning."

"But you've been crying."

"Yes, indeed I have."

His fingers touch his chin. "You certainly are involved in your work."

I smile and hurry past him toward the exit. And he doesn't once ask about the assignment. The day is turning out to be stellar after all.

chapter thirty-one

*Why do terrible days occur before wonderful days? Could it
be with life that, in order to savor the joy, we must dine first at
the table of despair? I don't pretend to know. What I do know is
that, as bad as the last several days have been, today has made up
for them and more. And, no offense, God, but it's about time!*

*When I walk in the door, the phone is already ringing. It is
Janet on the other end.*

"Janet? I was just going to call you."

"Queen's College of Cork."

"I beg your pardon?"

*"I found a record from the school for a Patrick O'Riley—he
attended the Queen's College of Cork in Ireland. He enrolled in
1926."*

"I won't ask how you tracked that down," I say.

*"There's more. He didn't graduate, but take a guess what he
studied."*

"Engineering?"

"Ding, ding. We have a winner."

The puzzle pieces are falling into place. Patrick O'Riley is growing into more than words on a page—he is becoming real.

Janet continues, "And you said he was in San Francisco in about 1931?"

"Yes."

"The last record of him at the school is in 1930."

"So, he's our man." I say, as I catch myself bouncing from foot to foot.

"Let me finish—there's more. You mentioned that your Mr. O'Riley worked on the Golden Gate Bridge, right?"

"Yes, he did."

"Well, in my digging, I learned that the Queen's College of Cork has a few famous graduates, among them a Mr. Michael Maurice O'Shaughnessy. Does the name ring a bell?"

"I think so. Let me try to remember." The name sounds familiar. It has something to do with the bridge, but I can't put my finger on it.

Janet interrupts. "Let me help. He came from Ireland to San Francisco to become the city engineer. Turns out he was one of the early advocates of building a bridge across the Gate. He was born in County Limerick, Ireland, which also happens to be the birthplace of . . . Patrick O'Riley."

"What are you saying?"

"In this business you make assumptions. Perhaps Patrick knew this guy or his family in Ireland. Perhaps this O'Shaughnessy is the one who convinced Patrick to come to America to work on the bridge. It's all plausible."

"Is there more?"

"That's all for now. The most curious thing is that I haven't been able to trace him after he arrived in the United States. Usually that's where we have the most success."

"I believe I can tell you why. We found a letter from him here at the university. He dropped the O' from his name. The family changed their name to just Riley."

"Of course!"

"Will that help you track him?"

"You know me. I'm the one who can't put down a crossword puzzle. Give me a couple more days, and I'll see what I can come up with."

"Janet, every time we talk, your wedding gift gets more expensive."

I don't expect to hear back from Janet for at least two days. Three hours later, she calls again.

"Are you sitting down?"

"Yes."

"Looking for the right name made all the difference in the world. Let me tell you about your mystery man. Patrick O'Riley was born in County Limerick, Ireland, in 1899."

I quickly do the math in my head and realize that when he started on the bridge, he was 32—older than I'd guessed.

Janet continues, "He married Anna Sullivan in Ireland in 1925. She was from a village called Claddagh. I have records of

Patrick at the university until 1930, but nothing in Ireland after that. That's the same time he pops up in San Francisco to work on the bridge. He's there until 1937. After that, it becomes tricky. I can track seven different Patrick Rileys during the years that follow. Interestingly, two are married to women named Anna. I found church records for one of the two Patricks in Portsmouth, Virginia. If he's our man, then he had three children—one son and two daughters. The other possibility is a Patrick Riley in Washington, near Tacoma. If that's him, then the news isn't so good. He had four children—one boy and three girls. However, I found death dates for his wife and the children, all on the same day. That means an accident or perhaps an epidemic. If he's your man, then when he died in 1959, he died alone and with no posterity."

My mind races. I recall reading about the bridge in Tacoma. Construction started shortly after the Golden Gate Bridge was finished.

"Let's assume, Janet, that my Patrick is the man in Virginia. What did you find out about his children?"

"The trail with the two daughters went immediately cold. That's common—they no doubt married, changed their names, moved away. The son is easier since his name stays the same. He was christened Robert Riley; personally, I wouldn't have named my kid Robert with a last name of Riley, but nobody asked me. It turns out Robert stayed in Virginia. He was Irish Catholic, like his father. He married a woman named Louise Skinner. They also had a son. Here's the bad news. Robert Riley died of a heart attack four years ago. His wife died two years later. I have an old address, but I don't think that will do you much good."

"So, where do I go from here?"

"Katie, it's me, Janet. I told you they had a son. Do you want his phone number?"

"You're serious?"

"Remember, it helps only if I've traced the right Patrick Riley. We still have the guy who moved to Washington. It's a fifty-fifty shot as I see it."

"Janet, what's his name? The grandson, I mean."

"Is your pencil ready?"

"Ready."

"His name is David—David Riley."

chapter thirty-two

I wait patiently in the office courtyard, watching the eleva-tors as they open and close, rehearsing what I'll say. There is a moment when I wonder if I have the courage, but then I remind myself that I need to find closure if I expect my life to move for-ward. An hour and ten minutes later, he walks into the lobby. He's staring at his phone and doesn't notice that I'm there. It's my chance to speak up—or walk away silent forever.

"Eric?"

He jolts to a stop at the sound of my voice, turns toward me, and stares. I watch his eyes drop, his head lower, his countenance crumble. He looks uneasy, even frightened. I hold my ground, not moving forward but not stepping back. I wait.

"Katie?"

"I saw you come into this building a few days ago. I live close by—I didn't want to keep avoiding the place."

When he speaks, he looks past me, as if there were someone standing in the distance. "Um . . . I'm . . . you know, of all the ironies, the company transferred me back here." He tries to laugh, but it sounds forced, unnatural. "I thought about looking you up, but I wasn't sure what the point would be."

I expected to be angry. I expected to feel pain. Strangely, I feel only pity. He keeps glancing down nervously, and it strikes me as odd that he seems so vulnerable. Has he always been so insecure? His foot twitches nervously as he waits for stinging words that don't come.

Instead, I watch, wait, and listen. After a minute, when it seems as if the silence will smother him, he speaks.

"Katie, it's just that . . . I'm sorry . . . I mean, I don't know what to say to you."

"I'm not here for an apology, Eric." I don't know if it's my words or my manner that surprise him the most. "How's your life been?" I ask.

He stutters, stammers, takes a breath. "It's been . . . okay, I guess."

Minutes ago I'd been the terrified one. Now that the moment is here, I find my words flowing with confidence. "Are you married? Dating?" I ask.

"No . . . I mean, I go out once in a while. I guess you're married, though. That's great. I'm happy for you."

His assumption catches me off guard. "No, Eric. I'm not married."

He looks bewildered, but he still refuses to look me in the

eyes. "I just presumed . . . well . . . you look good, Katie—a lot thinner than I'd remembered."

"Eric, there's something I need to ask you."

He takes another heavy breath, trying to anticipate what's coming. "Katie, listen, I don't have an answer. I don't know why I did it. I've been over it again and again. It wasn't planned. It just happened."

I can't help but smile. "Eric, that's not my question."

"Oh . . . I'm sorry. What, then?"

"I'm wondering about you, Eric."

"What do you mean?" He shifts his weight as I pick my words.

"If life could be rewound to that moment when you were in L.A. and I was driving down from San Francisco, and the woman you were with appeared again, from wherever she came from in the first place . . . would you do it again?"

My question seems to surprise, even stun him—as if he's never looked inward, never probed his own character. Moments pass before he speaks.

"I made a stupid choice. I never meant to hurt you like I did." He pauses, fidgets some more. "But I don't know that I could promise you, Katie, that I wouldn't make the same mistake all over again. How could I know something like that?"

It is a subtle realization, a pivot of understanding that, though slight, is also profound. In looking back, I find it interesting that such moments never come in the middle of the raging storm, but afterwards, in the gentle breeze of reflection and rebuilding.

When Eric proposed to me, I viewed him as a partner on a pedestal, someone to lift me up. I leaned so heavily on his strength that, when he cheated, when his pedestal crashed over and knocked me breathless to the ground, I was afraid my leaning may have pushed it over.

What I instantly understand, in an ordinary lobby on an ordinary day in an extraordinary moment, is that I don't want a hand up. Nor do I want a push from behind. I want someone who will climb mountains with me, side by side.

Despite my faults and weaknesses, despite my own insecurities, I deserve better.

There is little more to say.

"Thank you, Eric, for being honest. Right now that means a lot to me. Good luck."

I turn to walk away and he whispers his good-bye, visibly relieved that the ordeal is over. I am three steps away when I stop.

"Eric, wait." He turns, waits. "I'm curious why you thought that I was married?"

After the question is asked, he glances down at my fingers, and I realize that he is looking at my ring.

"It was your faith ring—you're wearing it with the crown turned out."

My blank stare is enough. For the first time, his laugh is genuine.

"You, of all people, a history major, and you don't know about Claddagh faith rings? There's an irony there somewhere."

"Can you tell me about them?"

*"You don't need me for that—the story's out there. You were
always an amazing researcher. I'm sure you'll find it."*

"But . . . how do you know about . . . ?"

*"Yeah, me of all people. My grandmother used to wear one.
She taught me."*

And with that, he shrugs and walks away.

• • •

*Claddagh. I'd heard the name from Janet—it was the town
where Anna was born. It doesn't take me long at my computer
before the legend of the Claddagh faith ring smiles back from the
screen.*

*I learn that while several misty fables surround the creation
of such a wondrous ring, the most common is of a man named
Richard Joyce who lived over four hundred years ago in the fish-
ing village of Claddagh, Ireland, which overlooks Galway Bay.
It is told that he sailed from the village to the plantations of the
West Indies only days before he was to marry his true love. He
was captured by Algerian pirates and sold as a slave to a Moorish
goldsmith, who trained him in his craft. In his captivity, Joyce
fashioned the now-famous Claddagh ring in memory of his only
true love, the one he'd left waiting in Ireland.*

*In 1689, Richard Joyce was finally released at the bidding of
King William III. The Moor offered him his only daughter in
marriage and half his wealth if he would remain in Algiers, but
Joyce declined and instead returned to the village to find his love
unmarried and still waiting. The ring was presented, the couple*

were married, and they lived the rest of their lives happily to-gether.

As I read the simple fable and the story of the ring, I can't help but picture Patrick and Anna, each so distant, each so con-cerned about reuniting again. The legend must have held a spe-cial place for each. Patrick's words are now so plain and evident. "With this crown, I give my loyalty. With these hands, I promise to serve. With this heart, I give you mine."

I discover that faith rings are still available today from many Irish jewelry shops. It is understood that if one wears the ring on the left hand, with the crown turned outward, it is a sign that the person is blissfully committed. If the ring is worn on the right hand, with the crown turned inward, then everyone knows that the wearer's heart is free.

Patrick and Anna are taking on depth and shape and life. He didn't disappear after the bridge was finished. They were reunited; they remained committed. Oh, there are still holes in the story—traits about the man and his wife that I am left to imagine. But if I do have the right Patrick Riley, I will have accomplished what my father couldn't. I will have found the rightful owner of Patrick's journal. All I have to do now is dial his grandson's num-ber.

I hold the phone against my ear, pick up my scribbled notes from Janet, and determinedly punch the keys. It rings once and then twice. On the third ring someone answers and I hear a voice.

"This is Dave Riley. I'm out right now. Please leave a number at the beep . . ."

chapter thirty-three

Rising in the majestic Rocky Mountains of central Colorado, the South Platte River flows 420 miles northeast, toward the central plains of Nebraska. As it has done for generations, the life-giving flow provides irrigation and hope to the many dotted towns sheltered along its valleys and basins.

As Dave followed the river, the countless towns blurred—North Platte, Sutherland, Paxton, Roscoe, Brule—small towns, hometowns. Five thousand people here, ten thousand there. Each a community harboring homes, farms, businesses, churches . . . and families. Sturdy names, solid names—Orchard, Hillrose, and Big Springs. Every town the same, every town unique. All loved, despised, appreciated, and scorned by those who called them home.

Just out of Big Springs, Nebraska, almost to the Colorado border, Dave pulled over to check his route. The battery on his phone was all but dead; thankfully he'd had the foresight to bring his printed maps. He traced the planned direction with his finger. The turnoff was just ahead to I-80 west into Wyoming. He'd gas up at one of the towns along the way, find a home-cooked meal at the local diner, then stop for the night when he reached Cheyenne. It was only June 30—he still had five days until the Fourth. It was a two-day ride—two and a half days at most—to the coast. He would make it in time.

Dave pushed the map back into his saddlebag and headed toward the freeway, accelerating up the on-ramp. Traffic was light—a far cry from New York or D.C., both of which felt so distant, in mileage and in memory. Two eighteen-wheel trucks ahead blocked both lanes of traffic as one passed the other. Dave slowed. He was on a Harley, so he could certainly roar around the left side and pass on the shoulder. But there was no point; he had time. He kept a steady pace behind the passing truck until it pulled over into the right lane to let him safely by.

A half hour later, when the sign read *Sterling, Colorado—48 miles,* Dave knew he'd taken the wrong road.

He pulled off the freeway onto the frontage road. He must have missed the turnoff when passing the trucks. Now, twenty miles too late, he had two choices: backtrack or head toward Denver, looping up north on I-25 to Cheyenne. Even with the unexpected detour, it was early afternoon; he could still make Cheyenne by nightfall. It was the long way, but no worse than retracing country he'd already seen. With plenty of time to spare, going forward seemed the best option.

A dot on the map—Liberty, Colorado—lay a few miles ahead. He would stay on the back roads and gas up his bike there.

The town was visible from miles away, its whitewashed water tower poking high above the thick canopy of green trees that staked out its existence. Running parallel to the road grew a mile-wide thicket of cottonwood, cedar, and spruce trees—a forest that snaked along with the river for miles in each direction, evidence that water runs not only over the surface but deep beneath as well.

Farms trimmed the outskirts, blanketing the area for miles with corn, alfalfa, and hay—each irrigated field adding lushness to an otherwise arid rolling plain. Even from a distance, Dave could make out the outline of a large grain elevator that companioned the town's water tower. They stood adjacent, as if sentinels, protecting the residents from intruders. Dave guessed the structures would mark the town's center, its main street.

The distant scene was picturesque, and Dave now congratulated himself for missing the turnoff. The only immediate problem was that he was starving. He hoped the town would have a diner with real food on the menu—mashed potatoes, chicken, vegetables. Fast-food burgers were wearing thin. The more his stomach rumbled, the harder he twisted the throttle and the deeper the bike crooned. He would finish with apple pie. All hometown diners served apple pie—it was a requirement. He shifted the gears again, adding five miles per hour more to the speedometer—and then the bike sputtered.

He twisted the throttle back and forth several times, but the bike continued to lose power. Dave checked for traffic behind and then pulled off to the side of the road. The fuel gauge showed a quarter of a tank. He removed the chrome gas cap and tipped the bike to see inside. The level looked about right, plenty of fuel to make it to Liberty. Bad gas at the last stop? That didn't make sense, since he'd been driving all morning with no problems. From Redd's maintenance lessons, Dave would have guessed the carburetor was at issue, but Redd himself had gone over the bike with a fine-tooth comb and pronounced it in perfect condition.

Dave set the kickstand, stepped off the bike, and glanced down the road in both directions. No cars in sight. The town was just ahead; perhaps some premium gas would do the trick. He fiddled with several switches, adjusted the carburetor, and then pushed the start button again. Instead of rumbling alive, the engine sputtered and chugged. The bike lurched forward. It was running rough, but at least it was running. With a little luck, he'd make it into town, where he could get help.

"With just a little luck," he repeated.

The engine stalled completely half a mile later.

Dave hated to leave the bike on the side of the road, and since the grade sloped gently toward town, he clicked the machine into neutral and started to push.

It took nearly thirty minutes to reach the first building, a plumbing-supply warehouse on the east side with a red pickup truck parked in front. Across the street, to the west, a community ball diamond waited. Dave opted east; they'd certainly have a phone. He looked both ways—still no cars. He was about to give his bike a heave to push it across the road when something ahead near the baseball diamond caught his attention.

It was built of polished river rock and stood about three feet high, adjacent to the three-tiered wooden bleachers behind home plate. It was a drinking fountain, the old-fashioned kind that had once dotted many city street corners before vandalism and city budgets put them on the endangered-species list. But it wasn't the structure that caused Dave to pause—it was that the fountain was spewing torrents of crystal spring water.

It was a call he couldn't refuse.

He pushed the bike forward close to the field, set the kick-stand, and beelined toward the water. The mountain air was dry, the humidity nonexistent compared with what he'd left behind. But the summer temperatures, coupled with the effort of pushing the bike, had left him exhausted and sweating profusely. His eyes locked on the stream that arched freely into the air and then down into a continuous splash, swirling in the cement bowl. As he approached, he mouthed a silent prayer: "Let it be cold, please let it be cold."

It was all he expected.

He gulped swallow after swallow so quickly he thought he might get sick. When he could drink no more, he lowered his head and let the stream cascade over his hair and neck. Every inch of him that the water touched wept with gratitude.

After several minutes of joy, he stepped aside and shook away the dripping water like a wet dog. With the bleachers adjacent, Dave found a seat to relax and let the water settle. For the first time, he noticed two young boys on the diamond behind the fence, one pitching balls to the other.

As Dave rested, he couldn't help but watch their play—once a coach, always a coach. They looked to be about eight and ten years of age, the younger of the two pitching to the older. Both had sandy blond hair, cut short above the ears. The single bat they shared was oversized.

When the boy swung, Dave cringed. His elbow was too low and his grip on the bat was not high enough for his height. Out of habit, Dave stood, stepped to the chain-link fence, and grabbed it with his fingers. Three more pitches, three more misses.

Elbow up, Brad, don't let him throw that garbage. Watch the ball, keep your eye on the ball.

Two more misses, then the youngster finally ticked one toward first base. With no one there to field the ball, he ran the bases. Rather than racing to home plate after retrieving the ball, the younger boy chased after the older one around second, then third base, then home. The run was scored; the younger boy never came close.

"I'm ahead by four," the older boy confirmed loudly.

"So? It's my turn to hit now."

They switched places and the game continued. His form was no better. He swung, he missed, he swung some more. Dave stayed at the fence.

A familiar ache was rising in his chest.

The pitch will come in high, Brad, watch the high pitch and remember you have a man on third.

Dave could feel his eyes begin to moisten. It was ridiculous. The young boys were having a great time—why get emotional now? Dave reached up to shield the sun and wipe his eyes.

"What's the matter? Don't you like baseball?"

The young voice startled him. He hadn't noticed the girl standing near the bottom bleacher watching the boys as well. Her hair was not just blonde, it was almost white, and it curled just below her ears. She wore Levi's with holes in the knees and a navy blue shirt. It was hard to guess her age—six, perhaps seven.

"Nothing's the matter, and yes, I do like baseball."

"Looked like you was crying."

Dave wasn't sure how to answer. "Not at all. It's just that those boys are holding the bat wrong. I was watching them and . . . never mind, it doesn't matter."

"Holding it wrong? How can you hold a bat wrong?" She was inquisitive, even amused.

"Look closely and I'll show you." He moved over to the bleacher and sat beside her. Both watched as the boys continued.

"See how his back elbow is pointing down? That means that when he swings, he will drift into the pitch, his bat will drag, and his timing will be off. The other boy is doing the same thing." She seemed truly interested, but bolted to her feet and ran to the edge of the fence. She hollered at them through chain-link openings.

"Jared! Glen! You're doin' it wrong!"

The boys' focus turned to the girl. It was the first time they'd noticed the stranger.

"We are not!" the younger of the two defended.

"Are so!" she shot back.

"Are not. You don't know what you're talkin' 'bout."

They stepped toward her.

"Are so," she repeated louder, this time pointing to Dave. "He said so." She waited for Dave, as if it were his turn to scream *are so* and defend her honor. Dave, more amused than embarrassed, wiped at his lips.

"Technically," he began, "she's right. Your power is great, gentlemen, but you're not holding the bat like you should."

Each boy scanned Dave independently, apparently sizing up the credibility of this sudden expert.

"Do you play?" the older one asked.

"I used to coach a competition team on the East Coast. We took the division championship, even went to state."

"Really?"

"Sure. Do you want some pointers?"

They cast a quick glance at one another. The younger one shrugged; the older one nodded. Dave winked at the girl, laid his jacket on the bleachers, and then walked around the fence to where the boys stood.

"So, who's Jared, and who's Glen?" Dave asked as they reached home plate.

"I'm Jared, my brother is Glen," the older one responded.

"And the girl, she's your sister?"

"Yeah, that's Gracie."

"Gracie," Dave repeated. It fit.

At the plate he spent some time helping each boy with his form. It felt good—very good—to be teaching baseball again.

"Look, you need to hold the bat higher—right here. Good. Now close your grip."

After a few minutes of instruction, Dave moved to the mound and pitched easy balls over the plate. Jared smacked one on his second swing. It rolled past second base into the outfield, the farthest he'd hit the ball all morning.

"Whoa!" Jared exclaimed. The boys stared in sheer amazement, a sight that made Dave grin.

"Are you going to run or not?" Dave yelled as he retrieved the ball. Jared ran the bases while Dave stepped back to the mound.

"Okay, Glen, your turn."

He played with the boys for nearly half an hour while Gracie watched patiently from the stands, clearly preferring spectator status.

It was Glen who finally asked, "Is that your motorcycle?" Dave had become so involved, he'd forgotten about his bike.

"Yeah, it sure is. I'm having some problems with it, though. Is there a bike shop in town?"

Jared answered first. "Ace Hardware sells bikes."

Dave forced away his smile. "Actually, I mean a motorcycle shop. You know, like a Harley dealer?"

After sharing a confused glance, the two boys shrugged.

"How about a phone, then?" Dave asked "My battery is dead. Any of you have a phone on you that I can use?"

While the boys' heads shook, Gracie's lifted. "We have a

phone at home you can use," she said. She pointed to a small house beyond the left-field fence, across an empty pasture.

Dave accepted. Not wanting to leave his bike behind, he opted to push it around the long way. The children didn't mind a bit—the two boys marched in front, and Gracie tagged along behind.

It was a one-motorcycle parade.

chapter thirty-four

When they had first moved into the area four years earlier, it had bothered Crystal to let the kids run free, to play by themselves. It was against her nature—her experience—to let them be so independent. Liberty was a small town, however, a safe town, and in time her worries abated.

Today, when she noticed the children approaching with a stranger, her pulse quickened. The closer they got to the house, the angrier she became. After all, she had just had the *stranger talk* again with Gracie last week—would that girl never learn?

Crystal waited on the front porch as the posse approached. Gracie was the first to speak. "Mommy! Look what we brought home!"

"Hello," Dave said as he extended his hand. She shook it curtly, then pulled her hand away. She hated to be rude in front of the children, but bringing a biker home? It was not acceptable.

"Is everything okay? Can I help you with something?" she asked briskly.

Gracie chimed in again. "He wants to use the phone. His motorcycle's busted." Then, without hesitation, she added, "And he showed Jared and Glen how to bat 'cause they were doin' it wrong and he's really good."

The boys shrugged sheepishly, both old enough to realize that once this guy was gone, they were toast. Dave stepped in, "I don't mean to bother you. My bike broke down a couple of miles from town. I pushed it to the ball diamond. The kids volunteered your phone. If it's too much trouble, I'll look somewhere else."

She had watched the news, seen the horror stories that occur when you let your guard down. She felt her pocket. It was empty. After another moment of hesitation, she cautiously relented. "It's fine, come on in. My cell is in the bedroom, but we have a landline in the kitchen."

Before opening the door, she spoke to the children. "Kids, you stay outside and play. Do you hear me?" By the look on her face and the tone of her voice, they knew she meant business.

She pulled the door open and pointed toward the kitchen. She let him step in first and then followed a few steps behind—close enough to watch, but at enough of a distance to run for the door if necessary.

"The phone is in there on the counter. My husband will be home soon, and he's pretty handy. Perhaps he can help fix your bike."

Dave walked down the short hall in the direction she had

pointed. A bathroom door hung open nearby; a full-length mirror covered the inside. He jolted to a confused stop when he noticed his reflection—wet shirt, hair sticking out in all directions, his face covered in a dark stubble.

"I look pretty scary, don't I?" he said.

She wasn't sure how to respond. "No—yes. Well . . ."

"And I probably smell just as bad?"

Her mouth was open, but no words would come out. Silence lingered in the air until both began to laugh.

"Yes, you do," she finally admitted, "you smell horrible." She extended her hand as if for the first time. "I'm Crystal Davis." Dave shook it again. Her icy stare thawed.

"I'm Dave Riley. And I promise, I don't always smell like this."

"It's the heat. Don't worry about it." Then she added, "And the phone is on the counter."

He hesitated. "I don't mean to be a bother, but do you have a computer? I need to find a number for the nearest motorcycle shop."

"I can grab my cell, but I can tell you already, the only shop in town that can work on motorcycles is Darin's RV. It's after six now; he'll be closed."

His eyes darted to the clock on the wall—he'd missed it by half an hour.

"If you don't mind, I'd like to try."

She grabbed her phone from the bedroom, tapped on the

screen to find the number, and then called. Both listened to it ring, then switch to voice mail.

"How about some premium gas? Is there a station close?" he asked.

"Believe it or not, we do have gas stations. Let me see if I can find an empty can and I'll run you down to the Texaco."

"Just point me in the direction, I can walk."

He looked rough and smelled worse, but even so, he was certainly the most polite biker she'd ever met.

"Look, it's not a problem—I can take you." She opened the door and waited for him to follow.

A metal can was located and the kids were loaded into the car. She waited for him to climb into the passenger's seat and then pulled out of the driveway.

"So what does your husband do?"

She glanced into the rearview mirror and checked the children. "He works for the school district. He'll be home a little later. Some days he works late." She understood he was just trying to be polite, trying to make conversation. In truth, his questions made her nervous.

"And how about yourself?" Dave asked.

She slowed at the intersection and pretended to look for traffic. There was none. Her answer was brief, bordering on curt. "I teach."

He didn't prod or push further, and with the exception of polite, one-word responses to questions from the children, he said nothing more.

• • •

Gracie pressed her hands intently against the inside glass of the family-room window. Her eyes shifted between Dave and his bike. Crystal found her behavior curious. Even more peculiar was the fact that Jared and Glen had both volunteered to help with dinner, though their motives were soon betrayed.

"Mom, can we get a new bat?" Jared asked.

"You already have a bat."

"Yeah, but it's too big."

"Too big? How can a bat be too big?"

"It is, Mom," Glen piped in. "Dave said so, and he coached a state team."

"Is that so?"

Both nodded, waiting for her response.

"Let's talk about it tomorrow. Now go wash up."

She turned toward the family room and called, "Gracie, go wash up for dinner." The little girl either purposely ignored her or was so intently focused on the subject outside that she didn't hear.

"Hello? Are you in there?" Crystal chided, raising her voice until Gracie turned in her direction. "Go wash up now—dinner is almost ready."

Crystal moved to the window next to where her daughter stood and glanced out at Dave. He sat motionless on the ground beside his bike. As she watched, Gracie posed the question she'd been pondering. "Mom, can we keep him?"

Crystal bit her lip to keep from laughing. "He's not a pet, he's a person. So, no, dear, we can't keep him."

Gracie's sigh was obvious. "Just 'til tomorrow?"

Crystal bent down and swatted her daughter lightly on the behind, then pushed her toward the bathroom. "Go wash your hands. I'll walk out and see how he's doing."

Dave was deep in thought staring up at the bike—or past it—when she approached.

"I've got some dinner ready." Her words startled him, and he jumped. "I'm sorry, I didn't mean to scare you."

"That's okay."

"No luck with the bike?"

He shook his head. "It's not the fuel—but I'm embarrassed to admit, I don't know that much about the engine. It just doesn't make sense. My friend Redd looked it over before I left and said it was flawless. I guess my best hope is to get it to a bike shop in the morning."

"Tomorrow?" she questioned.

"Is that a problem?"

"Not for me, but for them it will be—it's Sunday tomorrow. The only shop in town will be closed."

"Today's Saturday?" He looked at the numbers on his watch and then counted the days backwards.

"You didn't realize?" Crystal said.

"I guess I lost a day somewhere. And there's just the one shop?"

"The next closest would be in Sterling, but that's a good forty minutes away, and I'm guessing they'll be closed tomorrow as well. Look, I have dinner ready. You're welcome to join us and then figure it out afterwards."

Dave had been starving hours ago. Right now he would eat gravel.

"Thanks. It smells great."

Dave walked beside her to the house. On their way she began to apologize, "We don't always eat this late, so please don't think I'm a delinquent mother. It's just with summer, and it being light so late, well—anything besides cold cereal is considered a treat."

"Delinquent? Hardly. I used to coach kids. I'm a good judge of their character. Trust me when I tell you that you're raising some great children."

She accepted the praise with a smile, as if compliments were too few and far between to do otherwise.

"You know," she said, "it's nice to hear that once in a while. Do you have children of your own?"

His step quickened. His mouth pinched closed. He was slow to answer. "I have three," he finally said.

She nodded but didn't pry further. As they neared the house, Crystal motioned to the window where Gracie stood watching.

"Well, there's a six-year-old girl inside who is mesmerized."

When they neared the door, Dave reached out to open it for Crystal. At the sight of his own grease-covered hands, he jerked back.

"You think I smelled bad before, you'd better add oil and gasoline to the list."

She grabbed the knob to pull the door open herself and then

stepped past him. "That's okay," she answered dryly. "Gasoline is an improvement."

• • •

The food was delicious, the conversation light—even pleasant. The boys finished quickly and asked to be excused to watch TV. Crystal obliged. Gracie picked at her food, prolonging the event, as if not wanting to miss anything at the table. As Crystal and Dave continued their conversation, Gracie listened.

"So, what kind of work do you do?" Crystal asked.

"I work for a marketing research firm in Manhattan. How about you? You said you were a teacher?"

"Third graders."

"Bet that keeps you busy. And you said your husband works at the school district? Is he a teacher as well?"

"No, he's not." Crystal eyed Gracie, noticed her glass half empty, and poured her more water. Dave waited for an explanation, but when none came, he continued.

"Listen, I'm sorry. It's none of my business."

Gracie was trying her best to separate the food left on her plate into distinct piles. She didn't appear to be paying attention to the two adults.

"He often works late," Crystal replied. "It's just the way it is."

Her answer was rushed, like it had been in the car when Dave had first broached the subject.

Gracie set down her knife, then turned toward Dave, as if she'd been a part of the conversation the entire time. "Mommy's not married anymore." She met Crystal's glare with innocence. "Are you, Mommy?"

Crystal coughed, then flushed red.

"Not married?" Dave asked, as if a coup had been exposed right there at the table.

Gracie shook her head, causing her thin, white-blonde hair to flip from side to side. "Nope."

When Dave turned toward Crystal with a smile, she relented.

"I didn't mean to lie. It's what you're supposed to do when a stranger comes into your house."

"Especially a long-haired, smelly biker who hasn't shaved in a week?" Dave added.

She shrugged back. "Anyone ready for dessert?"

• • •

It caught Crystal off guard when Dave carried the dinner dishes to the sink. She appreciated the help, and he seemed like a nice guy—she just knew so little about him. And most troubling—how stable was a biker?

"Crystal, it was a terrific dinner. You've been very nice to me, but I'd better find a place to spend the night. Is there a motel nearby?"

Common sense battled loneliness. "They're building a new one on the far side of town, but it won't be done for several months. Fact is, most people don't stop here. They go on ahead to Sterling. Other than that, I think all we have is the Sundowner."

"That works."

She hesitated. "Well—"

"Is there a problem?"

"It's called the Sundowner for a reason. The sun set a long time ago on that place. It's kind of dumpy."

"It'll be fine. In fact, if you want to point me in the general direction, I'll walk."

"Oh, quit it with the walking thing. Your politeness is making me nervous. It's a five-minute drive. I'll take you."

She didn't mind dropping him off, but the thought of loading up the kids one more time was more than she could handle. She turned to Dave, "You're about to realize I'm not such a great mother after all." Then she called out to her kids, "Gracie, go get in bed right now. Jared, you're in charge. I'll be back in ten minutes."

Any other time, Jared would have complained. With Dave watching, he stood attentive.

Crystal continued, "You know the rules. Don't answer the phone. Don't answer the door. I'll take my cell phone. It will be just ten minutes, so you and Glen watch TV until I get back, then it's bedtime."

Gracie began her protest. "No fair! How come they get to watch TV and I don't?"

It didn't take much tonight to get Mom to cave. "Ten minutes, Gracie, that's all—then you get in bed, no questions asked. And I don't want to come back and hear that you were a pain. Deal?"

"Deal."

Dave grinned, as if perhaps the routine looked familiar.

While Crystal grabbed her keys, Dave retrieved a few personal items from his bike's saddlebags. When she pulled up the car, he climbed inside.

"So you won't report me to the authorities?" she asked.

"Actually, I am the State Child Inspector. I'm placing you under arrest."

They smiled together.

The motel was just a few minutes away, so while driving, Crystal offered up a little background. She explained that the complex had been originally built in the late 1940s to cater to fishermen who were expected to flock into the area once the levees upstream regulated the river's flow. The fishermen apparently had never materialized. Since then, the single row of eight dilapidated cabins had been strung together with a slipshod roof so they would be taxed as one building and not eight. Separate bathrooms had been added to the back of each unit in a "remodel" ten years later. No one in town could ever explain to Crystal why indoor plumbing hadn't been part of the original plan, except to say that fishermen prefer the great outdoors.

Tonight, as they approached, light from the almost-full moon was casting an eerie glow across the complex, though the buildings themselves were completely dark. While the place may have been described as quaintly rustic in its day, it hadn't approached rural charm in years.

Five of the eight cabin doors were wide open, with nary a soul in sight. Rugs and carpet had been pulled out of the units and were draped over the front railings. The light on the parking area's single pole was out as well. It was a parking lot normally covered with a hefty layer of gravel, but when Dave rolled down his window for a closer inspection, he could see moonlight reflecting off what looked to be a three-inch-deep lake.

"Just like you said, it is a bit—well—run-down, isn't it?" Dave commented dryly.

Crystal started to laugh. Calling the place a dive was too kind—it was a disaster area.

"I swear it wasn't like this a few days ago. It looks like they had a water leak or something."

"Or the dam broke," Dave added. "Now what?"

"Unless you're a good swimmer, you can't stay here," she said, stating the obvious. "The next closest place is almost an hour away, and I can't leave the kids that long."

"How about a campground?"

"You mean like a KOA?" she asked.

"Sure. Any kind, I'm easy."

"I can't think of one. We're not big campers." She paused for a moment, her head bobbing back and forth slightly, weighing the pros and cons of an idea that had been rattling around in her brain. "Listen, we have space in our front yard. You can roll your sleeping bag out there. You do have a sleeping bag, don't you?"

"I do, but I hate to impose."

"Under the circumstances, can you think of a better choice?"

He paused, obviously sorting his options. "I won't be a

bother, I promise. Now, you better get out of this lot before we're both stuck in this car for the night."

● ● ●

By the time Crystal had chased Gracie to bed, Dave had his sleeping bag rolled out next to his bike. He appeared to be looking at the stars.

Jared stepped to the window beside his mother and watched Dave for a moment with her. "How come he gets to sleep outside and we don't?" he whined.

She was losing her patience. "I told you to get in bed. Right now! I'm not going to tell you again."

Glen was still in the kitchen getting a drink of water. When he returned, she marched beside both boys to the bathroom and waited while they brushed their teeth. After they had been duly tucked in, she kissed them on the cheek and then offered her final threat, as if it would help.

"If you get out of bed, there will be extra chores in the morning. Hear me?" When they both agreed, she left to check on Gracie. Thank goodness one of the three was asleep.

Then, in stocking feet so the boys wouldn't hear, she slipped back to the window to watch Dave.

He was such a pleasant guy, though his appearance was still perplexing. He didn't seem as rough as he looked, as threatening as his image led one to believe. He simply wasn't your average biker. Or was he? She'd seen them riding in groups down the freeway from time to time. But as she thought about it, she'd never really stopped one. Were they all this nice?

Even from the window, she could tell he was awake; he kept shifting his position on the hard ground. The voices—the arguments—started once again in her head. Five minutes later, she stepped outside and marched toward him. She didn't bother with the typical *good evening*.

"Listen, if my mother knew, she'd kill me. If word gets around town, I'm done for. For the record, it's against my better judgment—but why don't you come inside and just sleep on the couch."

"Can I bring my guns and knives?"

"Sure, why not?" she answered. It had been such a long time since a guy had made her laugh.

Dave picked up his sleeping bag and a few things from the bike. Once inside, he rolled out his bag on the couch.

"Can I make you some coffee?" she asked.

"That would be great." He followed her to the kitchen, and while they waited for the water to boil, they sat at the table and talked. It was small talk at first, though it didn't take long to get to the questions each wanted to ask.

"No husband . . . does that mean you're divorced?"

She nodded. "He took off when I was pregnant with Gracie. Eight months pregnant, to be exact. He left a note—a note, can you believe that? Like I was a one-night stand."

"I'm sorry."

"It's okay—though to this day it amazes me that a person could be so cruel."

"Another woman?"

"There's always another woman. I haven't seen him, though, in five and a half years—since our last court date. I heard he moved to someplace in Florida. What kind of father would walk away from such terrific kids?"

Dave didn't need to answer. "Do the kids remember him?"

"The boys? Not really. Probably better that way. So, how about you, Dave Riley? I noticed you're wearing a ring, and you said you have three children—I take it you're married?"

He hated to go into detail, so he kept his answers short.

"My wife was killed in a car accident a few months ago."

She winced. "I am so sorry."

"That's okay. I'm still a little—well, confused about it, actually."

She was surprised when he continued. "I had three children—I lost them also. I'm sorry if earlier I implied otherwise."

"You're talking to the woman who told you her husband was coming home." More smiles. "That explains it, though," she added.

"Explains what?"

"Why you're great with the kids. You've had some practice."

The coffeemaker on the counter beeped as it finished draining. Crystal retrieved the pot and poured two cups.

After taking a few sips, Dave opted for a change of subject. "Is this your hometown?"

"No. We've been here four years now. We lived in Kansas City. I tried to keep the house there as long as I could, but it was a big house, and—well, things don't always work out like you expect, do they?"

"No, they don't. What brought you here, then?"

"Two things. A job, for one. The district had an opening, and I needed the work."

"And the second?"

"To get away from the memories—to have a place where I could start fresh, create my own life. Does that seem too weird?"

"Not at all."

After their cups were empty, Crystal poured more.

"The boys said you coached a baseball team," she said. "Tell me about that."

She found his company pleasing; he seemed to feel the same about her. They laughed at the same jokes, reflected when no words needed to be spoken. Each listened. It was one-thirty in the morning before she noticed her watch.

"Oh my, have you seen the time?" she asked.

"I'm sorry to keep you up."

"No, it was a pleasure. And I didn't mean to talk your ear off. With the three children at home, and then more during the day when school is on . . . well, I don't get much of a chance to carry on normal adult conversations."

Before she stood, she reached out and touched his hand resting on the table. It was a casual touch, a token of friendship, and yet a soft touch. As her fingers rested on his, his arm tensed, as if he wanted to pull it away but couldn't. She spoke sincerely while holding her grasp. "Really, thank you . . . for listening." When she let go, he moved his hand under the table.

"I have the same problem—and I don't even teach school."

"Well, good night, Dave Riley."

"Thanks again. Good night."

• • •

Dave could feel his quickened pulse as Crystal walked from the kitchen, down the hall, and into her own bedroom. He listened to the sound of her door closing before he clicked off the light and dropped back into the chair.

The sounds of her getting ready for bed permeated the small house. He looked down, then shook his fingers as if they were asleep, as if the blood had stopped flowing and he needed to start it again. The air was suddenly stifling, and he wished that he'd stayed outside beneath the stars. Still, he didn't move. He waited until her room was quiet, until the rhythm of his own breath had slowed, before moving to the bathroom to get himself ready for bed. He undressed in total darkness.

After he'd climbed inside his sleeping bag, he listened again for any further sound, any hint that anyone else was also awake. Nothing. His eyes burned. The sun would be coming up in just a few more hours, and he needed to sleep. Instead, his thoughts swirled in a tangled mix of confusion.

He didn't have time for this delay. He had to get his bike fixed. Most important, he had to get to the bridge.

chapter thirty-five

When Crystal entered the living room, Dave was sitting on the couch reading one of the books he'd picked up off the coffee table. Gracie sat at his side watching cartoons on the TV. Crystal did a double take. His clothes were clean, his hair was brushed back, and the beginning of a beard still cloaking his face was now neatly trimmed. It had been difficult to study his features the night before. Now she found herself not wanting to look away. He noticed the prolonged stare and stood.

"Good morning. I hope it's okay, I took a quick shower and . . ."

"Yes, I can see that. You clean up nicely, Dave Riley."

"Morning, Mommy!" Gracie beamed, proud to be the one at the side of their visitor.

"You're up early, kiddo. Are your brothers still asleep?"

"Guess so," she answered with a shrug.

Crystal turned back to Dave. "If you've already made breakfast, then I'll have to hurt you."

"I haven't. Thank goodness."

"Well, give me ten minutes to shower and then I'll come back and see what we have. Gracie, would you get your brothers up? We have church in an hour."

Dave had attended church with his family regularly. Since the accident, he'd been back just twice.

"You're certainly welcome to come with us, Dave. The service lasts a little over an hour."

"I thought you said people would talk if they knew that you had let a stranger stay."

"That's true; I did say that, didn't I? Of course, on the other hand, it would be a shame to waste a good shower and beard trim on just us."

"I appreciate the invitation, really, but I'm afraid I'll have to pass. I didn't bring any clothes for church. All I have are jeans and T-shirts."

She rolled in her lips but said nothing.

"What is it?" he finally asked.

"It's completely up to you if you come or not, but I was just wondering, will God really care what you wear?"

Then she walked out of the room to get ready.

• • •

They arrived at church late, and Dave was grateful. The only open benches were in either the very front or the very back. They opted for the back and slipped in through a rear door. Halfway to their seats, Gracie dropped her bundle of colored markers that she'd brought along to keep herself busy. The noise caused several heads to turn.

Dave expected a look of embarrassment from Crystal—instead, her mouth turned up slightly. She bent down as best she could in her skirt and helped Gracie retrieve them. Dave pointed the two boys toward the open bench and ushered them in to sit down. When Crystal arrived, she let Gracie enter the pew first to sit next to Dave.

The pastor was an older gentleman, but certainly none the worse for wear. He delivered his words with a balance of experience and passion, as if his own conviction would leech out to those listening. For some, it appeared to.

Even in such a small town, the place was full—surprising to Dave, who had come from a city many times the size but where filling only half the Sunday benches was the norm. There were drawbacks, however. Dave couldn't help but notice at least three ladies, all seated in separate benches, cast Crystal wondering glances. Small-town curiosity. It was only at the last minute that he'd grabbed his jacket—a futile attempt to dress up. From the expressions on the women's faces, it may not have worked.

Will God really care what you wear? He considered Crystal's earlier question—or was it an admonition? Either way, it was advice that could have come from Megan.

Meg. If she could see him now: sitting in a small-town church somewhere in Colorado, wearing his Harley jacket. He wasn't sure if she'd laugh hysterically or be appalled. It was a ridiculous question to even pose—she was gone and she wasn't coming back.

Since the accident, he'd found that by staying busy, by keeping his mind going, he could drive away thoughts of Megan and the children—trick himself into thinking about better times—forget the pain. It was hard to do, however, during quiet times, times of solitude, like last night in the living room, for example, or when riding on long stretches of open road. Sitting in church reflecting on his own existence, it became almost impossible.

He missed his wife—missed her desperately.

Gracie's touch interrupted his thoughts. She'd drawn a picture of his motorcycle and was presenting it to him. "I drew it green 'cause my black marker didn't work," she whispered up to him. Crystal watched with a grin.

"Thank you," Dave replied. He studied the image. Indeed the bike was green, and she'd drawn stick figures of a man and a little girl standing beside it. She grabbed another sheet of paper while Dave carefully folded the masterpiece and placed it in his front jacket pocket. Dave understood she'd drawn a picture of herself and him by the bike. How could she know the picture would remind him of his own daughter, Angel?

By now the pastor was in full swing. He was talking about giving our hearts to God, about living our lives according to God's will. Dave found himself wondering what the message meant for him, asking silent questions. *What should I do now that God has taken away my wife and family?* While he had the urge to stand and pose the question out loud, he didn't.

The sermon ended with no answers. Dave hadn't come expecting any.

On their way to the door, Crystal introduced him to half a dozen women who had meandered over. Dave couldn't remember their names. He didn't try. He offered a quick nod, a simple, "Nice to meet you, too." Soon they were in her car.

After a quick drive around to show him the town, they headed back to her place for lunch. Then, at the coaxing of the children, everyone walked over to the park.

"Show us some more batting stuff," Jared begged.

Dave was happy to help. They were younger than the kids he was used to coaching, but the basics remained the same. Dave added to the simple techniques he'd shown them the day before. He taught them how to grip the bat properly, how to make their swing level and consistent. He showed them how they could direct their power, increase their distance, by working on form and follow-through. It was baseball, and all three were in heaven. After an hour, the boys would have followed Dave to the ends of the earth.

Crystal watched with curiosity while Gracie played on the bleachers. Despite the intent direction he was giving Jared and Glen, he found himself casting glances back in Crystal's direction.

Once the boys were hitting consistently, Dave yelled over to the two spectators, "Okay, it's time for a game. Let's go!"

At first Crystal glanced behind her, as if he were speaking to someone else.

He clarified. "Yes, you. I'm talking to the two blondes."

"I'm not very good," Crystal responded.

"Well, practice can't hurt then, can it?"

Crystal grabbed Gracie's hand, and they walked out onto the field. Dave surveyed the talent. "Okay, it'll be me and Gracie against you three."

Both Glen and Jared protested that the teams were not fair.

"What? You want Gracie as well?" Dave inquired. They weighed the offer but clearly realized any trade negotiations at this point would be in vain. The teams were divided and the game began.

Crystal and the boys took first ups. Dave pitched; Gracie stood near first base; Glen batted. The batting lessons had apparently helped. On the first pitch he smacked the ball past Gracie and out into right field. Gracie watched the ball soar by, then gave Dave an *I'm-not-gonna-go-get-it* look. Everyone laughed as Dave ran to the outfield to retrieve the ball. By the time he returned to the pitcher's mound, Glen was firmly planted on third base.

Jared was next. He missed the first pitch, but on the second he hit a solid grounder past third. Glen ran home to Crystal's cheers while Jared slid into second.

Next up was Crystal. When she stood up to the plate and took the bat, Dave couldn't help but grin.

"Okay, what's so funny?" she asked.

"Nothing, really. Except for the fact that you bat like, well . . ."

"Don't you dare say *girl*," she threatened.

"Okay, how about *rookie*?"

"I don't believe that's meant as a compliment."

Dave pitched the ball as gingerly as possible over the plate. Crystal swung late. Jared called the play from behind.

"Strike one."

She pulled the bat back into position, ready to try again. Dave's brow furrowed. Her batting form was hideous, painful to watch. He thought about giving her some pointers, but instead pitched the ball.

She swung soon enough this time, but several inches high.

"Strike two," Jared called.

"Whose team are you on?" Crystal mumbled over her shoulder.

When she pulled the bat back for her third try, it was more than Dave could handle.

"Time-out! We have a training time-out on the field." He stepped toward Crystal, who lowered her bat and waited.

Dave continued, "Okay, I realize this is helping the opposing team—but, quite frankly, you're killing me." He took the bat from out of her hands and began to give pointers.

"Am I that bad?" Crystal asked.

Dave hesitated, then confirmed. "Yeah, that bad. You need to follow through with a full swing, not swat at the ball." He gave Crystal a quick demonstration, then handed her the bat to try again. She looked as if she were fighting off an attacking mugger—and it wasn't pretty. Dave's wince let anyone watching know: she just wasn't getting it.

"No," Dave replied, "not like that at all." Crystal began to laugh. Dave grabbed the ball and tossed it to Jared. "Go about halfway to the mound and then toss a few easy ones over the plate. Glen, you play catcher." He moved with Crystal to home plate. "This will have to do for now, but really, you need a smaller bat."

"That's what the boys said. Is this a conspiracy?"

"Get them a size twenty-eight, perhaps even a twenty-nine, but nothing bigger. When they grow out of it, you can use it to keep stray bikers away."

"Good idea, I'll do that."

"Look, take the bat in your hands—grip it like this." After letting her watch him grip the bat, he handed it to her and then stepped behind. He reached an arm around each side to help her grip it as well.

"Okay, now feel the motion as I swing through." Dave swung the bat, showing her the path it should follow. "Can you feel the difference?"

She exhaled, letting her body relax and drop slightly back against his. "Do it once more," she said.

He swung the bat again, more slowly this time. With the slower swing, his tone hushed as well—somehow an innocent situation was becoming something more.

"How was that?" he asked.

When she answered, her voice had softened. "That was better," she replied.

He turned to look in her eyes, to see if the moment was

imagined, but her face was too close, their cheeks almost touching. Her words now were almost a whisper.

"Yes, that was definitely much better."

He could feel her breath against his neck; his arms stayed wrapped around her body. It was innocent, unplanned, but when Dave recognized what was happening, he wasn't sure if he should pull away or pull her closer. The feeling was warm, yet awkward, pleasant, yet painful.

When he did finally let go, confusion edged in between them. With both at a loss for words, neither he nor Crystal spoke.

Jared came to the rescue. "Are you gonna stand there all day, Mom, or bat?"

"Yeah," Dave added, his sarcasm masking a still flooding river of emotion. "Are you gonna stand there all day, or bat?"

Crystal smiled contently as she pulled the bat back into position. Dave took over for Jared, who moved behind home plate. Gracie, her interest long since gone, was picking dandelions on the far side of first base.

Dave pitched. Crystal swung. Jared called it from behind the plate.

"Strike three—you're out!"

• • •

The game was a massacre. Though Crystal struck out more than she hit, the boys made up the difference. Dave could smack the ball far into the outfield, but Jared and Glen quickly developed a system for getting the ball back to home plate before Dave could run the bases. With Gracie to follow, they were usually able to force Dave out at home and still manage to tag their sister out as well.

After an hour Crystal called the game, and everyone headed home.

It was one of the most pleasant Sundays Dave had spent in months.

After dinner, while the children were getting ready for bed, Crystal stepped to the couch where Dave was calculating routes on his phone and then checking them against his printed maps.

Crystal stepped close and whispered almost covertly, "The shop for your bike opens tomorrow. Tonight's our last chance to talk. I'll meet you for coffee at the kitchen table in fifteen minutes."

Dave nodded his agreement, then watched her slip into Gracie's room to help her get ready for bed. He couldn't deny he was enjoying his time here—despite feeling uneasy about getting sidetracked. He finished a few more calculations, folded up his map, then started the coffee. When Crystal entered, he'd already poured the cups.

"Are you okay?" she asked, sitting beside him. "You seem a little tense."

"I didn't sleep much last night, and I guess I'm worried about fixing my bike."

"I had a hard time sleeping as well. We should've stayed up to talk."

He smiled at her humor. It was familiar. "Yeah, we should have."

"Listen," she said, "these kitchen chairs make my butt sore. Let's sit on the couch."

He agreed, and soon they were seated next to each other in the family room. Tonight they skipped the small talk.

"Why are you so worried about the motorcycle?" Crystal asked. "Where are you off to in such a hurry?"

"In a hurry?"

"Well, you seem a bit apprehensive—as if we're keeping you from something."

"You're perceptive."

"It's a woman thing."

She waited for his answer. He paused, deciding how best to explain.

"This probably won't make sense, and I'm sure afterwards you'll think I'm unstable, but the truth is that I'm going to the Golden Gate Bridge to look for answers."

It was a thoughtful pause. "I can understand that." Her voice was calm, sincere. He waited a moment for her next question, the follow-up question. It didn't come.

"Don't you want to know what answers?" Dave finally asked. "I mean, that's the next thing everyone asks."

"I know exactly what answers."

"Really? That's surprising, because even I'm not sure myself most of the time."

"Yes, you are—you just don't realize it. You're looking for the same answers that everyone looks for in their life. Let me take a guess—questions like, why me? Why not me? How do I make the pain go away? Will I ever find love again? How do I get up and survive tomorrow after everything that I've been through today?" She paused. "So, how am I doing?"

"How do you know these things?"

"Because they're the same questions I asked myself when I packed up the children and moved here—some of the same questions I still ask myself. I am curious about one thing, though."

"What's that?"

"Why did you choose the bridge?"

"I think it chose me. I've been told that my grandfather considered it a special place. I figured if the bridge worked for him, it might work for me."

He watched her lips press together, her head nod forward, her eyes narrow, as she seemed to agree. He had never met anyone, except perhaps Megan, with such empathy. And Crystal was not only perceptive, she was charming—and beautiful, in a girl-next-door sort of way. As he studied her, he realized that she returned his gaze, that she was looking directly into his eyes, yet not saying a word. He wanted to turn away, but he couldn't—or didn't.

Like an actor on stage, on perfect cue, she leaned over in the dim light of the night and kissed him. He kissed her back.

You have your whole life ahead of you, Ponytail Man. I'm just happy that I'm the one you've picked to share it with.

The feeling was strange—exhilarating, yet profoundly confusing. His pounding heart was being stabbed by tiny pins, and

271

yet he couldn't discern if the emotion was excitement, guilt, or sorrow. Either way, she was the first woman he had kissed—truly kissed—since Megan.

I love you, honey. Have a wonderful birthday! And, remember, no matter what, I'll always be younger.

In the past, when he couldn't take the pain of memory any longer, he would force the thoughts away, compel himself to think of other things. In an instant, as Crystal kissed him and he kissed her back, he realized that he was consciously forcing thoughts of Megan from his head. When he recognized what he was doing, the whole notion made him nauseous. He pulled away and looked down.

She followed. "I'm sorry. I shouldn't have done that."

"It's okay." The shakiness of his words betrayed the ache now swelling in his chest.

"It's not okay. I'm so sorry."

He wished that he could retract the moment, change the past—but he knew that such hopes were wasted. Experience had been a meticulous tutor.

"I have to leave early tomorrow. I need to get some rest," he said as he stood, trying to not act cold but knowing he was failing miserably.

"I understand. I'll see you in the morning." She excused herself and headed to her own room.

Dave readied himself for bed and climbed into his sleeping bag. For the second consecutive night, he lay on the couch with his eyes wide open. The walls in the house were thin, and as he contemplated his departure in the morning, he wondered if the muffled sound coming from the back bedroom was that of someone crying.

• • •

In the morning he was gone. She was sure he didn't realize it, but leaving the way that he had, without saying good-bye, caused a flood of familiar and painful memories to surface.

She fixed breakfast for the children in silence and then readied them for the day. With school out for the summer, Crystal worked three days a week at the district office while the kids played at a day-care center across the street.

Today, instead of going in to work, she dropped the children off and then drove back home. She'd hoped to see his bike parked out front. Nothing. She walked around the outside of the house and glanced past the field and over toward the park. No trace— nobody there. It was as if he'd been a dream, as if she had imagined the whole encounter. She also knew from painful experience that hoping would never change reality.

She reached for her keys, considered driving to Darin's RV to find him. She wanted to tell him again that she was sorry. She stepped to her car and kicked the tire in frustration before looking heavenward.

I had to go and kiss him. What was I thinking?

She weighed heading back to work. They would wonder why she was so late. Instead, she walked inside, called in sick, and then dropped onto the couch. By eleven-thirty, she still hadn't moved. She couldn't.

At the sound of the approaching bike, she jerked upright, bolted to the door, took a breath to collect herself, then stepped quietly onto the porch. She watched him pull into the driveway, drive up onto the walk, and stop just short of the steps. He turned off his bike and removed his black helmet.

"I see you got your bike fixed," she said.

"It was the carburetor."

"I would have driven you down to the shop. You didn't have to walk."

"That's okay. I had to push the bike down anyway—and I was up early."

"Well, I'm glad they could help—glad you could get it fixed."

He nodded. "I'm relieved that I caught you. I was afraid you would have already gone."

"I called in sick today." She hesitated, then added, "I need to tell you again, Dave, that I'm sorry about last night."

He held his finger to his lips. "Please, not another word. I think last night I may have sorely overreacted."

She waited, didn't answer, let him continue.

"I didn't mean to run out so quickly this morning. It's just that if I don't go now, I won't make the bridge in time. I need to make it by the Fourth of July."

She didn't understand his urgency, why the date should matter, but she accepted that it did. "Be careful."

"Crystal, if this was another place or another time . . ." He paused, taking obvious care to choose his words. "But the thing is—I just don't have anything that I can offer you right now. I'm not sure that I ever will. I don't know if that makes sense."

"I understand," she replied, even though she didn't.

"I'm sorry."

"Gracie missed saying good-bye. I wasn't sure what to tell her."

Dave cringed. "It was early and she was asleep." Even now his excuse sounded hollow. "Please tell her that I'm sorry."

"Okay, if that's what you'd like."

Then silence let each know that it was time. He had mounted the Harley and started to put on his helmet when she spoke. "I hope you find your answers, Dave Riley."

He stayed on the bike but reached out his hand toward her. She took it, held it. A quick hug followed—a brief embrace—the kind you might give a friend or a relative. It would have to be enough.

"Thanks, Crystal. I won't forget you."

"Nor I you."

Two days earlier, when Gracie had asked if she could keep Dave Riley as a pet, Crystal had had to bite her lip to keep from laughing. Standing in the driveway saying good-bye, she bit her lip again, for a different reason.

She watched as he buckled down his helmet, started the bike, and rumbled out of the driveway. As he passed out of sight, she dropped onto the porch, leaned her head against her folded knees, and wiped at her watery eyes.

chapter thirty-six

I've been trying his number, but with no success. Every time I call, no matter day or night, the machine picks up. I've left three messages. No response.

The day Janet gave me his number, I felt relieved. I was sure he was the descendant of my Patrick O'Riley—he just had to be. Now, with more time that passes, with days ticking by and still no contact, doubt chews at my heart.

Tonight, after I dial for the second time since arriving home, I sit down at the computer and run a search on his name. At first I find nothing new, only the same information Janet has already provided. I keep clicking, continue looking. Several pages into my search, I come across a website for a marketing research company, Strategy Data International, in Manhattan. The search engine pulls up the page because among its listed employees is a man named David Riley. The address of the business is not terribly distant from the home address I have for Mr. Riley, and I wonder if he is the same man. On the company's personnel page, he is listed as a senior vice president. I click the link and, to my surprise, a picture flashes onto my screen.

His short hair is dark, and a look of confidence radiates in his eyes. I smile because he looks like he might be posing for the cover of a magazine—a mental picture so different from the one I've developed for Patrick, a bridge worker. As I study his features, I wonder if the two men resemble one another. Did the man who penned such wisdom in his engineering journal look like the person staring back at me from the computer screen? Are their features similar?

I find myself dropping into my interrogation mode, my park-bench game. This time the questions are different.

"Mr. Riley, do you know about your grandfather? Do you realize he spent years of his life alone, building a bridge, so that he could find hope for his family in America? If I send you this priceless journal, will you cherish it or toss it aside? And, Mr. Riley, do you still hold dreams in your heart?"

My questions end without answers as I pick up the phone and dial his number again. On the third ring, the machine clicks into its hired service. But as I stare at the picture of David Riley smiling back from the computer, it dawns on me that I now have another avenue. It is too late today—no one will answer after hours—but first thing tomorrow I will call the offices of Strategy Data International. First thing tomorrow, I will finally talk with Mr. David Riley.

Dave headed west. He didn't look back.

In the distance, miles over the horizon near the coast, a wall of cool ocean air, heavy with moisture, was sweeping inland. It was moving rapidly toward a blanket of warm desert air that had stagnated midland. Before long the two layers would collide over the San Bernardino Valley, causing the temperature to drop several degrees in just a few minutes. The billowing mass of majestic cumulus clouds was just beginning to thicken and churn near the base of the mountains.

In the distance, a massive storm was forming.

The phone rings only once.

"Good morning. Strategy Data. How may I direct your call?" The young voice is polished and professional.

"I'd like to speak to Mr. David O'Riley, please." I notice a pause.

"Do you mean Dave Riley?"

I chuckle. I've been calling Patrick by his last name, O'Riley, for so long that it sounds wrong pronounced any other way. "Yes, my mistake. May I please speak to Dave Riley?"

"Let me transfer you."

After a few clicks, the phone is answered again. This time the woman sounds older, less mechanical.

"I need to speak to Dave Riley, please."

"I'm sorry, Mr. Riley is out on . . . an extended leave. It could be several days, perhaps longer."

It's odd that they don't know when he'll be back. I wonder what message to leave. *"May I give you my number? I presume he'll be checking for messages?"*

"He hasn't. I'm sorry, I don't know if he will."

It's a peculiar way to run a professional corporation. But then again, I work at a university. *After I recite my number, she asks,* *"And may I tell him what this concerns?"*

I could tell her that it's a personal matter, but that won't give me answers. Instead I decide to respond with a question. *"Do you know if Mr. Riley had a grandfather named Patrick?"*

Her silence tells me it's a question that she's never been asked.

"I'm sorry. I wouldn't have that information."

It was worth a shot. *"If Mr. Riley does check in, please have him call me immediately. I have something valuable that may belong to him."*

Brock was on the phone when Ellen entered for the third time that morning. She waited patiently—not her usual character—until Brock finished.

"Anything?" Ellen asked.

"I talked to a guy named Redd down at the bike shop, a friend of Dave's. He spoke to him yesterday. I guess Dave was having some bike problems in Colorado, but according to Redd, he got them fixed and is now heading toward the coast."

"And you tried his cell number again?"

"I did. Either the battery's dead or he's not answering. I get nothing."

"Seriously? How can he not answer?"

"Don't blame him for that."

Ellen ignored the comment. "Look, just keep trying, and if you hear something, anything at all, let me know." She turned and headed out of the office, mumbling.

chapter thirty-seven

I've been working on the report for days—with just five more to go until it needs to be finished. That will be a problem, since I'm currently only a fraction of the way through. It's not that it's difficult work. The facts are there; the numbers are there; and, in the name of research, I can plagiarize just about anything. The problem isn't the information, the problem is the flow. No matter how I try, I can't get my words to read with any genuine conviction.

The professor has called twice in the last two days. To say he's nervous would be an understatement. It is, after all, his reputation that's on the line. He even invited me over tomorrow for a Fourth of July barbecue—I'm guessing to interrogate me in person about what's been going on. I'm sure he suspects something is amiss.

I turned him down. I told him I was working feverishly to finish the report. At last, my response was truthful.

The worst part is that I still haven't been able to get in touch with Dave Riley. I call his home number about every two hours, but all I get is his machine. His office won't give me his cell number, and they even claim they don't know when he'll return. I have something of such incredible value for him, and the man doesn't realize it exists. As I go through the motions, as my mind drifts while I work, the whole situation causes me to question and wonder: Where are you, Dave Riley, and why don't you call?

A roar of thunder followed each flash as streaks of light divided up the darkness of the western desert sky. It was more than just a light show—a pelting torrent beat against the ground.

For the time being, Dave was protected by the overpass off of I-80 where he'd taken refuge when the intensity of the rain had become dangerous. He pulled himself out of his sleeping bag for the third time and clicked on the flashlight that lay beside the bike. He removed his map from the open saddlebag, held it flat against the bike's seat, and again calculated the mileage. The numbers hadn't changed.

He flashed the light onto his watch and registered the time. It would be light in an hour. By his calculations, time was running out to reach the coast by tomorrow—and he had to get there tomorrow.

Ride across the bridge on the Fourth of July, the sun at my back, the wind blowing through my hair. That was what he'd told Meg so many weeks ago—that was how it had to be.

In a fit of frustration and fury, he tore the pages into pieces and threw them into the wind. He wouldn't need the map. He'd checked it so often over the last few hours that he had the thing memorized.

He knelt down and rolled his sleeping bag, then stuffed it into the empty saddlebag on the bike. Next, he pulled on his helmet and mounted the machine. The rain continued to pour. He pushed the ignition and let the bike rumble to life. In controlled frustration, he rolled it toward the open side of the overpass where the assaulting rain strafed at the road just outside the bike's reach. The sun should have already started to illuminate the eastern sky—instead, it remained dark and cold.

He revved the bike's engine and waited.

It had to be by the Fourth of July.

• • •

Redd was in the middle of rebuilding a carburetor when Jenny, the receptionist, buzzed his phone.

"Redd, there's a man here to see you. Could you please come out right away?"

He looked down at his grease-covered hands, at the coil spring he held in place. He called back through the speakerphone, "Jenny, I'm right in the middle of a rebuild. It'll be a little while before I can finish. Can someone else help him?"

She sounded nervous. "Umm—no. He specifically asked for you. He's talking with Chuck while he waits."

"Chuck" was Charlie Holden, the owner of the Lakeshore BikeHouse franchise. This would be serious.

"That's fine, Jenny. Let me get washed up and I'll be right there, 'bout three minutes. Can you tell me who he is?"

"I'm embarrassed, Redd. When he first came in I didn't recognize him. I mean, I should have known him from his picture on the annual report. It's Mr. Wiesenberger, Redd. Mr. Jim Wiesenberger, BikeHouse's CEO. He's here in our store in person and, Redd, he's asking for you!"

chapter thirty-eight

The Fourth of July is almost over. While it has poured for most of the day, I hoped the rain would clear enough so I could watch the fireworks over the bay after dark. I had planned to stretch my legs then—it's a celebration that I never miss.

At dusk, however, a TV news reporter announces that the firework show has been canceled due to inclement weather. It's news that I'm sorry to hear. After having been cooped up all day with the dreaded report, I really need to get out.

At times it still makes me want to scream—nothing like a few days ago when I tossed my first pages, but it remains dreadful; my heart is simply not in the work. Oh, the information is accurate, the history is there. It's just so meaningless, so void of heart. It's my job to make it more than informative, to add significance— I just can't get all the pieces to fit together.

It will be a miracle if I can pull it off in any form. But even if I do, the professor will read it and know that I've let him down.

Even after all the late work, he'll see through it and be disappointed.

I decide to go to bed and get an early start in the morning. As I head to my bedroom, I see my phone resting contently on the edge of the kitchen table. Almost out of habit, I pick it up and dial the number for Dave Riley. It is too late to call someone in San Francisco, let alone in Virginia. It doesn't matter. I already know that no one is there to hear it ring.

Before I climb into bed, I check the weather out the front window. The rain has let up, and in the darkness it looks as if part of the sky is clearing. I should be tired, but instead I feel anxious and restless as I pull the sheets around me.

After several minutes of tossing, I get up and glance outside again. It is a spur-of-the-moment decision, much like running out to the store late at night to buy rocky road ice cream. Although the bridge is usually closed at night to pedestrian traffic, it will be open tonight due to the holiday. So I decide to do something that I haven't done since finding the journal. At a few minutes before eleven, I get dressed and head out the door to have a talk with my father at the bridge.

A ghostly blackness enveloped portions of the bay as the bike crested the hill on US-101. Intermittent flashes of lightning in the low-lying clouds, coupled with rolling power outages in the city, caused a jagged patchwork of light to blanket the valley. The bridge remained lit in the distance, though the thick storm clouds that continued to thunder allowed only a partial view. A light rain was starting once again.

Dave paused for a moment to take in the eerie scene before gunning his bike toward the lights on the bridge. Drops of rain streaked across the faceplate of his helmet as he neared the structure. Traffic was unusually heavy near the bridge; perhaps the holiday crowds had been delayed by the torrent that had rolled through the city just hours earlier. With each car or truck that passed, a pasty mixture of water and greasy road film splashed onto him and his bike. Though his leather jacket was waterproof, it proved no match for the constant barrage that had pelted him for the last many miles. He could feel water running freely against his skin, mixing with his sweat. Though the air was still relatively warm, the wind and moisture were causing him to chill.

As he approached the bridge entrance on the north side, he slowed his bike to stare at the rising towers that stood like sentinels guarding the way. A car, following too closely behind, hit its brakes to avoid a collision, then darted around the side of the bike. The window shot down and a voice yelled obscenities.

Dave glanced toward the angry driver but could see no face in the darkness. The car bolted ahead, passing dangerously close and smattering Dave with a grimy spray. He steered over to the far right side of the bridge in an attempt to get out of the way of moving traffic. The rain was falling harder now.

He'd expected this to be a day of finality—a day of answers. Now, as the bike rumbled slowly across the bridge's massive span, he felt nothing but emptiness. All the while, his mind darted in a futile attempt to outrun the memories.

I enjoy my art, but honestly, I can paint anytime. Watching my kids grow up, being there with them, with you—I'm living my dream.

He thought of Megan, Brad, Brittany, and Angel—but for many miles he'd also thought of Crystal, of her two boys, and of Gracie.

I hope you find your answers, Dave Riley, I hope you find your answers.

Every thought of Crystal also brought guilt—guilt for remembering the color of her eyes, guilt for laughing at her coy smile, guilt for admiring her determination—and regret for having walked away so coldly.

I just don't have anything that I can offer you right now. I'm not sure that I ever will.

The lights on the bridge were waging a determined battle against the rain and clouds, one hoped to illuminate the structure, the other worked feverishly to cover it. At the bridge's midpoint, Dave noticed an opening in the metal barrier that separated the pedestrian walkway from the vehicle lanes. An eight-foot-wide section had been removed for repair. He steered his bike through the gap and popped it up onto the sidewalk. If anyone was watching, no one stopped him. He parked near a lamppost next to the railing—out of the way, out of sight. He killed the engine and lowered the kickstand.

The walk to the railing was short. He leaned against the

metal, letting it provide support. It was slippery and cold—like everything that surrounded him, reminding him. He stood alone in the darkness. The hiss of the waves, the smell of the salty ocean air carried voices—whispered echoes that taunted and beckoned.

You're not getting old, honey. I'll always love you.

He'd hoped for peace, for closure, for answers. He waited.

Nothing came but rain.

Did Mom tell you who I like now? Jason Wilson. He's so hot!

He listened again. The only real sound was the wash of holiday traffic rolling wetly behind, battling the elements.

What had compelled him to visit such a miserable place? It took a few moments in the darkness to remember, to recall the words of his father. "Your grandfather said he found answers there; he called the place magical."

Dave felt water coursing into his socks. He leaned farther over the railing.

I enjoy the bridge at night, perhaps because there are so few people around. But tonight, despite the announcements of the canceled fireworks display, a large number of people still linger about the entrance.

I find a spot and park my car near the Vista Access on the south shore. It's a short walk across the structure to my favorite spot. As I stroll, I begin to speak to my father. "I can't sleep, Dad. I have this assignment that I'm supposed to finish, and I can't get it right."

I wait, as if to give him time to respond. He doesn't.

"There's something else, Dad," I tell him. "I think I've found him—the grandson of Patrick O'Riley. I won't know for sure until I speak with him, but his name is Dave Riley. Can you believe it? He changed his name—that's why you couldn't find him. I hoped you'd be proud of me."

A security guard passes and nods in my direction. I nod back. I catch him from the corner of my eye as he turns around to take a second look, probably wondering why I'm on the bridge alone this late at night, wondering why I'm talking to myself as I walk.

The temperature is dropping, and I know from experience that the bay—including the bridge on which I'm standing—will soon be shrouded in a swirling, dank, drizzle-laden fog. Warm air rising from the inland valleys creates a vacuum that sucks the cool, heavy ocean air inward through the gaps in the coastal mountain range. The Gate is the broadest and lowest of these gaps, and each summer it is the same—wildly fluctuating winds, moisture, and vacillating temperatures boil together in a cauldron of instability. As the Pacific high pressure moves north, the swell of chilled ocean water off of San Francisco increases in size, generating a rolling, massive wall of fog that can drop the temperature thirty degrees in just a matter of minutes—instantly reducing visibility from miles to just a few feet.

The rain begins again, and it causes the people who remain on the expanse of the bridge to scurry to its ends. I'm already at my destination, so I open my umbrella and do what I do best— watch. I watch as the droplets spatter into oily puddles on the

pavement, sending concentric rings of fractured light into danc-
ing patterns that scurry to the outer edges. It's fascinating, even
hypnotizing, but the circles are ruined every time a car passes.

I turn my gaze to the drivers of the cars and begin to play one
of my people-watching games—the one where I divine their lives
solely by their appearance.

A man drives by in a Mercedes and I can see his suit and tie.
Late at the office on a holiday, with his secretary . . . won't his
wife be surprised when she finds lipstick on his collar?

A couple in their late teens follow close behind in a red
pickup truck. The young woman is sitting so close to the guy
driving that they almost occupy the same space. She has her arm
around his neck; as they pass, he has taken his eyes off the road to
gaze at her. Certainly an accident waiting to happen. Rather than
make something up, I question their young love. Will it last? Will
they stay together forever, or will tonight be the last time?

As I watch and wonder, the wall of fog rolls over and engulfs
the bridge, just as I had predicted, bringing my people-watching
game to an abrupt end.

I shiver in the damp air and decide to head for home. As
I walk along the bridge toward my car, I resume my discussion
with my father. With fog blanketing the bridge, no strangers will
stare or interrupt. "It's me again, Dad. I forget. Where were we?"

I'm waiting to form my thoughts when I see a dark figure
ahead. A patch has opened in the fog, as it often does. The glow
from the overhead lamp bathes the area in a gauzy, orange light,

and for a second or two I see a dark-clad man standing near the rail, perhaps a hundred feet away.

Unlike others on the bridge who are rushing to their destinations, this man is motionless, leaning his head against the light pole. He has no umbrella and makes no attempt to shield himself from the rain. I can see him taking deep breaths, his shoulders heaving, and I wonder if he may be crying. I feel for the pepper spray in my purse and then move closer.

He was here to find out for himself, to see whether his grandfather had told the truth about the bridge or if it was a big lie, a cute story. He'd said a person could find answers here. If not direct answers, how about a hint of direction, some small ray of hope?

As Dave waited, a fog rolled over the structure. It should have provided comfort, sheltered uncontrolled emotion, masked moments that he might later regret having let the world see. Instead, it enveloped him with a terrible loneliness, a hollow, empty blackness. He needed someone to talk to—anyone. Instead, he stood isolated and alone.

He could hear the waves laugh below, mocking his despair, posing fractious questions.

What had he done to deserve such misery? Why had these things happened to him? Void of hope, his mind began to drift into another dimension, a darker dimension. Reason began to blur. Why *had* he come here?

You aren't going to jump, are you? He'd laughed at Brock's comment; it had been ludicrous at the time. Even during his most miserable moments after the accident, he'd never considered ending his life. Now, shrouded in loneliness, he wondered why it would matter. Who was left? Who would care? Since getting on his bike more than three thousand miles away, he'd determined to hold in the tears. Now, in the darkness, leaning against the angry steel of an unforgiving bridge, he began to sob openly.

The fog, the rain, the emotional destitution, it all continued—unrelenting. The heinous summons of the distant waves grew louder and more insistent.

Though I know that we are both standing still, he seems to undulate, moving closer and then farther away in the patches of fog that roll past. I watch as he shifts his weight and turns his back to me. I'm quite close now and can see that he is wearing a black leather jacket. Farther down the bridge I see the barely visible outline of his motorcycle leaning against the railing. I don't need to wonder anymore—this man is a biker.

I inch closer, a baby step at a time, as the rain worsens and the patches of fog gel back into a dense cloud. My people-watching game has morphed into a surreal, almost dreamy exercise. I am close enough now that if this stranger turns in my direction, he will see me—but he doesn't. For long moments, he grips the railing. There is no movement other than his labored and deep breaths. I am motionless as I continue to observe. When he turns,

I look for tears. If they exist, they are drowned in the drizzling rain.

As I watch, I wonder about his hard life . . . wonder if he's part of a gang, if he's been in jail or ever killed anyone. Does he have a wife and family at home? My thoughts are interrupted when he lifts his head, leans over the railing, and stares down into the dark abyss.

It is late, very late. I've been up working for hours, and as a result my mind and reflexes are slow. As I watch him now, as I watch his heaving, as I watch him draw closer to the rail, I sense his misery. My veins pulse and adrenaline begins to pump through my chest. For the first time, I realize what is about to happen.

The man is going to jump!

chapter thirty-nine

Dave pulled the jacket tight to keep the rain from running inside. As he did, he felt something crumple in the front pocket. He reached in. It was the folded picture that Gracie had drawn in church—the picture of her and Dave in front of his motorcycle. He unfolded it the best he could, its edges damp and curled. The brown and green ink swirled together as new raindrops moistened the page, then dripped away in a muddy trickle.

He was sobbing now, unable to control the swirl of emotions, the grief that clouded his decision. Hope was gone, driven out by despair, replaced by fear. He was exhausted by the loneliness, the emptiness, the memories. It would be so easy to forget everything. *Everyone.* Forget the pain, forget the sting of separation that he faced every morning, forget hope.

He opened his fingers, letting the paper slip out from his hand and flutter away. He watched it disappear into the depraved shadows of the bridge.

He could follow. It would be so simple . . . so easy.

I don't know what to say, how to even begin. I don't want to startle him, but I don't want to watch a man end his life in front of me, either. I wonder how my father would have handled the situation—what he would have said. I wish he were here instead of me. He would certainly know what to do. My lips barely move. I don't want to make any noise. The words form in my mind as I begin to speak to my father once again.

"Dad, help me to know what to say. Help me, please."

I need my father to answer, but I hear nothing. His answers are always my answers, those that I make up in my mind. I hope this time it will be different, and so I wait and hope for his words.

Silence.

I know that I need to say something soon or let a man die, but I can't do it on my own. I simply can't. I ask again.

"Dad, you helped save twenty-eight men on this bridge. I need you to help me with just one more. Just one more, and then I'll move on with my life—I'll do better. Please, Dad, help me now to know what to tell this man in order to give him a second chance. Dad, I want to give him hope."

I wait again, and again in the darkness nothing happens. No words come, no images flash into my mind, nothing. I'm confused and helpless, and except for a man standing just yards away—a man who has no idea that I'm even here—I feel so very alone.

That's when an extraordinary and inexplicable thing happens. I say extraordinary because it wasn't what I'd asked for. It wasn't what I'd hoped would happen. It wasn't what I'd expected. I don't know if it was an answer or an accident, and if I explain it to others later, I'm sure they'll think I've been spending too much time alone in the fog on the bridge. But it does happen. At the exact moment when I'm going to slip back into the darkness, just as I'm about to slink away and leave the stranger all alone to fend for himself—

I sneeze.

His body tensed at the sound. He swung around; instinctively, his fists tightened and his senses sharpened. Whoever it was had been so close, so hidden. He readied for the attack that was certain to come.

It didn't.

As he peered into the fog, he spied a woman standing directly in front of him. She didn't move, didn't say a word; for a moment, she looked as startled as he. How long had she been there spying? He turned his back toward her. A spectator was the last thing he needed right now. He just wanted to be alone.

Though he tried to ignore her, she inched forward—and then she spoke.

"My dad worked on this bridge. He loved it—thought it was a terrific place. I mean, some people will say it's just a bridge, and at times, I guess I'd certainly agree. But then there are other times, times like tonight, when it feels like there's more going on here—times when it seems like there might be something else happening in the universe, like someone is watching over us—too much magic, if that's the right word, to have this be a normal place. Does that make sense?"

Dave was speechless. In the middle of the fog and drizzle on a wretched night when it didn't seem possible for his life to get any worse, a crazy woman now stepped out of the fog to ramble on about the bridge. Was she on drugs, delusional, a wayward tour guide? She'd asked him if she made sense, and then she had waited as if he was supposed to answer. She made no sense; he felt no need to address her.

She continued to babble. "It was important to my dad because he saved the lives of twenty-eight people here. Because the bridge meant so much to him, I learned to love it as well. I apologize for rambling like this. I was just out on the bridge tonight walking around, thinking about him, thinking about how important he was to me, thinking about the lives that he saved. Then I noticed you, and even though you're a stranger and you didn't know my father, I wanted to tell someone, you know, let someone else know what he did for them . . . and what he did for me."

She paused again. Dave didn't speak; he had nothing to say. Instead he stepped to his bike, grabbed the handlebars, and threw his leg over the wet seat. He pushed a step forward, stopped, and stared at her again. She seemed sincere, friendly. Tonight, however, he was simply too tired and confused to care.

He'd been having thoughts—dark, terrible thoughts—at least she had interrupted those. He wished he could stay, perhaps help this woman, listen to her problems. It was great for her that she was in love with this place, but to him it felt utterly miserable, the cold steel and dismal fog unrelenting, unforgiving. He was starting to shiver; it was time to leave.

Before he could start his bike, she spoke again.

"I'm sorry; I didn't mean to interrupt your thoughts. I know you were busy. I just wanted to tell someone about my father, and I happened to see you. Thanks for listening. I appreciate it. Sorry again for the bother."

When she finished, he whispered something to her, though he guessed she wasn't close enough to hear. It didn't matter. He couldn't help her, certainly not now. Drenched and miserable, he'd decided to finish what he had come here to do.

Dave didn't look at her again. Instead, he started up his bike and, in the last handful of minutes remaining on the Fourth of July, he finished his ride across the bridge to the south, then returned back the way he'd come from the north.

He rode on into the darkness . . . away from the towers, away from the cables, away from the lights and the fog—away from hope.

I'm sure my sneeze startled me more than it did him. He was a bit tense at first. Of course, what else could be expected when I just kept rambling on? He must have thought I was the crazy one. As I look back on the experience, I'm surprised that he didn't pick me up and toss me off the bridge just to shut me up. I didn't have a clue what to say, so I just tried to be myself. I told him about

my father, about the selfless man that he was; I told him about the bridge.

I can't say that I helped him. I'll admit he appeared tired and lost even after I finished. But when he got on his bike and rode away, I'd like to think that he took at least a small glimmer of hope. In thinking back, I guess I should have asked how I could help. I should have asked for his name and given him mine. I should have done more than just talk. I should have listened. Life is often like that—a lot of time spent wishing we'd done things differently.

Mostly, I can't help but wonder about the sneeze. If it hadn't happened, I don't think I'd have had the courage to stay. It's just so strange that it would happen when it did. I know that some will think me a foolish and naive girl, but I think that my dad may have been there after all.

I used to imagine that when my father talked people down from the bridge, the right words would pop into his head—that he would always have the perfect solution. I'm guessing now that it wasn't that way at all. I'm guessing that, like me, he often felt confused and alone, that he didn't always have answers. I'm guessing that, instead, he just tried to be himself. I'm thinking that perhaps what my father said to the people on the bridge wasn't as important as the fact that he was there to say it. I think he was just trying his best.

I remember him telling me from time to time about the people he had saved. His only regret was that, out of the twenty-eight, not a single one had ever come back to express any gratitude. And yet, he still kept going out, still kept saving everyone he could.

I don't know if the man I met on the bridge would have actually jumped. Perhaps he doesn't even know. It's just that if my father was really there, if he was helping me, then it seems like such a fitting end. You see, after the man in the black leather jacket climbed onto his bike, just before he rode off into the darkness across the bridge, he whispered two words that my father would have appreciated.

The man on the bridge looked up at me and said, "Thank you."

chapter forty

Dave didn't stop—didn't look back. The dark feelings were like a demon, and he wanted to create as much distance as he possibly could. Ten miles past the memories, he approached a dimly lit sign: *Golden Tower Motel—Vacancy*. It was sleazy, but for tonight it would do. He was too tired and wet to continue—and where was he to go? He was on a journey now with no destination, no end.

He steered his bike into the parking lot and stopped near the office. When he pushed open the door, the lobby was empty. The place reeked of rancid smoke and mildew. What looked to be a secondhand shower curtain hung between the front office and a back room. A TV blared behind the curtain.

Dave pressed the bell on the counter and waited. Within a few seconds the curtain parted, and a heavyset woman, dressed in a nurse's uniform, waddled through the opening. Her makeup was thick and her voice low—almost the tone of a man. With steely eyes she surveyed Dave and the trail of water he'd tracked through the door. Next, she glanced toward his bike waiting in the rain.

"Can I help you?"

"I need a room, please."

She moved close to the counter, her eyes reading the stranger.

"All I have left is two double beds."

"That'll be fine."

"It's $145 plus tax."

The price was ridiculous for the run-down dump, but Dave was too tired to argue. "I'll take it."

She pushed a guest sheet fastened to a clipboard in his direction. "Fill this out."

Her tone was demanding, and under other circumstances he would have turned and walked out the door. Tonight he took the clipboard, scribbled in the information, and pushed it back to her.

"Here you go."

She scanned the scrawled answers. "How do you want to pay?"

Dave reached into his back pocket and removed his wallet. It was soaked completely through—the bills were matted and pressed together into one lump. Rather than create a spectacle by separating them now, he pulled out his American Express Gold card and dropped it in front of the woman.

She snatched it from the counter, her eyes darting from the name on the card to the sheet that Dave had filled out. She then studied the picture of the man on the card. It had been taken two years earlier. It showed a smiling man with short hair, a clean-shaven face, and an expensive suit. She compared it to the biker standing before her—dirty, long hair, stubbled beard, and blood-shot eyes. She looked suspicious; he didn't care.

She moved to the machine and swiped the card. Her fore-head lifted in surprise when the approval flashed onto the screen. She scribbled the number on a pad and then reached under the counter and into a box of keys.

"I don't want any problems," she said as she slapped a key onto the counter and slid it over. "Room 107, around the cor-ner. You've only paid for a single, so no one else is allowed in the room—no other bikers."

Too exhausted to respond to the mistrusting woman, Dave grabbed the key and headed out the door. He pulled his bike around the corner in the direction that she had pointed and found Room 107 on the lower floor. He shoved his key into the lock and then pushed himself inside. When he clicked the light switch, nothing happened. In the darkness, he moved to the out-line of a lamp on the desk near the bed and fumbled for the knob. As it turned, the light flickered on.

The room was cleaner than he had expected, though the fur-niture was certainly dated. He slumped onto the nearest bed and pulled off his boots and socks. His feet were red and swollen. He walked barefoot to the bathroom and twisted on the shower before moving back to the bed to peel off the rest of his saturated clothing. Since there were two double beds, he sat down on the one closest to the door—the one where he'd left his wet boots and socks. It didn't matter if the bedspread got soaked through with his wet clothing, he reasoned—he would sleep in the other bed. It would serve them right for overcharging customers.

He pulled off his jacket and draped it over the chair near the space heater on the wall. He turned the temperature dial to the hottest setting—the fan kicked on. Next he stripped off his shirt and undershirt and tossed them beside his boots.

A wave of exhaustion was rolling over him—not just physical, but mental and emotional fatigue as well. He sagged onto the edge of the bed, thoughts of Megan still resonating. He pushed them away . . . not now, no more pain today.

Steam billowed from the bathroom door. He didn't care—there would be plenty of hot water, it would wait. He started to undo his belt and felt his wallet in his back pocket. He pulled it out from his pants and removed its saturated contents. Too exhausted to consider otherwise, he peeled apart the wet bills and credit cards and laid them across the bedspread to dry.

The slamming knock at the door startled him. He didn't move. Again, several loud raps rattled the door.

Most motel rooms had a small viewer that allowed the person on the inside to see who was standing on the outside. This one didn't. Dave shot a glance at the security door chain that dangled loosely against the doorjamb. It had not been set. He moved to the door and touched the knob. He listened intently, not sure if it was safe to open.

The door rattled with knocks again—this time he heard voices.

"Open up the door, now. This is the police!"

• • •

Dave twisted the knob and pulled the door open a crack. Outside a drawn firearm was aimed at his head.

"Down on the ground, now!" the officer yelled.

He obeyed and dropped to the floor.

"What's going on?" Dave grunted as his arms were twisted behind him and a pair of handcuffs tightened into place around his wrists. "Look, there's been a mistake, you have the wrong guy."

A second officer entered the room, his weapon drawn, to sweep the place for additional suspects. He dashed toward the steaming bathroom and burst inside.

The first officer held his gun in place and began to read Dave his rights.

"You have the right to remain silent. You have the right to an attorney. Should you choose not to—"

"I told you this is a mistake. You have the wrong person," Dave interrupted. "I just checked in—ask the lady at the front desk."

The policeman, unfazed by the interruption, continued his monologue.

" . . . Knowing and understanding your rights as I have explained them to you, are you willing to answer questions without an attorney present?"

"Of course, but like I told you . . ." Dave turned his head to see the office lady standing outside the open motel room door, watching the events unfold. Upon hearing the commotion, half a dozen other spectators had exited their rooms and were gawking as well.

The second policeman returned from the bathroom, his gun now replaced in his holster.

"The place is empty. He's alone—at least for now." Then he noticed the rows of neatly laid out bills and credit cards spread incriminatingly across the bed. He moved closer and picked a card up, the same one that Dave had shown the motel clerk.

"My, oh, my, what do we have here?"

Dave, with his face against the floor and hands cuffed behind his back, remained confused. "Please," he pleaded, "what's this all about?" He arched his head to meet the policeman's glance.

"Crackdown on fraud and burglary," the man in blue replied. "Seems we've had a bit of a problem with bikers running an identity theft ring—and this neighborhood has been ground zero. So, it begs the question, when are your friends arriving?"

"Friends? I'm alone. I promise. I'm not involved!"

The man studied the photo and then glanced to Dave on the floor. "Of course not," he said, his words sopping with sarcasm.

To Dave it was becoming clear: the nervous glances when he was checking in, the comparison of the pictures.

"Look, those credit cards are mine. I swear."

"Really? Will you pinky swear?" His tone mocked.

"I promise I—"

The man cut Dave's sentence in half, didn't give him time to continue. The closer he leaned, the more aggravated he became. "Look, buddy, I've been on shift for ten hours now, and I just can't listen to any more of this crap. I don't know where you come from, but stealing credit cards is a crime in California." He turned to his partner with disgust. "Nick, load him in the car!"

Dave was jerked to his feet and herded out of the door.

"Let me at least get dressed," he pleaded, still barefoot and with no shirt.

While the first officer stuffed Dave into the backseat of the squad car, the second snatched Dave's shirt from the bed, his wet boots from the floor, and the leather jacket from the chair. He rolled them into a bundle and then tossed them into the back of the waiting squad car.

• • •

Dave arrived with the officers at the Corte Madera Police Station on Doherty Drive, north of San Francisco. The thought of putting back on the wet shirt was repulsive, but once his handcuffs had been removed so they could fingerprint him, he stretched it back onto his body. He was cuffed again, his mug shots were taken, his statement was noted, his record filed. He tried again to plead his case with the intake sergeant but found him even less caring than the two officers who had brought him in.

After the booking was complete, he was led by two more men down a long, narrow hall and past two security checkpoints.

At each one, an armed policeman behind thick Plexiglas buzzed them through self-locking steel doors.

Once inside, they approached a row of holding cells. All held at least one accused perpetrator, some two. A steel-barred door opened with a buzz and a clank at the same time that Dave's handcuffs were released. He was escorted inside, and the door locked behind him.

"How long will I be here?" he asked as the escorting officers retreated from the direction they had come.

"You'll be the first to know," one guard replied to the other, rather than addressing Dave. "The first to know." Both laughed at the comment, then vanished behind the locked steel door.

• • •

The man lying on the cot was big. Dave presumed he was sleeping, but once the officers had disappeared, he rolled over and sat up on the edge of the bed. His eyes were cold and bloodshot, his stare icy.

Dave stared back, not sure how to respond or what to say. Only the man's eyes moved, sizing Dave up, like a wild animal assessing the fight in its prey.

Without saying a word, Dave backed to the cot on the opposite side of the cell and sat down. He kept his eye on the man, who was still staring, perhaps still deciding what move to make next.

When the man finally spoke, his voice was like steel.

"What are you doing with my jacket?"

Dave wasn't sure that he'd understood. "What?"

"Are you deaf? I want my jacket back." The man stood. He was about Dave's height, perhaps slightly taller. His shoulders were broad.

Dave stood as well. "Look, this jacket was a gift from my wife. It's not yours."

"You calling me a liar?" The man took a step toward him.

Dave held his ground.

The man's eyes burned with hatred. "I'm telling you for the last time, give me my jacket. *Now!*"

It was not just a jacket. It was a gift from Megan, a piece of her—one of the last pieces he held. Vicious threat or not, there was no way he would part with it.

Dave took a step forward, now just inches away from the man. He stood tall and with broadened shoulders, hoping to intimidate. "I'm telling you, man, this is my jacket, not yours, and I'm not giving it to you, or to anybody, for that matter. If you want it, you'll have to take it, but it'll be over my dead body!"

He hoped his aggressiveness would cause the guy to back down, even frighten him. Regardless, his words weren't an act. When he said *over my dead body,* he meant each and every syllable. Whatever it took, he was keeping the jacket.

"Dead body? You saying I'll have to kill you first?" The man didn't seem fazed by Dave's boldness. He turned back toward his own cot. As he did, Dave breathed a silent sigh of relief.

The man's next move was so quick it caught Dave completely by surprise. In one motion the man jolted back, his clenched fist catching Dave in the lower jaw. "Killing you won't be a problem," he said as a second fist pelted Dave in the abdomen. The blows stunned. He gasped for air, not able to breathe in or out. He was dazed—shocked—bent over, but still standing. The man continued to growl, but it was hard to make out the garbled words.

" . . . kill you? If you want me to kill you . . . I'll kill you . . ."

The next blow caught Dave in the face as he fought for air. He dropped to the concrete floor in a crumpled ball beside his cot as everything in the room faded to black.

chapter forty-one

The sun was shining as he rode over the crest of the hill, the ocean waves coming into full view. The rays warmed his face— a refreshing change from the terrible rainstorms that he'd just ridden through. He slowed his bike to bask in the warmth and to admire the surroundings. The low rumble of the engine beneath him was sweet and solid. The valley around him was green and lush, with plants—strange plants—blanketing each side of the highway.

He could see the bridge in the distance, and it was stunning—just like he'd remembered as a child. The pillars towered, huge orange skyscrapers reaching heavenward, roped together with strands of massive twisted cable.

The road should have been crowded with people coming to enjoy the splendor of such a day, the majesty of such a bridge— and yet today the path lay vacant and deserted. The sky above the bridge was an astonishing shade of vivid blue, with only a few wispy clouds on the horizon that served to contrast the deepness of its color.

As the bike rolled on toward the grandeur before him, Dave could feel and smell the ocean air blowing in from the bay. It was fresh and cool—the perfect mixture of salt and sea. His hair blew in the wind.

It was just as he had imagined it.

The bridge—the bridge to freedom—lay majestically before him, beckoning. The view was grand, and he found himself wishing Megan were with him to share in the moment.

No sooner had the thought entered his mind than the sound of another bike startled him. As he turned to look behind him, Megan pulled up to his side. It was peculiar to see her riding a motorcycle . . . so out of character. And yet she looked comfortable on the bike—at peace, and enjoying the beauty of the day.

It had been so long since they'd been together, so many months since they'd had a chance to talk. He wanted to speak— to touch her—to hold her—to tell her how much she had been missed. He knew the rumble of the engines would drown out his words, but he found himself speaking them anyway.

"Meg, I've missed you."

He was startled to hear her answer—whispered, and yet as clear as if they'd stood in a quiet room alone. "I've missed you as well, honey."

Her voice was sweet and soft, her smile radiant, her face and body so full of life.

"It's been so hard without you," he said, not knowing if she had known the turmoil in his life.

She smiled her understanding—a smile that let him know that she was aware, that she cared. "You've been doing fine, Pony-tail Man. Just fine."

He'd never felt fine, not until today. His thoughts turned to the children.

"What about Brad, Brittany, Angel—how are they?"

No sooner had he spoken their names than the sound of another bike resonated behind them. He turned to see Brad pull up adjacent to Meg. He was riding his own bike, a dark blue Classic Swift Tail with shimmering chrome—a smaller, easier-to-handle bike. Dave recognized the model from the showroom at Lakeshore. Brittany sat in back, her arms wrapped tightly around Brad's waist.

Brad gave Dave a thumbs-up sign before he spoke. "This is the coolest, Dad—absolutely the coolest!" Brittany's braces glistened as she beamed her approval of the journey as well. With a slight acceleration of the throttle, Brad's bike pulled ahead, taking the lead in their excursion toward the bridge.

"And Angel?" Dave asked Megan once Brad had passed. As he spoke her name, Dave noticed a sidecar attached to Meg's bike. Strange that he hadn't seen it before. Angel was seated in the side-car, surrounded by a few of her favorite toys. She held a flower in her hand from which she was pulling the petals and leaves and letting them go in the wind. Watching them flutter away made her giggle.

"Still precocious?" Dave questioned.

"Afraid so," Megan responded with a laugh—a laugh that was rich, warm, and familiar.

The bridge was drawing closer, the pillars rising high into the sky as they neared its entrance. The purring sound of the engine on Dave's bike changed—a quick sputter, a sudden loss of power. He twisted the accelerator, hoping it would help. The engine continued to falter.

It was the carburetor—the same problem he'd just had outside of Liberty. He reached down and tapped the side of the bike. The sputtering worsened.

"Meg?" His heart quickened at the realization that he might not be able to keep up. She slowed her speed to match his, aware of his trouble and concern. "Meg, it's the carburetor," he continued, pointing down at the engine. "It gave me some trouble a ways back, near Liberty. It needs an adjustment. I need to stop and fix it, but I can't be left behind."

Her tone was understanding, her voice full of reassurance. "Honey, it's okay. I think that you should stay here and get your bike fixed—do what you need to—get things taken care of—then catch up to us later. I'll ride up ahead with the kids. We'll wait for you on the other side of the bridge."

He wanted to protest, to change her mind, to convince her and the children to stay. She continued, "Everything will be fine. We'll be waiting for you—I promise."

The sputtering worsened. Meg's bike pulled slightly ahead.

"I love you," he called to her.

"And I love you too, Ponytail Man."

A warm fog enveloped the bridge. It rolled soundlessly across the structure, its piers and anchorages, its cables and towers. As Dave's bike coasted to a stop on the side of the road, he watched Brad and Brittany enter the bridge first. He could hear their laughter, feel their anticipation.

Next he watched Megan and Angel approach the structure. He wanted to feel sad—sad that they were leaving, sad that he was being left behind—but for the first time in months, he didn't.

She was distant now, but he thought he heard her voice one last time. *I love you, Ponytail Man.*

He watched Meg glide onto the bridge—the bridge of magic, the bridge of hope—and then slowly disappear into the mist with Angel by her side, still throwing petals into the wind.

chapter forty-two

Dried blood caked his face, and his head pounded. He tried to open his eyes, but they were covered with dirt and blood. He pushed himself up into a sitting position. He'd been passed out on the concrete floor; his muscles were stiff and sore. He focused first on the filthy sink in the corner, and then on the cot on the opposite side of the cell. Dave wished he could rinse the blood from his face, but he feared that he might disturb his cellmate, who was asleep and wearing the tight-fitting leather jacket.

The buzz of the steel door sounded, and the man on the cot stirred. Dave could hear voices, but none that he recognized.

"Get him out. Get him out now! The boys upstairs have done it again."

The cell door rattled open, and three uniformed guards stepped inside. The tallest of the three appeared to be in charge. He directed the others, who moved to Dave's side to help him up.

Dave's joints ached as he attempted to stand. He spoke softly. "I swear it's me in the picture."

The guard in charge turned toward the other two. "Oh, they're well aware of that now. Down here we're just wondering why the hell the *city's finest* couldn't figure it out last night."

Dave's cellmate, who'd been watching from his cot, now sat up. The guard motioned Dave toward the door.

"So I'm free to go?" Dave asked.

"Of course. That's a nasty cut on your eye. Did that happen last night?"

Without a word, Dave glanced at his cellmate. The man on the cot shrugged, spat on the floor, then leaned back against the wall.

The two men at Dave's side reached out to help him walk. He shrugged off their assistance and stepped ahead alone. He paused at the door and then turned to address the tallest of the guards. "Are you in charge here?"

"Down here, I am. Paul McGuire." He held out his hand. Dave reached out and shook it.

"Mr. McGuire, can I ask a favor of these men?"

"I guess that depends on what you have in mind."

Dave leaned over and whispered to the circle of men.

Paul McGuire was the first to speak. "I think that's doable." He turned toward the two guards and nodded his approval. "Gentlemen," he directed.

Dave stepped back into the cell with the uniformed men and

toward the burly man sitting on the cot. As they approached, he stood.

"I'd like my jacket back," Dave said politely.

The man grunted a response—Dave took it as a no.

With as hard a punch as Dave could muster, he drove his fist into the man's stomach. Instantly the man buckled over, though he remained on his feet. He lunged toward Dave, but the two guards had already stepped forward. Each grabbing an arm, they stripped the jacket from him, pushed him back down onto the cot, and then handed the jacket to Dave.

"Thank you," he said to the still-gasping man. "I knew you'd understand."

Then, accompanied by the three uniformed men, he turned and walked through the cell door a free man.

• • •

The sky was still cloudy as Dave retraced his path across the bridge, but this time he could see patches of blue dotting the horizon. He slowed down when he reached the structure's midpoint. The pillars, the cables, the towers—everything looked different today. Everything felt different.

He didn't stay long—he didn't need to.

A few miles down the road, he pulled off at Citrus Heights to eat. After he'd finished, he called Redd.

"Redd, it's Dave. How are you?"

"Dave? Good to hear from you. I'm doing fine. How about yourself?"

"I'm okay."

"How's the bike working?"

"Just the one little detour; otherwise she's been great."

"Glad to hear it. Listen, you may not want to hear this right now, but I've had a bunch of visitors around here this last week."

"Visitors?"

"Well, yeah. First, your friend Brock and his boss came by. Then, the next thing I know, the CEO of BikeHouse himself shows up—asking for me. You should have seen my boss's face. I think my job security is at an all-time high."

"So, what's up?"

"Well, they came asking for me, but only 'cause they need to find you."

"Me?"

"Yes, sir. Seems you stood up in the middle of an important meeting, said to hell with it all, and walked out—just so you could take off on your new motorcycle."

"I guess I did—and they're still mad?"

"Mad? They want to make you the BikeHouse poster child. CEO wants to meet you. Their ad people have been going crazy. They're thinking of re-creating the whole thing for their TV commercials. A highly paid executive who chucks it all to ride off on his bike to find life's answers—you have to admit, it has possibilities."

"You're serious?"

"Oh, they're convinced this approach will sell more motorcycles than *Easy Rider*. Problem is, they'd like your permission. Oh, you've got a slew of people looking for you, all right."

Dave was stunned. He could only imagine the look on Ellen's face.

Redd continued. "And here's the best part. I'm chatting with the CEO and he starts asking me questions. He wants to know what I think. Can you imagine . . . the CEO asking what *I* think?"

"Congratulations, Redd."

"Thanks. So—" Redd hesitated, as if not sure how to ask, "what should I tell them?"

"Nothing yet. If you'll wait to tell them that I called, I'd appreciate it."

"No problem. And Dave . . . how did it go?"

"On the long stretches of road, Redd, I still think about her and the children. I still remember her smile, her voice, the highlights in her hair from too much time in the sun, the way she'd touch my hand . . . but it's different now. It's better."

"It's so good to hear you say that. What are your plans? Are you heading back this direction?"

"You'll be the first to know, Redd, the very first to know."

It's been nine days since I met the stranger on the bridge. Since then I've hardly slept. I've scarcely quit typing. My assignment for the Society is all but complete. Who knows? The professor may be proud of me yet.

I tore up the work that I'd started and began fresh with a clean sheet of paper. I've started fresh in many ways. I realized that there's a more important story to tell than to recite a history of the bridge. I wrote it for the Society instead. It's a story that's been held captive inside, trying to find a means to come out—and it found a way. Once it started, I couldn't get it to stop. Ideas and phrases and words poured into my mind so rapidly, I was terrified they would slink away before I had time to get them all down on paper. The story I've created for the Society is one of a man who kept a journal about a bridge. It tells of a cable and a selfless ironworker and the lessons they taught to a young girl. It's a story about pain and fear turning into courage, and about not giving up on life. It's a story about giving of ourselves to save others.

I've pasted a picture on the cover of my assignment. It's a picture of the bridge—my picture, the one I painted long ago. It's a house with a chimney and a white picket fence. There are cows and pigs and a pasture blended with bushes and trees and small yellow flowers covering the yard. Next to the house and connected to it are the tall golden and orange spires of a bridge that springs forth from the ground.

I used to think it was odd that there was no ocean in this picture—odd that, rather than spanning a treacherous strait, the bridge connects to a house and a family. I realize now that the picture is profound, that only as a child was the truth so plainly evident.

I'm grateful that it recently came flooding back, that it has again touched my life. You see, I'm beginning to remember, to realize that it's not the cable or the steel or the concrete; it's not the design or the engineering; it's not the structure itself or even the turbulent ocean that it spans. What matters is that it connects people and families—that lives come together because of it, that they touch each other, become stronger. That's the real magic.

I've changed the title of the report. I didn't ask for permission.

A Forever Bridge, by Patrick O'Riley and Kade Connelly, as told by Katie Connelly.

It's a story everyone needs to hear.

The best news is that I finally spoke to Mr. Riley. He called me at home yesterday. He got my number from his secretary. As I hoped, he is the correct David Riley. He confirmed that his grandfather, Patrick Riley—or Patrick O'Riley, if you prefer— did work on the bridge as a younger man. Mr. Riley was more reserved than I would have guessed from his picture on the Internet, but he seemed thrilled, even overwhelmed at the news. I have Patrick's journal, letter, and Anna's ring all packaged up and ready to send to him.

Giving up the journal and especially the ring will be difficult. They mean such a great deal to me. But they're not mine, and I sense—at least I hope—that they will mean as much to Dave Riley.

It's okay that I won't have the journal in my hands to hold. I've instead placed its lessons in my heart.

My father taught me that people are like strands of cable, and he's right. But I also think that love is sometimes like that piece of cable as well. If it's not held tightly, if it's dropped, it can break apart into a tangled pile on the floor.

I'd been expecting someone else to show up and put the pieces of my cable back together. Perhaps I should have started on my own. The main thing I think I'll remember is that once my cable is together, once it's strong, I'm going to keep the ends tightly wrapped.

chapter forty-three

He stopped at a small-town barbershop in Kearney. It had a striped pole out front and an old-fashioned leather and chrome chair inside. It was quaint; Megan would have loved the place. The barber was friendly, even nosy—no doubt a small-town job requirement.

"That's a nasty scar above your left eye, young man. Still a bit red."

"It looks great now," Dave replied. "You should have seen it a couple of months ago."

"Well, I won't ask what happened." The man's curiosity was evident.

"My old barber slipped with his scissors," Dave replied. "That's why I came here." He laughed. It felt good to joke.

The barber laughed as well, accepting the teasing answer without pushing further.

"So, how do you want your hair cut?"

Dave considered the question. "I used to keep it short, but I've been wearing it longer lately—I like the look. Just trim it up a little, take off a couple of inches or so, and it'll be fine."

The barber nodded his understanding and began to comb and snip. He chatted politely as he worked. "You're obviously not from around here?"

"No, I'm from Jamesburg—it's on the East Coast."

"You're a long way from home. Are you coming or going?"

"Coming, I guess. I've got a business meeting in L.A. I'll get there eventually."

"Eventually?"

"Yeah, I have a stop to make in Liberty, Colorado. Have you been there?"

"Liberty? Of course. It's what—four or five hours west? Yes, I've been to Liberty many times. It's a nice little town."

"I agree."

"Yeah, Liberty," the barber repeated. "I had a great-aunt who lived there once. So, you have relatives there?" Nosy again. His job, his nature.

Dave didn't immediately reply. It was a stop that he'd been weighing for weeks now, prodded by a note in his Grandpa Patrick's journal. *We can't know 'til we travel the road.*

The old barber stopped snipping and waited for Dave to answer.

"I'm going to Liberty because of some kids."

The old man raised an eyebrow. "Kids?"

"Yes, sir. I need to teach some kids how to play baseball."

• • •

The park was empty when Dave approached. He'd expected to see two boys hitting balls, with an inquisitive blonde girl umpiring from the bleachers. Instead, the place was deserted.

He parked his bike near the stands and climbed up to the second row to sit. The wood was still weathered, the fountain still spewed gallons of fresh water, the late-autumn air was still dry—the place still felt inviting.

It was a quaint town, and again, Megan would have loved it. He thought of her often—remembered her voice, her smile, the sparkle in her eyes. But the memory was no longer painful—not since his final visit to the bridge. Her voice now seemed to reassure, to coax him forward.

He felt a little uneasy about coming back, not sure what the reception might be like, considering his coldness when he had ridden away so many weeks prior. But mixed with his anxiety—indeed, woven into the same fabric—were whisperings of hopefulness, longing, and desire, all edging him forward.

"Hey, you cut your hair!"

Gracie had snuck up on him again, approaching while his mind wandered elsewhere. Her white-blonde hair wisped in the breeze as she climbed the steps and stood beside him.

"Just a little bit—and I shaved. Do you like it?"

She studied him for a long moment before nodding her satisfaction. "Yeah, I guess so."

"Well, that's good. You want to sit down?"

The little girl sat beside him.

"Jared and Glen got a new bat," she announced, as if the news may have made the town paper.

"They did? Did your mommy buy it for them?"

"Yep. She had to go to Greeley."

"Can they hit better with it?"

"Guess so," she shrugged.

"I figured they'd be out here playing."

"Nope. They're doin' chores."

"You're done already?"

"Yep."

She chatted as if they'd been friends for life—as if he had never left without saying good-bye.

"So, is your mommy home?" he asked.

"Yep." Her standard answer, though in her own observant way she added, "She's gonna be surprised to see you. She was sad when you left."

"She was?"

"Yep."

While they talked, Dave glanced across the field to see two boys approaching with a bat and glove. They were walking slowly, but when they noticed Gracie sitting next to Dave on the bleachers, they began to holler and run.

Not far behind them Dave noticed someone else—her blonde hair, like Gracie's, reflecting the autumn sun. She walked slowly at first, as if she didn't believe what the boys were hollering back at her, what her eyes were soon telling her. Dave sat up on the battered wood. He couldn't help but watch her approach, admire her confidence. He stepped down from the bleachers and waited as she neared.

Crystal approached haltingly and spoke in a dry, sarcastic tone. "I told the kids to leave the bikers alone—and damned if they just won't listen."

He shrugged. "Kids will be kids."

"So, are you just passing through again—on your way to somewhere?"

"I guess that depends. Is there a bike shop in town?"

Her finger touched her chin. "The mechanic at Darin's just moved to Raleigh. His brother opened up a shop there. There's always Darin, the owner, but he mostly works on the RVs."

"That's too bad. I guess I'll have to stay a while, then." He thought he noticed a smile, though it was slight and quickly vanished.

"That could be a problem," she said.

"It could?"

"Sure. The Sundowner's been condemned, and the new motel isn't open yet."

"Is there a campground?"

"Not that I know about. Hmm . . ." She put her finger to her lips, pretending to weigh a decision. "I do have a spot in my front yard—but it will cost you."

"I'll take it."

"Okay, then." She reached out and took his hand. As she did, she turned serious. "Honestly, Dave, I'm surprised to see you."

This time he held her hand tight and didn't let go. "The truth is, after I left here—I couldn't quit thinking about you."

She was startled by his blunt response. "You couldn't?"

"No, not at all. I mean, your batting stance was terrible. You really need some practice."

"I see. And you're here to help me?"

"Absolutely. It's what I do."

She pulled away, reached out and took the bat from Jared, and held it out upside down, by the fat end. "Like this?" The boys' grins nearly touched their ears. Even Gracie showed a smile.

Dave stepped beside her, took the bat, and turned it around. He touched her hands, held them for a moment before placing her fingers around the bat in the proper grip. He then stepped behind her, reaching around her body to hold the bat with her.

She relaxed, let him hold her—and it felt familiar, more acceptable, more certain.

"Are you ready?" he asked, as he helped bring the bat back into position.

"That depends," she replied. "Are *you* ready?"

He considered the question. "This time I am." He swung the bat with her—together. "Did you feel that? Did you feel the difference?"

"Yes," she answered. "It does feel different."

Dave drew the bat back once more as he asked, "Are you ready to try it again, then?"

Crystal pulled away. She turned her face to look him in the eyes.

"We are talking about the same thing, aren't we?" she questioned. "I mean, I just need to be sure that I understand what you're asking."

"I'm talking about a second chance, Crystal—another shot."

"Are you positive?"

"I am."

Hers was a smile that she couldn't hide.

He asked again. "Do I get a second chance?"

"Yes, okay," she answered. "You absolutely get a second chance."

Dave turned to Glen, Jared, and Gracie. "Did you hear that? I really hate to lose, and so your mom says I get a second chance. The teams are me and Gracie against you three. Now, if everybody's ready—let's play some ball."

I've come to the bridge one last time. My car is overloaded with all my things. I rented a trailer hitch, the kind that bolts onto the bumper, and pulling the tiny U-Haul trailer is about all this little car can handle. There was only room for my father's desk and a box or two of my things. I'll come back in a few weeks to sell the rest of the furniture. The real-estate agent said she expects the house to move quickly.

I'm not sure what it says about me, being able to pack everything I own into my trunk and a small trailer, but I think I'm finally on the road to figuring it out.

In two weeks I begin teaching history to high school

students—eleventh graders, to be exact. The principal called and offered me the job without even requesting an interview. He said we'd already met, the evening he listened to me speak to the crowd at the Society banquet—the night I broke down and cried like a baby. He called Professor Winston, who sent up my file along with a hearty recommendation. I wish he would have asked me first, though I certainly won't complain. I never do. It turns out that the principal is from the high school in Crescent City, where the Society will debut my material about the bridge. It seems like a great place to begin.

I must say, the thought of standing in front of a class of high school students scares me crazy—even worse than standing before the gray-haired Society ladies. Kids tend to be brutally honest. Then again, it's a trait that I think I'll appreciate.

The Society is ecstatic with my final report, my lessons from the bridge, and while I'm glad they like it, mostly I'm ready to share it with others. I'm frightened, sure, but at the same time I feel an energy that I've never known. It's like I finally have something to give, something to pass along—lessons that deserve to be treasured.

I said good-bye to the professor. He claimed that he was glad to finally be rid of me, but he did get teary-eyed when we shared a last hug. As usual, he got in the final word. He shouted to me from the window as I climbed into my car.

"I thought you should know, Katie," he yelled, "the principal who hired you up in Crescent City—he really likes you and he's single!"

I'll miss the professor.

I spoke to Dave Riley again last week. He thanked me for sending the journal, said it meant a great deal to him. He asked for my address so he could send a thank-you gift. I assured him that there was no need, that coming to know Patrick and Anna was certainly payment enough. He insisted, and I received the box from him yesterday.

It wasn't Anna's ring—he certainly cherishes that—but it was strikingly similar. He ordered it from the village of Claddagh, in Ireland. Isn't the Internet amazing? Along with the ring came a paper reciting the legend and the words I've grown to love: "With this crown, I give my loyalty. With these hands, I promise to serve. With this heart, I give you mine."

I wear my ring proudly on my right hand, with the crown facing out. My heart is indeed free. The ring, the words, the lives of those before—they all reassure. Yes, I was betrayed, but not all men are betrayers. Yes, I was hurt, but not all relationships cause pain. If I ever forget these truths, I'll take a walk and have another conversation with my father.

Mr. Riley gave me his new address in Colorado. He said he was no longer working or living in New York. I look forward to meeting him someday, but there's not time for me to drive all the way to Colorado—not with a loaded-down car pulling a trailer, not with eleventh graders waiting . . . but perhaps someday.

I leave the bridge in peace; we part as friends. I take so much of her with me and leave so much of myself behind. I think that's what life must be about—helping others, leaving pieces of us with them, in return fitting borrowed pieces from them into our own voids, each person helping others along the way.

Yes, I'll finally be leaving this crazy old bridge, but I leave with hope in my heart. I'll try not to miss the place too badly.

She is, after all, just a bridge.

epilogue

Memorandum

From: Shaun R. Safford
Vice President, Marketing
BikeHouse Customized Motorcycles

To: Dave Riley
Vice President, Market Research
BikeHouse Customized Motorcycles

Dear Dave,

I've just been handed the latest sales figures generated from the ad campaign that features you and your bike. The numbers look very good. If sales continue at this pace, then we can all look forward to the best year in the company's history. Congratulations!

Also, I want to tell you again that it's been great having you on board as part of my team these last five months. I was concerned at first with you living in Colorado, so far away from company headquarters. When you told me you would ride your Harley over once a quarter for the company meetings, I was skeptical. Then I realized that attitude sums up the whole message of the campaign, the whole genius behind it. With email, phones, and video conferencing, one can live just about anywhere these days. I wanted you to know that it's working out well, and it's been a pleasure having you on board.

I look forward to seeing you again in April.

Sincerely,
Shaun

P.S. Congratulations on your engagement. Please give my best to Crystal.

author's note

Since the Golden Gate Bridge was finished in 1937, nearly 2,000 people have leapt to their deaths from its girders, making the bridge the most popular location to commit suicide in the United States.

In April 2017, after years of debate, construction on a suicide-deterrent system was started: steel nets to span the bridge's length on both sides. It's an effort that officials believe will save many lives, including those of the ironworkers who volunteer their time talking down potential jumpers.

For additional information, including other works by Camron Wright, please visit AuthorCamronWright.com.

acknowledgments

Although *The Other Side of the Bridge* is a work of fiction, it's natural for a writer to stitch bits of real life into his or her narrative. In this case, it includes the adaptation of an experience related to me by an acquaintance whom I'd not seen in thirty-five years. As a young man, he shared with me a sliver of his own life that I've never forgotten. It seems that, as a teenager, he got the notion into his head that the day he would ride across the Golden Gate Bridge on his motorcycle would be the finest day of his life. He longed for it, lived for it, finally saved enough to buy a bike, and then headed west. When he arrived, instead of the day being sunny, warm, and wonderful, it was cold, rainy, and emotionally miserable. As I remember it, he'd just received word from home that a good friend had passed away. It meant that an experience he'd hoped would represent a pinnacle of satisfaction turned instead into heartache, sorrow, and tears—and yet it proved to be a critical turning point in his young life.

As I've thought about his experience over these many years, it's helped me to deal with my own sorrows and disappointments—and I believe therein lies the lesson: Take time to interact and share with others. In our Facebook world, brimming with people who are starved for honest communication and contact, we may never know how our in-person words and kindness will touch another.

Deserved thanks for this story must also go to my wife, Alicyn. She loved this story every time I dug it out, dusted it off, and revised it. She continually encouraged me to do something with it, and for her perseverance, I'm sincerely grateful.

Information about the bridge was culled from several sources, the most important being *The Gate: The True Story of the Design and Construction of the Golden Gate Bridge,* by John Van Der Zee. It's a book I highly recommend. Thank you, Mr. Van Der Zee, for your fascinating work.

Thank you as well to the various editors whose technical expertise and insight always help to improve my writing. (There are many and you know who you are.)

I also owe a hearty thank you to Adam Rosales, an MLB player with the Arizona Diamondbacks, who graciously corrected my baseball dialogue. His foundation, Sandlot Nation, uses the love of baseball to teach youth about the importance of education, teamwork, and sportsmanship. Visit him online at SandlotNation.org.

Last, thanks must deservedly go to you, the reader, both individuals and book groups. Without you, I wouldn't have the opportunity to write. You are truly my heroes for reading my books and then sharing them with others.

reading guide

1. In Emily Dickinson's opening poem (the book's epigraph), she describes faith as a bridge without piers or supports. Is that a fair description of the way many in the world view faith? At the same time she calls it *bold* and having *Arms of Steel* that *join behind the Veil.* What do you think she is implying with this phrase? What parallels can you draw between the concept of faith and hope in the poem and then in the story?

2. In reminiscing about her father's death on the bridge, Katie wonders what part fate played. Do you believe that accidents are fate—that they are meant to happen? Or are they, as their name implies, simply *accidents?*

3. In one of Dave's visits with Dr. Jaspers, his grief counselor, she tells him to "be careful about chasing dreams that are only wispy puffs of hope not based in reality." Is this wise advice? Have you ever chased a dream and wished you hadn't? On the

other hand, have you ever chosen to not chase a dream but later wished you had? How can we know if our dreams and desires are worthy of chasing?

4. Redd shares an experience with Dave that he had at the Vietnam Memorial when he heard the voice of Leslie Harris, his friend who was killed in the war. Have you (or someone you know) ever had an experience when you saw, heard, or felt the presence of someone who had passed? If so, how did it impact your life? Researchers in a University of Milan study suggest the phenomenon is common, reporting a "very high prevalence" of what they call "post-bereavement hallucinatory experiences." Are these experiences simply a way people deal with grief, or do they represent something more?

5. Katie enjoyed creating "people-watching games." Have you ever done the same? Have you ever caught someone watching you in a people-watching game?

6. Were you disappointed that when Dave and Katie met on the bridge, neither realized there was a deeper connection between them? Do you believe these types of encounters happen often in our lives? How would we know?

7. There appear to be endless quotes posted on social media about bridges—building bridges, crossing bridges, burning bridges. What is it about bridges that makes them so prevalent as metaphors in our lives?

8. Early in the story Katie ponders the role of chance, particularly something as trivial as the timing of a sneeze and its

potential to dramatically alter the course of one's life. Is her worry valid? Did Katie's sneeze near Dave at the bridge happen by chance? Should we worry about the timing of sneezes in our own lives (for either good or bad)?

9. The reality of Dave's ride across the bridge played out differently than his vision. Instead of the day being warm, sunny, and uplifting, it was dark, rainy, and emotionally draining, an experience that easily could have ended in tragedy. Have you been in a similar situation, when reality dashed your expectations? In the end, after some time had passed, did everything work out for you?

10. When Glen, Jared, and Gracie brought Dave home, their mother, Crystal, was horrified—and perhaps rightly so. If a smelly, long-haired biker came to your door asking to use the phone, would you let him in? How do you draw the line between kindness and caution? When you see a tattooed biker with a ponytail and a leather jacket, what is your first impression? If you could wave the person down and chat for a few minutes, do you think your impression might change?

11. Did you know much about the building of the Golden Gate Bridge before reading this book? What did you learn that surprised you?